T0279109

The Ghost of You

THE GHOST OF YOU

Michael Gray Bulla

Quill Tree Books
An Imprint of HarperCollinsPublishers

Quill Tree Books is an imprint of HarperCollins Publishers.

The Ghost of You

For information address HarperCollins Children's Books, a division of HarperCollins Publishers, 195 Broadway, New York, NY 10007.
www.epicreads.com

Library of Congress Control Number: 2023944819
ISBN 978-0-06-309175-7

Typography by Laura Mock
24 25 26 27 28 LBC 5 4 3 2 1

First Edition

To Erica

June

1

THE FIRST TIME I SAW Ghost was at my brother's funeral reception.

The funeral itself was a blur. I sat numbly through the burial, staring ahead at the coffin as it was lowered into the ground. Earlier, at the open-casket service, I had only managed to look at Jack's body for a few seconds before I had to turn away. I couldn't handle seeing his still frame just lying there, the blank expression on his motionless, unnervingly pale face. But the image had already impaled itself onto my memory, and even when I stared down at the graveyard's summer-green grass, there was Jack's body, overlaid like an afterimage.

I didn't feel like myself. None of this—Jack's sudden death, my grief and my parents' grief, the funeral—felt real. Despite the sunshine, the world seemed to be covered in a fog, everything a little hazy like something was missing, something was off. It was all *wrong.* My brother was supposed to be alive. I was supposed to start my junior year of high school in August, and Jack would go back to his college campus for his Film Studies program, and he would come home to visit for Thanksgiving, for Christmas, for New Year's. We were supposed to have so much more time together. He shouldn't have been buried under the ground, his body already beginning to decompose. This was wrong. This wasn't—*couldn't* be—real.

I was thinking this as I sat in the back of my parents' car on our way home from the funeral, and I was thinking it as we got to our house and everyone else arrived, as food was served and tearful hugs exchanged, as I escaped the crowd to sit on the back porch alone.

There were two rocking chairs on our porch, handmade gifts from my grandfather. Jack and I used to sit out here and rock in them, talking about nothing. Now, I sat in one and started to rock absentmindedly, staring out at the trees in our backyard. I kept the door open, leaving just a screen between me and the living room, and I could still hear the chatter from inside.

Jack's funeral had been well attended. Most of our neighbors—including my childhood best friend, Tanya, and her parents, Mr. and Mrs. Gupta—had shown up, along with a lot of my extended family: my grandparents, most of my aunts and uncles, a few first cousins. At the service, I'd seen a group of Jack's friends, but I'd avoided speaking with them, and none of them seemed to have followed us to the reception, instead slipping out right after the burial. Almost everyone else had chosen to join us, though, and now the house was filled with low murmuring and somber-but-polite conversation. From my spot on the porch looking out at the yard, I heard Tanya speaking with my parents.

"Do you know where Caleb went?" she asked.

"I'm not sure," I heard my mom say. "Maybe out on the porch?"

I didn't hear Tanya's response because something in the distance caught my eye. In the trees, I noticed a small black cat prowling around. My family hadn't had a pet in a long time—I was told that we used to have a cat when I was really young, although I didn't remember much—but I'd always loved animals, so I got up and took a few steps closer.

At my movement, the cat looked up. He was still far enough in the distance that I couldn't see his face well, but I got the feeling that he was looking at me anyway.

I crouched down and held out my hand. "Here, kitty kitty."

The cat stood completely still, then, after a long moment, began to make his way toward me. He was slender and muscular like a small panther, and his tail swished as he walked. The closer he got to me, the more I noticed that something about him seemed—off.

I'd assumed the distance had made the details of his face blurry, but as he approached, I realized he wasn't coming any more into focus. Where his eyes, mouth, and nose should have been, there was just darkness.

But it didn't seem like he didn't have a face *at all*—it was more like my brain couldn't process it, like I'd already forgotten what his face looked like even as I stared directly at him. His form seemed almost smudged out, as if someone had tried to erase him but couldn't quite get all the way there. I felt the hair on my arms stand up, and even though it was almost a hundred degrees out, I suddenly felt very, very cold.

Behind me, the screen door slid open.

"Caleb?" Tanya said.

I turned to look at Tanya, blinking at her. "Did you see that cat?"

She scanned the porch and backyard, using her hand to shield her eyes from the direct sunlight. She shook her head. "No. Was there a stray running around here?"

I looked back at the trees. The cat, of course, was gone.

"I guess so," I mumbled. I sat back down in the rocking chair.

Next to me, Tanya shifted her weight from foot to foot. "Do you . . . want company?" she asked gently, almost hesitantly.

We'd been best friends for as long as I could remember, and in all our years of friendship, I didn't know Tanya to be gentle or hesitant when it came to us. We were always so blunt with each other, never pulling punches or tiptoeing around each other's feelings. Hearing her sound so unsure was yet another way that things were off now that Jack was dead.

That was when it started to sink in for me—from now on, everything would be different. Nothing could go back to the way it was before.

"I think I just want some alone time right now," I said quietly.

She nodded. "All right. . . . Well, um . . . I'll be inside if you need me, okay?"

"Okay. I'll head inside in a bit."

She nodded again. I didn't watch her go back inside, but I heard the screen door open and shut as I stared out at the trees, still scanning for any sign of that black cat.

November

2

FIVE MONTHS AFTER JACK DIED, I went to a house show with Tanya.

"Deck of Fools is having a show to celebrate their one-year anniversary," she'd said the day before, while I drove us both home from school. "I'm gonna go if you want to join . . . ?"

The question trailed off, almost like she was nervous asking it, and I knew she was expecting me to say no. It had been a long time since I went out with Tanya and her friends. For almost half a year, I'd declined every invitation—roller skating, the movies, yet another concert or house show or party.

But it was November now, fall already starting to come to a close and winter fast on its way. I figured it might do me some good to get out of the house for once. I figured I could—*should*—be able to handle it. So, to both of our surprise, I said yes.

When we got there, Nathan, one of Tanya's friends, greeted

us at the door. He was a tall white guy with dusty blond hair, and when he saw Tanya, he smiled to reveal straight, pearly white teeth. The two of them had started hanging out last spring semester, but I still wasn't particularly close with him.

"Hey! You made it!" He beckoned her into a hug, and when they pulled away, she was smiling, too. Even from here, I could smell the liquor on him, and I wondered if he was drunk already.

"Of course," she said. "Wouldn't miss it for anything."

After a moment, his eyes slid to me, and he gave me a polite smile. "Nice to see you, man."

I nodded back. "Yeah, you too. I'm, uh, glad I could make it."

"Me too! It's gonna be one hell of a show." He grinned, then seemed to realize we'd been standing in the entrance this whole time and gestured behind us. "Do y'all wanna head to the back? The band isn't starting until nine, but it's way quieter out on the patio."

Tanya nodded. "That'd be great."

Nathan led us through the crowd with more grace and expertise than I would've thought possible for a maybe-drunk teen in a room full of very-much-drunk teens. The house was large and crowded, and the air was filled with booming music I'd never heard before.

To be fair, I should've expected this; it was a house show, after all. But it wasn't just *any* show. It was one for Williams School of the Arts's own up-and-coming punk rock band, Deck of Fools—aka, Nathan's best friends, and Tanya's and my new friends by association. They were somewhat popular at our school for the local, albeit mild, celebrity they'd amassed over the past year from playing a few gigs around Nashville, but I hadn't seen them perform yet. Tonight would be my first time, although it wouldn't be Tanya's. She must have invited me to a dozen Deck of Fools shows over the past few months.

When we finally made it out to the patio, Nathan slid the door shut behind us, and the noise immediately became more bearable.

"I'm gonna check on the band real quick, so I'll see you two in a few," Nathan said, giving us one last dazzling smile.

We waved our goodbyes, and then watched him walk over to the group of people trying to set up equipment for the show. Their "stage" was a black tarp on the ground, a handful of amps and speakers, a drum kit, and a mic on a stand. A safe distance away from their makeshift stage was a heated pool, where kids were swimming and drinking and laughing.

Tanya and I found some vinyl patio chairs, and we sat there for a moment, listening to the music bleeding out from inside and the loud chatter from the pool, not saying anything to each other. I leaned back and watched the people around me, bodies moving through the water, a small group in the corner passing around a joint, smoke curling into the sky. All the patio lights were turned on, and the whole area was covered in a fluorescent haze.

Tanya laid a hand on my arm gently. "I think I saw some pizza in the kitchen. Want me to get you a slice if there's any left?"

"Yes, please."

She smiled and rose from her seat. "Back in a sec."

While she went inside, I crossed my arms, then uncrossed them, then checked my phone even though I knew I didn't have any notifications. I couldn't get comfortable. No matter how I sat or what I was doing, my body felt wrong. Out of place. We'd only been here for twenty minutes and I already wanted to go home.

There had been a time when I was able to do this—be with people. My sophomore year, I went to parties with Tanya whenever she asked, with only mild discomfort. I talked to friends-of-friends, like Nathan, with relative ease; every now and then, I even drank a few beers or smoked weed with Tanya and whatever acquaintances were offering; I sat in the corner without feeling like I was going to crawl out of my skin. I used to be able to *do* parties. But it seemed like I just couldn't anymore.

A loud, shrieking laugh pulled my attention back to the pool, where a girl was slung over a guy's shoulder.

"I swear to God, if you—"

"In you go!"

She was flung into the water, scream-laughing all the way, and the resulting splash just barely missed my feet. The guy high-fived one of his friends before jumping in, too.

I couldn't help it; I was irritated by them. Maybe it was petty, but I resented them for having fun, for being loud, for not sharing my discomfort and anger and sadness.

I didn't want to feel this way. I wanted to disappear into a version of myself that could forget everything that had happened in the past five months—forget Jack's death, forget the cat-creature I'd been seeing, forget it *all*.

But I couldn't.

After the first sighting on the porch, I began noticing that black, faceless cat everywhere, until one day, only a week after Jack's death, I realized he was following me. He (or she? It was unclear) wasn't much more than a dark feline form, a smear in the corner of my eye, but I knew he wasn't going to leave me alone.

The first time he appeared in my room, it was in the middle of the night while I was trying to fall asleep. It was pitch black, no moonlight filtering in through my curtains, so if it hadn't been for the sudden drop in temperature and the prickling feeling at the back of my neck, I probably wouldn't have noticed something was wrong at all. But as it was, I blinked my eyes open, and there, on my windowsill, was the faint silhouette of the cat.

Panic bubbled in my throat, but I just stared at him, staying completely still, like I was paralyzed by his presence.

I lay like that for what felt like hours before I eventually fell asleep from exhaustion, and even though he wasn't there when I woke up the next morning, I knew right away that it was real. There was no way it could have been a dream.

After that, I named him Ghost. That was what he had become to me—a haunting.

His visits became more frequent, more startling, more intense. At first, he'd only visit me when I was alone, but slowly, he started popping up when I was with my parents or friends or out in public. Tanya and I would be hanging out, talking about something innocuous, and I'd look around for just a second, and suddenly Ghost was there on the other side of the room, sitting back on his haunches as if to watch us.

No one else could see him. No one ever mentioned a black cat following me around, let alone a faceless one. I was completely alone in seeing Ghost.

The summer passed me in a haze, the days somehow both dripping by like syrup and steamrolling over me so that I woke up on the first day of junior year wondering where all that time had gone. My days were a blur of sleeping in until late afternoon and avoiding as much contact with my family or friends as I could.

Tanya and I went to the same arts school in Nashville—Williams School of the Arts. Some days, Ghost sat in on classes with me. Other times, I managed to go entire school days without seeing him, and then I'd get in my car to go home, and he would be in the back seat, lying down comfortably.

Even as I tried to anticipate when and where he would show up, I never got comfortable seeing him appear somewhere in public. It always derailed the rest of the day. It didn't matter how well anything else was going; the moment I saw that smudge of black in the corner of my eye or felt that prickle at my neck, I knew my day was going to be ruined.

And here, at this party, I knew Ghost would make an appearance. I hadn't felt his presence yet—usually, I could anticipate when he would show up, my body somehow sensing he was nearby—but it was just a matter of time. It always was.

I tried to go back to fiddling with my phone, hoping I looked more comfortable than I felt, when a plate of pizza was set in front of me.

"Nathan said Deck of Fools should be starting in a few

minutes," Tanya said, sitting down next to me, already digging into her slice.

I nodded and picked up my pizza. She'd gotten me two pieces, one pepperoni and one cheese, just how she knew I liked. "Thank you," I said.

"No problem." She took a sip from a red Solo cup, no doubt filled with jungle juice. I kind of wished I could get my own drink—*maybe it could help calm me down*, I thought—but I was our driver for the night.

Things were quiet between us for a moment. Tonight, Tanya was dressed in an orange romper, her eyeliner thick and sharp. Physically, the two of us couldn't have been more different: Tanya, tall and skinny, her black hair thick and shining, her brown eyes only a few shades deeper than her skin; me, short and round, with dirt-blond hair and brown eyes, my pale skin covered in freckles and acne scars.

I wiped my hands on a napkin and asked, "So, what should I expect for tonight?"

"In terms of music?"

I nodded, and she *hmm'd* as she thought about it. "Well, sometimes they do a cover or two, but I think it'll probably be mostly their stuff, since this is for their anniversary."

"You said they have an EP out or something?" I asked it casually, but I could admit there was a part of me that was . . . well, jealous. I hoped to record and release my own music someday, but I wasn't sure how or where to start.

"Yeah. I think they're working on their second one right now, though."

Tanya looked toward the stage, so I followed her eyes to see

Nathan talking to Emmett—another of Tanya's new friends and the lead singer of Deck of Fools. Emmett and I were both in the music conservatory at WSA and in the same Intro to Songwriting class, along with sitting at the same table at lunch.

I sat with Tanya and her friends every day at school, but I didn't say much most days. Her friends were nice, but I wasn't close with them the way I was with Tanya. And I was sure they didn't feel particularly close with me, either. We were more like friendly acquaintances.

On the stage, Nathan passed Emmett a black electric guitar, and they grinned widely as they took it, saying something I couldn't make out as they plugged it into the amp. Emmett was white, androgynous, and almost as tall as Nathan. Their bleached blond hair was shoulder-length with dark brown roots grown out, almost as if they'd bleached it once years ago but gave up after that, and they wore ripped black skinny jeans, a gray tank top, and lots of silver jewelry.

The amp buzzed before they strummed a few experimental chords. At the noise, the people smoking in the corner turned their attention toward the stage, and into the now-working mic, Emmett said, "How's everyone doing tonight? Y'all enjoying the party?"

From the pool, the guy who'd thrown that girl in earlier shouted his agreement.

"Yes! That's what I wanna hear!" Emmett laughed and ran a hand through their hair. I wondered if they were nervous at all, or if they were really as laid-back as they looked. I wondered how many shows like this they'd done. "Welcome to the one-year anniversary show for Deck of Fools!"

The crowd cheered. Other people were starting to trickle out from inside the house, finally catching on that the show was beginning.

"If you don't already know us, I'm Emmett—"

A pause for cheers. Tanya cupped her hands around her mouth and hollered her support.

"Logan is on bass—"

Another pause for cheering while Emmett gestured to their right. Logan was a Chinese American boy with a dark undercut, big in both size and stature, and he held a blue bass guitar. He waved for the crowd.

"—and Dima is our badass drummer!"

In the back, Dima—a small Lebanese American girl with wavy brown hair cut in a choppy bob—sat behind a large drum set. She offered her own wave.

I glanced at my phone as the cheering died down: 9:13 p.m.

"Tonight, we're celebrating the formation of the world's greatest up-and-coming punk rock band," Emmett said, flashing a grin, "which, as I'm sure you all know, is us. This first song is something we wrote when we first got together, so without further ado, here's 'I Don't Forgive You.'"

Dima counted them off, and they jumped into it. Tanya watched with her lips turned up in a smile as the music played. I sat back in my chair and ate the rest of my pizza.

The band was pretty good. Emmett sang in that voice that almost all punk or emo artists seemed to have—that half-shout, half-sing, almost-whine-but-not-quite thing—and they stomped their feet too much while they played. They were way more into it than anyone in the audience was, but the melodies were catchy, and the lyrics were interesting. Plus, Emmett wasn't, you know, *bad* to look at, so . . . At the very least, there was that.

After their second song faded out, they launched into a spiel about the journey Deck of Fools had been through so far and how excited they were to keep playing, et cetera, et cetera. I turned my attention to the crowd, pulling my knees up to my chest, heels resting against the edge of my chair.

There were a decent number of people still in the pool, but a lot of them had gotten out to dry off or sit on the pool steps as they listened, beer bottles or red Solo cups in hand. When the third song started, this time a cover of "Wonderwall" (I couldn't tell if the choice was meant to be ironic or sincere or some combination of the two), the crowd sang along loudly.

The group in the corner was still smoking, passing around what must have been their second or third joint by then, and the thick smoke curled around them, lingering in the air. I could smell the weed from here, intense and pungent. The smoke kept accumulating, and the shadows from the patio lights threw everything into half darkness.

As the joint was passed between hands, I stared at the red burning, the small ember in the crowd of bodies, and I had a flash of memory—an image of Jack sneaking home late at night, his messy steps up the staircase, his bloodshot eyes.

The back of my neck prickled, and I felt, suddenly, like I was being watched.

I looked behind me, and just as I expected, there he

was—Ghost, sitting at the archway that led from the patio out to the packed driveway, the creature I couldn't escape from. He was perched at the feet of strangers, his black paws resting in front of him, his twitching tail somehow avoiding contact with anyone even as people drunkenly swayed to the music.

Emmett sang about blinding lights and winding roads and Ghost's dark frame flickered, and I felt my whole body convulse with a sudden intense heat until my chest was constricting and there was only the creature—only Ghost—and the bass of the song, and the heavy smell of smoke, and that red burning down, and somewhere distantly, Emmett's voice and Tanya singing along.

Panic built.

I needed to get out of there.

I stood without telling myself to stand, pushed through the crowd and out into the driveway and away from all the noise, and plopped down in the damp grass, my head in my hands.

The panic rolled over me, my hands shaking, and no matter how tightly I shut my eyes, I couldn't stop the flashes of images—Jack's slurred speech, his body in the casket—and I let the tears fall, let the tremors move through me, my heartbeat thumping in my ears, my breaths ragged.

When the anxiety attack was finally finished with me, I was exhausted, as if all the energy had been sapped out of me. I looked up; Ghost was sitting only a few feet away. He had followed me out here.

"Of course you did," I mumbled. There really was no escaping him.

Tanya found me sitting out in the driveway a few minutes later.

"What happened?" she asked, a hand already on my shoulder. I could still hear Deck of Fools playing, the world moving on around me.

"Nothing," I said. "I just . . . I don't feel good."

She frowned, then glanced around us before turning back to me. "Was it . . . Ghost?"

I paused, then nodded. Tanya knew about Ghost. She was the only person I'd ever told about him. Even my parents didn't know.

She bit her lip. I could already tell she was about to start blaming herself for asking me to come tonight. I knew what she was thinking: *I shouldn't have made you do this. I should've known that it wouldn't be okay. I should've known that you weren't in the headspace for it.*

But I had *wanted* to do this. I had thought I was ready for things like this again. I had thought that Ghost's presence wouldn't bother me this much. I had thought I would be okay.

"It's fine. He's gone now anyway," I lied. "I'll just stay out in the car and rest until you're ready to go." I'd driven us here in my car, a hand-me-down from my dad. Tanya, who was a grade below me, had turned sixteen in October, but she didn't have her license yet.

"Caleb—"

"I don't want you to miss the show."

"I'm not gonna make you sit in the car while you're feeling bad just to listen to the band," she said. "It's okay. I'll tell

Nathan that we had to leave early. It's not a big deal."

But it *was* a big deal, because I always managed to mess up her plans, because this was the millionth time I'd kept her from enjoying herself, because this wasn't the first time I'd been the reason she left early from something, this wasn't the first time I'd let Ghost get in the way of my life, or even Tanya's life, because my brother was dead, because I was seeing this thing no one else could see, because I was the world's most fucked-up person—

But I knew if I said that, she'd just keep insisting. Her mind was made up. I couldn't convince her of anything else now.

"All right," I said finally.

She went back to let Nathan know we were leaving. While she was gone, I sat there, feeling someone—something—staring at me. That faceless gaze. The judgment.

I kept my eyes on the ground.

3

WHEN I GOT HOME, MOM was in the living room watching a late-night talk show. Dad must have already been in their room asleep.

She turned the volume down when she heard me enter. "Hey, honey. How was the show?"

I'd told her about the Deck of Fools show, not because she was particularly strict or wanted to know everything I was up to—but because I wanted her to worry about me a little less. I wanted her to know I was doing better. Healing. Returning to "normal."

That was one thing I was slowly realizing I kind of hated, though: the idea of "getting back to normal." We would never return to life before Jack died—we couldn't. But it felt like no one around me really understood that. Or at least like they didn't want to acknowledge it.

"Fine," I said. "The band was pretty good."

Mom nodded, and after a moment, I just stood there, watching the TV over her shoulder. The talk show host cracked a few jokes about the state of the economy, and the audience laughed in agreement. For some reason, I thought about those kids in the pool at the show tonight, and I was suddenly irritated by the man on the TV, his canned smile, the studio laughter.

It seemed like everything was grating to me these days. The smallest things could set me off.

"I'm gonna head to bed," I said, shuffling toward the stairs.

"All right. Love you. Get some sleep."

"Love you, too."

In my room, I wriggled out of my binder, threw on some pajamas, and curled up in bed, wrapping myself in my comforter with all the lights turned off.

I got out my laptop and searched through Netflix for a horror movie to watch. I wanted to erase the night's events from my head for a while, replace them with something theatrical and scary, something with blood and guts and tears, something even worse than what I was going through.

I turned on *Scream*, one of my all-time favorite movies, but I couldn't focus on it. My mind would inevitably wander back to the show: Emmett's grin under the patio lights. Tanya's voice over the crowd's chatter. The glowing ember of the joint.

Ghost.

I was barely past the iconic opening with Drew Barrymore's character before I paused the movie, frustrated, and checked my phone. I had one new message.

Tanya

thanks for coming with me tonight! how r u feeling?

Sent five minutes ago.

Caleb

fine. just tired

Tanya

i'm sorry for making u go. i shouldnt have pushed u

Caleb

its okay. you didnt MAKE me go. i wanted to

and im glad i did. i had fun

She sent a heart emoji—the pink one with the sparkles. It was her favorite.

The two of us had always been close. Tanya's parents, both from India, moved to the US right after she was born. My parents were some of her parents' first close friends, so we basically grew up together. I knew her before she was this cool, tall, beautiful girl who got invited to parties by cute guys. I knew kid Tanya and preteen Tanya and every other iteration of Tanya there had ever been, all the good with the bad, the fascinating and beautiful along with the ugly and embarrassing—and she knew me, too.

Three years ago, when I was in eighth grade and she was in seventh, we both realized we were trans within a few months of each other. I thought it was fitting, almost poetic, that we got to go through our transitions together; somehow, it just made *sense.* And there was something special about having each other's backs through that, about having my best friend right there with me the whole time. We were never alone through it all.

All of our parents were supportive, thankfully, although mine were slower to accept me than hers were. Some people seemed surprised when they found that out. They assumed that, since Tanya's parents were Indian, they would automatically be less accepting than my white parents. In reality, it was Mr. and Mrs. Gupta who were there for me when my mom and dad didn't yet understand how to support me.

Being so close our whole lives, and then supporting each other through our transitions on top of that, meant that we'd opened up to each other about everything. I hadn't waited long to tell her about Ghost.

I locked my phone and set it on my bedside table. When I turned back around, Ghost was sitting at the foot of my bed.

"What do you want?" I snapped. Like usual, he didn't respond. I didn't think he could talk, but sometimes I got the feeling that he understood what I was saying.

Ghost got up, stretched, and jumped down from my bed. I didn't hear it, but I thought I could feel his weight leaving. I wasn't sure if he had mass, if he was tangible or just a specter. I didn't think he'd ever touched me, and sometimes it looked like he just passed through the world like his namesake.

Other times, though, I could feel how he interacted with the space, when he jumped on my desk and managed to just barely crumple a sheet of notebook paper, when he gently batted a sock around my bedroom floor, when he settled on my windowsill and gazed out across the backyard. Sometimes, he would sit in my bedroom as I did homework, lounging on the carpet as if everything was fine and his presence was normal. It was times like those that I forgot he wasn't just a stray who took a liking to me.

But then he would do something else: disappear from my vision, reappear in the corner of my eye, show up around school, find a space for himself wherever I went, no matter what.

Sometimes his body would become fuzzy, weird, and I couldn't look at him for too long, otherwise it would start to feel like I was watching something I shouldn't be, and then there would be a gap in my memory and time would slip away and Ghost wouldn't be there anymore when I returned to myself, and all that was left was a pounding in my head.

That was when I would remember I didn't just have an ordinary animal following me around. That was when I remembered that Ghost was more creature than cat.

In songwriting class on Monday, our teacher, Mr. Russak, announced that our final would be a six-week-long project where we'd have to cowrite and record at least four songs with a partner, and I knew immediately that I was fucked.

Guitar and songwriting classes were what I was most excited for when I decided to audition for Williams School of the Arts. I'd been playing guitar since I was ten, banjo since I was twelve, and writing songs since I could remember—but before coming here, everything I knew about music was entirely self-taught. I was excited to learn from an actual teacher, to become a better musician, to write better songs.

And for the first two years here, I was doing good, improving. I wasn't a prodigy, but I kept at it, practicing consistently, and I had steady As and Bs in almost all my classes.

But that was before Jack died.

These days, I hadn't written a new song in months. Every Friday in this class, we had a song due, and I managed to get by all of August and September turning in old ones that I'd written in my freshman and sophomore years. But the backlog had ran out, and now I was far behind. I couldn't even write *one* song by myself; how was I going to manage writing *four* with someone else?

He gave the class five minutes to figure out our partners, but I stayed in my seat, staring at my notebook and trying to avoid eye contact with anyone as the people around me migrated to their friends. Emmett was in this class, but I didn't move to ask them to work with me. They probably had someone else they would rather partner with, I figured.

I felt a prickle at the back of my neck, and when I looked up, I saw Ghost on the other side of the room, sitting under someone's desk. After a second, I realized it was Emmett's, and that they hadn't gotten up to find a partner, either—instead, they just sat there, scribbling something on a sheet of paper. They were completely oblivious to Ghost's presence.

I stared at Ghost wide-eyed, trying to will him to go away. He didn't move.

"Caleb?"

I jumped at Mr. Russak's voice. "Jesus—um, I mean, yes, sir?"

He chuckled a little. Mr. Russak was in his early forties, his brown beard just starting to show gray. He was a songwriter and a guitarist, and taught classes on both. He definitely wasn't the worst teacher I'd had, and he never called my deadname while taking attendance, which was much better than some of my other teachers.

Even though I had been out as a trans boy for my entire time at WSA, I wouldn't be able to change my legal name for a while, so I still had to let all my teachers know at the beginning of the year that they should avoid saying my legal name during roll call. Some teachers remembered and respected my request, like Mr. Russak. Others seemed to forget frustratingly often.

"Sorry to sneak up on you," he said. "Are you having trouble finding a partner?"

I glanced back at Ghost. He had lain down, his chin resting on his inky paws, and, a moment too late, I realized that Mr. Russak had followed my line of sight to Emmett.

"You know, Caleb, if you want to work with Emmett, I'm sure they wouldn't mind," he said. "They don't seem to have found a partner yet, either."

"Oh no, Mr. Russak, that's okay—"

But I was too late; he got up and headed over to Emmett's desk. Ghost still sat there, refusing to move even as Mr. Russak approached. I watched as he said something to Emmett, and when Emmett's eyes flickered over and briefly met mine, I quickly looked away, hoping my face wasn't as red as it felt. *Shit.*

I was still actively refusing to look their way when Mr. Russak came back, a satisfied smile on his face like he'd done me a great favor. He tapped my desk twice. "Why don't you go and join Emmett?"

I nodded and started gathering my things. Only then did he leave my desk to talk with another pair about their project.

Ghost was still sitting under the desk when I looked over, and this time, I didn't avert my eyes quick enough to avoid meeting Emmett's. They offered a smile, but it seemed a little uncomfortable, maybe even forced. I doubted they actually wanted to work with me on this; Emmett probably only agreed because they felt obligated.

I sighed and headed over to their desk.

When I got home from school that afternoon, Mom was crying in the living room, Dad holding her.

"I've got you," I heard him say, rocking her as her tears kept coming. "Shh . . . I know . . . I've got you."

For a moment, I stood in the doorway, listening to my mom's quiet grieving. Sometimes I had dreams about her crying—the loud, shaking sobs she would let out those first few weeks after Jack's death. It was the only sound I'd never been able to get out of my head. I had a feeling I would remember it for the rest of my life.

I slid past my parents and up the stairs to my room, trying to go by unnoticed. When things like this happened, I always ended up feeling useless and inadequate, unsure how to give comfort. A month ago, the sight of them breaking down would've made me burst into tears, too, and join them on the couch. But I just didn't know what to do anymore.

I cried constantly the first few months after Jack died. Up until the three-month mark, it felt like there was a blanket of despair covering everything, and I couldn't go a day without tearing up. Then, something changed, and I got angry instead. It wasn't like I hadn't felt *any* anger about Jack's death before this—but it had been buried under sadness and confusion and just trying to find my footing again.

Now it was like I'd started poking my head out of that despair, and what I found instead was raw anger and frustration and a low, constant thrum of hurt. I felt prickly and exposed all the time. Everything seemed to set me on edge.

It was early November. Soon, it would be six months since my brother died. Six months since Ghost first appeared. Six months since everything in my life had fallen apart.

In my room, I quietly closed the door and tossed my backpack on the floor before changing from my school clothes into an oversize T-shirt and sweatpants. I left my binder on, even though I was getting close to having it on for the recommended maximum of eight hours. If I was worried about binding safely and not accidentally hurting myself, I should've changed out of it and given my lungs and ribs a break. But to be honest, I usually wore my binder for way longer than I was supposed to.

Tanya often fussed at me about it, and in return, I fussed at her for tucking for too long, and too frequently. But neither of us really listened most of the time. I think, for us, it felt worth the physical risk if it meant we had a few more hours of comfort in our bodies each day.

My phone buzzed, and I flopped down on my bed before seeing it was a text from Emmett. We already had each other's numbers from the group chat that Tanya had made between us, her, Nathan, Logan, and Dima—but this was the first time Emmett and I had texted one-on-one.

Emmett

hey caleb, it's emmett!

i know we didn't have much time to talk about it in class, but have you thought any more about what to do for our project?

Caleb

not really. you?

Emmett

idk, kind of

i came up with a few ideas but i dont know if theyre any good lol

Caleb

better than no ideas at all

Emmett

lol fair

well i was thinking that, since we have to do at least 4

songs, we could have them relate to each other in some way
like maybe they all have the same themes or they tell a story
or they represent a group of 4 (like seasons, elements, etc)

Caleb
i like the idea of having them relate in some way
so maybe we should come up with themes/groups of 4 that we could do and decide from there

Emmett
sounds good :) i'll start brainstorming!

I wasn't sure what to say after that, so I just "liked" the message. I locked my phone and lay back on the bed, staring at the ceiling.

There was a knock at my door, and my dad appeared. "Hey, kiddo."

I sat up. "Uh, hey. What's up?"

His glasses had slid down his nose, and he pushed them up now. Jack had been almost a carbon copy of Dad, with the same blue eyes, long face, and pointed nose. It was hard, sometimes, seeing Dad these days, because the resemblance was so close. Sometimes I looked at him and just saw the outline of Jack.

If I was honest, I had been sort of avoiding my parents the past couple of months. I wasn't sure why, except that every time I talked to them for longer than a few minutes, we always found a way to return the conversation to Jack. And I got it—I knew that they were grieving, too, I knew they just wanted to keep his memory alive—but I thought about Jack so much already that I just wanted one place where I *didn't* have to think about him.

So, it felt easier, sometimes, to just . . . not talk to them. To stay in my room all day. To come home late enough that they were already heading to bed.

"Just wanted to see how your day at school was," he said. He pushed the door a little farther open but didn't move into the room.

"Fine," I said. "It was . . . you know. School."

He nodded. "Did you learn anything interesting?"

"Not really."

I saw the way he deflated, and I realized I was shooting him down. Leaving no room for an actual conversation.

I felt guilty, but I also didn't know what else to say. I didn't want to talk about the songwriting project; I didn't want to talk about Ghost following Emmett around and distracting me during class; and I definitely didn't want to talk about the moment Mom and Dad were having when I got home. So, I was at a loss.

"Was there something you wanted to talk about?" I asked instead.

"Yeah, actually." He shifted his weight from one foot to the other—a nervous habit that I remembered Jack also having. "Mom and I were thinking . . . well, you haven't been to group in a few months, and they're having a meeting this Wednesday, so we were thinking maybe it would be nice for you to go?"

Back in August, my parents found a support group for teens dealing with loss and convinced me to attend. It was run by a therapist named Tom, and the group met twice a month. It was . . . okay, sort of. Tom was nice. But I'd skipped September's and October's meetings.

"It's up to you," Dad continued when I didn't say anything. "We just thought it might be helpful. Maybe it would be good to hear from other kids your age who are going through something similar. . . ."

I wondered how much he wasn't saying, what had led him and Mom to even think about this in the first place. I'd been trying to not make my parents worry about me, pretending like I was fine, like things were normal, like I was coping and functioning and at least *relatively* okay.

But if they wanted me to go again, then maybe I was worse at convincing them than I thought.

"I'll think about it," I told him.

He smiled, one of those close-lipped, slightly uncomfortable smiles, and nodded. "All right. Sounds good. Just let us know what you decide to do."

"Okay, I will."

He left, closing the door behind him, and I heard his footsteps retreating as he went back downstairs. I wondered if I should have said something about him and Mom. If I should have asked if they were all right.

I lay back down, staring again at the ceiling, and felt a gentle pressure next to me; Ghost had decided to make an appearance again.

After the incident in songwriting, he had left me alone for

most of the day. A part of me wished he would stay around all the time instead of disappearing in and out of existence (or whatever it was he did). At least when he was around consistently, I knew to expect him. I just didn't like surprises.

Once, a few years ago, Tanya and I were bored at a sleepover and playing Would You Rather, and she asked me if I would rather experience one huge instance of pain once in my life but never have to feel any ever again, or a small amount of pain every single day forever. At the time, I chose the first option. I thought it seemed easier.

But I knew better now. No huge pain was ever just once. A pain like that—a pain that size—would stay with you long after you thought it was gone. It would linger. Maybe even for the rest of your life.

4

WHEN JACK AND I WERE little, we used to make home movies. For Christmas one year, our grandparents bought Jack this old, vintage camcorder—nothing too expensive or huge, but he loved it, and after that, he and that camera were inseparable. He recorded everything; you couldn't even eat breakfast without Jack pulling out his camera and trying to film you. If you covered the lens with your hand like you were shooing away paparazzi, it just made him want to keep filming even more.

But he didn't record everything *just* to record everything. He wanted to make films. He'd write out these scripts and barge into my room with his camera held high and demand to use my Barbie dolls for one of the scenes. He did this enough times that I think, eventually, he just decided it made more sense if I helped him from the beginning. Or maybe Mom and Dad asked him to let me in on his projects, to make me feel included. I was always trying to tag along with him and his friends when they came over. Jack was five years older and four grades ahead of me, and I didn't even really like his friends all that much—they teased me in ways that Jack never did, and when he was around them, he was meaner, more willing to pick on me—but, still, I didn't want to be left out.

I must've been around seven years old when Jack actually started hanging out with me. I was never sure what changed that year—maybe I was just grown enough to not be *as* painfully annoying to him and his twelve-year-old friends?—but suddenly, we were getting along more. We spent Saturday mornings taping bedsheets to his bedroom wall as our backdrop and angling the camera just so, and it didn't seem to matter to him how many times we messed up our lines. We had fun. God, we made so many videos. None of them were any good, but it wasn't about that.

In the weeks following Jack's death, Dad dug up all the old home movies he could find. Some of them were so old they were on videocassette tapes and had to be played on our somehow-still-functioning VHS player, while the rest had been excavated from the files on our old desktop computer. He asked Mom and me if we wanted to watch them with him, and I agreed.

I didn't really *want* to watch them, if I was honest with myself—but my dad had looked so hopeful, had seemed so happy about the idea of sitting down and watching old home videos and reliving better memories together as a family, that I didn't feel like I could say no.

One Saturday in early July, we sat down in the living room and hooked my dad's computer up to the TV. We scrolled through file after file, eventually settling on one titled "Christmas with the Stones 2005"—this was from before I was born, and when Jack was only two. I watched tiny Jack on the screen toddling around, carrying a toy monkey. Behind the camera, Mom cooed at him, asking what he was up to.

It was strange watching a version of my brother so foreign to me, but it didn't move me to tears yet. It was only when I heard my dad sniffling and looked over to see my mom wiping tears away that I realized how much it was impacting my parents. That was when my own tears came, but I tried to bite them back.

I sat quietly through the rest of the video. It was only twenty minutes long.

"I think . . ." my dad said, once the video had stopped. "I think that's enough for tonight. Don't you?" He turned to Mom and me, offering us a painful, watery smile.

I wasn't sure why, but I suddenly hated *everything*—these old videos for upsetting my parents, myself for not knowing how to comfort them, my dad for wanting to watch them in the first place, my brother for dying.

I hated these feelings. I hated the hole that had opened up in my chest, I hated the ghost that was haunting me, I hated that I hated anything at all.

"I'm . . . I'm tired. I think I'm gonna go to bed," I said, standing abruptly. I couldn't be there anymore. I just couldn't.

As I ran back up to my room, I could still hear my mom sniffling on the couch and my dad's attempts to comfort her.

"Caleb, can I talk with you after class?" Mr. Russak asked on Tuesday morning. His expression was neutral, which meant something was definitely wrong.

When the bell rang, I waited until the other students had mostly filtered out before going over to his desk. It was covered in trinkets—a glass figurine guitar, a tiny model boat, a rock with Mr. R painted on it. I focused on them as he spoke.

"So, Caleb . . ." he started, sitting forward in his chair. "How've you been?"

I shrugged. "Fine, I guess."

"And . . . your family?"

I knew what he meant, but there was nothing I would've rather talked about *less*. I kept my eyes on the model boat, its sails tiny and bright white. "They're fine." A standard, safe, undeniable answer.

He sighed softly. "Listen . . . I know things haven't been easy for you this year. . . ."

This again. I was sick of this speech, this sympathy dance people felt the need to do. It was like no one could go longer than two seconds without reminding me that Jack was dead. I stared at the boat and counted the number of sails. Fifteen.

". . . but we're coming up on the end of the semester, and you're pretty far behind in the class. At this rate, I don't know if you're going to pass."

I wasn't sure how I felt about that. I had known my grades were bad. I hadn't been doing any homework, after all; of *course* I was failing. It shouldn't have been a surprise.

But . . . I guess I'd thought I had time. I thought I could fix it.

"Is there no way for me to make it up in time?" I mumbled, avoiding his eyes.

He sighed again. "It's possible. I'd be willing to accept some of your missing assignments, but you'd get points off for being late. You'd also need to stay on top of the work we're currently doing, so it wouldn't be easy. . . . You're only a junior, so if you fail the class, you can take it again next year, but it won't look great on your college applications, and I'm sure you don't want any added stress with applying. . . ."

In truth, I hadn't even thought about college yet. I took the ACT in October, and I'd gotten okay-ish scores, which was better than I'd expected considering I hadn't really prepared for it at all. But beyond that, I hadn't given it any thought.

"That being said," Mr. Russak continued, "I'm not your advisor, so it's not up to me. But as of right now, you're failing; no matter what, something needs to change."

I nodded, but I didn't say anything.

"I was at your audition, you know," he said.

I remembered him there, back at the end of eighth grade, when I first came to Williams to audition for the music conservatory. Mr. Russak and two other teachers in the department watched me perform a song I'd written onstage in the auditorium, and I still remembered how it felt under the bright, warm lights.

It was the first time I'd ever performed one of my own songs, and I had been nauseous with nerves. The school felt like a dream back then, or like something from a movie, with its colorful murals and eclectic sculptures decorating every hallway, dancers practicing in leotards and theater students hauling props to and from the studio—it was everything I'd ever dreamed of. Everything I'd ever wanted. And I'd wanted it *so badly* standing on that stage, blinking against the spotlight. I would've done anything to get in.

"You're talented, Caleb," Mr. Russak continued. "I mean that. But talent can only get you so far if you refuse to do any of the work."

Refuse. The word rang in my ears.

"I understand," I said, staring at my hands in my lap. "I'm gonna fix my grade, I promise."

There was a pause. For a moment, I thought he was going to say something else, but he excused me to my next class. I left quickly, not looking back as the door slammed behind me.

Refuse. Refuse. *Refuse.*

Had I been *refusing* to do my songwriting homework?

I didn't know. I didn't think so, at least. It wasn't like I sat down every day, stared at my assignments, and thought, *I refuse to do this.* It wasn't like I thought, *I don't want to, so I won't.* It never felt like *won't* to me. It felt like *can't.*

When I sat in my room, guitar or banjo in my lap, and tried to find a chord progression, tried to find a melody, I just . . . couldn't. I felt disconnected from myself. These days, it felt wrong to play anything. My parents would be in their rooms, or downstairs, or just getting back from work, and I would be in my room with my guitar, while Jack's room sat empty next to mine, untouched, door closed—and it felt *wrong.*

Other times, I would sit down to do my work, and I couldn't get my body to move. I would think, *I should do this homework, I* need *to do this homework*, and try to will myself to move, but I was stuck, like my limbs wouldn't listen to me anymore, like my body wasn't mine.

Maybe to other people this looked like refusing. Maybe it

was refusing. Maybe I just needed to get my shit together. I wasn't sure.

All I knew was that there was no joy in it anymore.

"Some days are . . . harder than others," said Candi, a girl a year older than me with bleached blond hair. Tom's office included two couches across from each other and three chairs, all arranged in a circle, and Candi sat across from me on a couch, picking at her nails. It was Wednesday night.

Not including Tom, the group consisted of six people: me, Candi, a boy named Raúl, a girl named Katherine, a boy named Garrett, and a genderqueer person named Jewel. I was thankful to not be the only trans person in the room, even though I barely knew Jewel.

I barely knew any of them, honestly. I remembered a little bit from the last meeting I went to—I knew Candi had lost her mother about a year ago, and Garrett was a sophomore at Hume-Fogg, a public school in Nashville. But other than that, they were all strangers to me. I thought I remembered a few different people attending the last time I was here, but I guessed the roster changed sometimes.

"I know that sounds so obvious," Candi continued, still looking down at her nails. "Of course some days are better or worse than others, right? But I never realized before just *how* hard it can get. . . . And how suddenly it comes up. . . ."

Tom nodded. He had a clipboard in his lap, but he hadn't written anything down since the beginning of the meeting. "How suddenly *what* can come up? What specifically, I mean?"

Candi glanced up, casting her eyes around the room for a

second, before she looked back down. "Everything, I guess. Sometimes I'll just be talking with my friends completely normally, just going about my day, and it's like, all of a sudden, I remember that my mom is dead, and it feels like I'm losing her all over again, and my day is just . . . ruined."

"I know what you mean," Raúl said quietly. He was short, only a few inches taller than my five foot one, and his dark hair was styled in a buzz cut.

Tom looked around the room. "I think all of us in here know what you mean," he said. His eyes landed on me, and he subtly raised his eyebrows, as if to ask if I wanted to speak.

I stuck my hands under my thighs to keep them warm. It wasn't the November cold that was chilling me—it was Ghost's presence, his dark form lying on the rug, right in the middle of the circle. He'd shown up as I pulled into the parking lot, and he'd trotted alongside me into the building, never falling out of step with me. It was like he knew exactly what I was doing, exactly where I was going.

To Tom's look, I didn't say anything.

"It feels . . . weird, sometimes, that I almost seem to forget," Candi said. "And then when I realize that's what's happened, I feel like a horrible person for just being able to forget that she's gone."

"I wish I *could* forget," Garrett said, his voice scratchy. "I would give anything to not have to think about it every fucking moment of every fucking day."

Candi opened her mouth, then closed it again, and even I could sense how she deflated a little. Tom laced his hands together.

"To your statement, Candi," Tom said, "you aren't a bad person for being able to take your mind off of your pain. Everyone deserves moments of peace, even when things are tough. And Garrett, it makes sense that you want a break from constant grieving."

"It's not even that it's constant grieving," Garrett said. "I'm not always breaking down or anything. But it's like—no matter what I do, it's always *there*."

I looked at Ghost on the floor in front of me. "Like something's always following you," I mumbled.

There was a pause. I wondered if anyone was surprised that I'd spoken. Other than the introductions at the beginning, I hadn't said anything the entire meeting.

"Would you like to elaborate on that?" Tom prompted.

"I just mean . . . for me, it feels like I have this . . . thing . . . following me." I shifted in my seat. "Sometimes—or most of the time—it feels like I can't escape it. No matter what I do or where I am or who I'm with, somehow, the fact that my brother's dead is just *there*. And it's like it takes up so much space in the room that . . . that I can't see or think about anything else."

Garrett nodded, his eyebrows furrowed. "Yeah. It's like that for me, too."

"I felt that way the first few months," Jewel said. "Now I can have some days where it's not on my mind, but . . . I don't know what made that feeling stop. If it was just time, or . . . something else. . . ." They shrugged. "These days, it's mostly when I'm asleep that I can't get away from it. I have dreams about my dad dying constantly."

Candi looked at Jewel. "Me too. . . . I . . . I have these horrible nightmares almost every night about my mom. In them, she's always asking me to help her, begging me to figure out a way to bring her back to life, and . . . I know that it doesn't mean anything, I know that it's just a dream, but sometimes when I wake up, I swear it . . ." Her voice cracked at the end. Jewel passed her a tissue box, and she took it gratefully, wiping a tear away. "It feels like she's really there," she finished softly.

I felt a chill go up my spine, and when I looked at Ghost, he'd stood up and walked the few feet over to Candi. He sat down in front of her, but his head was facing me, as if asking me to look in that direction. I frowned at him, but, of course, it did nothing to deter him.

"When we lose someone," Tom said gently, "sometimes our brains can play tricks on us during the grieving process. A lot of people, especially immediately after a loved one's death, report seeing them or feeling their presence."

"But what if it's not a trick?" Candi asked quietly. "What if she actually . . ."

I wasn't sure, but I thought I could guess what the end of that sentence would be: What if Candi's mom actually *was* trying to speak to her through her dreams? What if, when she felt her mom's presence after waking up, it was because her spirit had actually been there? What if there was something more than we could explain going on?

Five months ago, I never would've said I believed in ghosts or spirits or anything else supernatural. I would've bet my life that all of it was complete nonsense. Before, whenever people told me stories about their grandma's haunted attic or the weird experiences they had in an old graveyard, I secretly thought they were exaggerating, making things up for a good story, tricking themselves into belief.

But now . . .

Now I wasn't sure *what* I thought.

After the meeting, we filtered out of Tom's office as a group. I noticed a few people's parents were in the waiting room when we got out, ready to take them home. I lingered behind everyone as we headed down the elevator and toward the parking lot. I could hear Garrett and Raúl discussing basketball, and someone who might've been Katherine's mom asking what she wanted to eat for dinner. Beside me, Ghost trotted along calmly and confidently, as if he were a normal part of this scene, as if his presence made perfect sense.

Once outside, we all separated to go to our cars, but Ghost swerved instead of following me. I frowned as I watched him drift toward Candi, who was getting into her car with no awareness of the cat behind her.

"Ghost," I hissed, trying to keep my voice down. "*What* are you doing?"

He turned his head to me but didn't move, as if in challenge.

"Jesus Christ." I shifted in place anxiously but didn't make a move toward him. Candi got into the driver's seat and the engine roared to life, but Ghost stayed there, as if trying to tell me something.

Was it about Candi? Was he trying to get me over there to

talk to her? Did he just inexplicably decide he liked her? Ghost occasionally took an interest in people other than me. At the party and at school a few times now, Emmett had seemed to be the target of Ghost's interest, and there was a time at the beginning of the school year where Ghost had behaved similarly to a few other people in my classes—a girl in AP Language and Composition who I was pretty sure I'd gone to middle school with, a guy I briefly sat next to in physics before our seats were moved. But other times, he completely ignored people, like they were invisible.

Somehow, in my gut, I felt that Ghost had reasoning—I *knew* there was a purpose to all this, a goal. There *had* to be.

"Come back here," I tried again, waving him over.

He turned his head toward the car, then to me again, before moving in my direction. I thought he was finally going to walk over to me, but the car started backing up, and before I knew it, Ghost had flickered out of existence without a sound.

I huffed. Of course he would cause a commotion and then disappear into thin air. Like any cat, it seemed he was incapable of listening to me.

After that, I was alone as I drove myself home, no Ghost anywhere in sight. But I kept thinking about him, about the eager way that he followed Candi and the intent in his movements when he plopped himself down at Emmett's desk.

There was something going on. I just needed to figure out what.

5

DURING SONGWRITING ON THURSDAY, MR. Russak gave us time at the end of the class to work with our partners on the final project.

"So, uh, I came up with some themes we could use," I said after Emmett sat down across from me, my notebook open.

Emmett pulled out their laptop, and I got a good look at the stickers that almost entirely covered their case. Some were band stickers, including ones for the Mountain Goats and Sorority Noise, but the rest seemed to be things Emmett must have just picked up somehow over the years. One particularly faded sticker read, "I got my ears pierced at Piercing Pagoda!" with a cutesy cartoon bear underneath it. I noticed that Emmett's ears were, in fact, pierced.

"All right." Emmett nodded. "Hit me. What have you got?"

"Well, going with the group of four thing, I was thinking it could be cool to do, like, the four elements, or the four horsemen of the apocalypse. . . ."

From the corner of my eye, I saw a smudge of black. I turned as subtly as I could to catch a glimpse of Ghost, but I didn't see him anywhere.

I cleared my throat and looked back to Emmett, trying to play it off. "I was also thinking that we could try to do more of a story-ish thing, where maybe we write songs based off of folklore or classic narratives."

"I like that idea," Emmett said. "I already like writing songs based off of characters or inspired by stories, so that would be right up my alley."

"All right, so we should do something with that. Now we just need to figure out what story or characters we're doing. . . ."

We rattled off ideas for a little while, but I was still thinking about Ghost. I hadn't seen him at school today, though the back of my neck had started to prickle, and I knew he was around. And then I was thinking about Ghost's presence at the group yesterday, and I thought about all those people also trying to cope with death, and my dad holding my mom as she cried the other day and those home videos that we kept returning to and Jack's body in his casket—

"Does that sound good with you?" Emmett said.

"What?"

They frowned. "Character archetypes? Maybe we go with that theme?"

"Oh!" I could still feel Ghost watching me, but I tried to ignore it. "Um, yeah, that's fine." I looked down. "Sorry. I didn't mean to space out. . . ."

"You're all good." They smiled.

"So, uh, I guess that means we should get started on the

songs," I said. I started writing examples of character archetypes in my notebook, more so I could look like I was doing something than to actually remember them.

We talked for a little longer about what archetypes we'd write songs off of; Emmett mentioned the lover archetype, and I thought of writing about the outlaw character, but I already dreaded having to sit down and write these. I worried that no matter what I wrote, it would turn out shitty and forced.

Emmett didn't seem outwardly thrilled about the project, but they also didn't seem to dislike it, either, and I wondered if they ever dreaded songwriting. If they ever felt like garbage after playing or reading their own music, or if they ever stared at a blank page for hours, unable to think of anything at all.

As the class ended, Ghost came trotting out from underneath Emmett's desk. I stared at him—had he been there the whole time as we talked? He circled around Emmett's legs, somehow avoiding touching them, and finally acknowledged me by coming to my side.

I would never get a day away from him. I'd known that for months now. But sometimes it hit me how I would probably have to live like this for the rest of my life. Every day. Every moment. It felt inevitable that this would just become a part of my normal.

For a second, anger flooded me, and I hated Ghost. I hated him more than I'd ever hated anything. I wanted to tell him to fuck off, leave me alone, stop following me, stop stop *stop*.

But I pushed that down. I couldn't get mad *here*, in the middle of class, so I took a deep breath. The bell rang, and students started filtering out into the hallway.

"See you later," Emmett said.

But I was still thinking about Ghost, and I couldn't help how my frustration slipped through when I mumbled back, "Yeah, see you."

Emmett glanced back at me, but I avoided their eyes. They left without another word, and, thankfully, Ghost didn't follow them.

A few hours after I got home from school that afternoon, I texted Tanya.

Caleb

i need to talk to u

(its not an emergency though so if ur busy its fine)

Tanya

meet u at the creek in 20?

Caleb

see u there

Tanya and I lived only a few roads down from each other, in the same suburban neighborhood located a few miles outside Nashville.

When we were kids, I would walk to her house; she never walked to mine because her parents were strict about her going out unsupervised. But sometimes, when her parents let us play outside, we'd go to this playground only a few minutes away from her house, and behind that playground was a creek. We used to spend hours there, skipping stones, dipping our feet in the cold water, trying to catch frogs. It was *our* space. A sanctuary for us only.

As I made my way over to the creek, the sun was just beginning to set. Since getting home, I'd been thinking about Ghost's behavior. I needed to talk with Tanya about it—she would know how to make sense of this. Or, if she didn't, she would at least understand why I was weirded out by it.

There was a small bridge above the creek, and Tanya was sitting on the ledge overlooking the water by the time I got there, her legs crossed and her hair pulled into a small bun at the nape of her neck. She was texting someone, so she didn't seem to notice me coming up behind her until I said, "Hey."

She jumped, clutching her phone tightly to her chest. "Shit, Caleb! Are you trying to give me a heart attack?"

I couldn't help but laugh; she was so easily startled, and she always had the most animated reactions. "Sorry," I said, sitting next to her. The bridge was only a few feet above the creek. As kids, we used to dare each other to jump off it. The one time I finally did, though, I sprained my ankle, so that was sort of the end of that.

"Who are you texting?" I asked, trying to get a glimpse over her shoulder.

"No one." She pulled it away from me before I could see anything. "You're so nosy."

"I like being in the loop."

"Trust me, if there was anything to keep you in the loop about, I would tell you." She sent one final text, then locked her phone and put it in her pocket. "So, what'd you want to talk about?"

I looked down at the rushing water. It had been raining a lot lately, so the creek was almost overflowing. In the setting sunlight, the rocks under the water glittered like jewels.

"I think something is going on with Ghost," I said.

I felt her demeanor change, heard the frown in her voice when she asked, "Did something happen?"

"Kind of." I paused. "It's just—it seems like Ghost is . . . acting out or something."

"What do you mean?"

"Lately, he's been . . ." How did I even describe this? I struggled for the words. "He's been showing an interest in other people? Like, yesterday I went to my group therapy, and he was acting strange about this one person there. And then in class the past week or so, he's been sitting near Emmett's desk. And there were a few times at the beginning of the semester where he seemed interested in random people in my classes. . . ."

Tanya thought about it for a moment. There was a breeze, and I shoved my hands in the pockets of my hoodie for warmth.

"How does he show interest?" she asked.

"I guess mostly he sits near them." I shrugged. "But sometimes it seems like he's trying to lead me toward them. Like he wants me to talk to the people or . . . something." I thought about when he sat near Emmett in songwriting on Monday, how my reaction to his behavior inadvertently caused us to become partners. Had that been his intent the whole time? Or was it just a coincidence?

"Hmm." Tanya frowned. "That's weird."

I laughed. "I'm being followed by a cat-ghost without a face that apparently only I can see, and *this* is the weird part."

Tanya smiled but went quiet and looked down at her lap, her hands laced together.

"Hey." I nudged her gently. "What's wrong?"

"I'm just worried about you," she said quietly.

Hearing that sent anxiety shooting through my body. Flashes of my parents' crying, their despair—Mr. Russak's voice when he said *refuse*—Tom saying in group that our minds can play tricks on us.

"You don't need to be," I said, a little too harshly, my anxiety turning to anger, frustration, defensiveness. "I'm fine."

Tanya bit her lip and nodded. "If you say so."

We sat in silence for a few moments while I let my irritation dissipate. The sun was almost finished setting, the sky blooming from bright orange to a dark blue.

"So, what do I do about Ghost's behavior?" I asked finally. "Like, *why* is he even interested in these people in the first place?"

She uncrossed her legs, letting them hang over the side of the bridge, and leaned back on her palms, her head tilted toward the sky. "I don't know," she said, "but I think we need to figure it out." She thought about it for a moment. "You said he has an interest in Emmett, right? So, why not talk to Emmett?"

I gave her a look. "And how is that conversation going to go?

'Hey, person I only sort of know. I'm being haunted by a faceless cat and for some reason that cat's taken a liking to you. Would you happen to know why?'"

"Of course you wouldn't say it like *that*," she huffed. "But there's got to be a reason, right? Maybe there's something drawing him to Emmett. Maybe it has to do with his 'unfinished business.'"

I laughed. "His unfinished business? He's a cat, Tanya!"

"Don't laugh! You never know!" She shoved me playfully, grinning. "I think if you got to know Emmett more, you could figure out what's going on."

"You're just saying that because you want us to be actual friends," I said.

Ever since Tanya and Emmett started hanging out last year, Tanya had been trying to convince me that we would get along well if only we'd hang out more. But Emmett never made an effort to do that, and *I* certainly wasn't going to reach out first, and then my entire life got derailed last summer, so Emmett and I never quite got there.

"Well, yeah, duh," she said. "But even outside of that, I think getting to know them more and seeing how Ghost reacts to that could maybe answer some of your questions."

I thought about it. Get to know Emmett more? It wouldn't be impossible, I guessed. We sat at the same lunch table every day with Tanya, Logan, Nathan, and Dima, and we were already doing this project together now, so it wouldn't be hard to find time to hang out.

Plus, they were one of the few other trans people at our

school, along with me and Tanya, and maybe it *would* be nice to have more trans friends. . . .

"But isn't it a little weird if I get to know them with, like, an ulterior motive?" I asked. "Is that, like, bad of me?"

"People get to know each other just 'cause they're curious all the time, Caleb. It's not like you're trying to 'use' them for something; you just want to see what they're like and how Ghost reacts to you two talking more."

"I guess. . . . Still feels a little weird, though."

"Then I guess you'll never find out why Ghost is interested in them," she said, shrugging.

I groaned. "Ugh, fine. Your idea is smart and you're a good and helpful friend. There, are you happy?"

She grinned. "Yes."

We stayed at the creek for another half hour. By the time we left, it was dark, and we had to use our phones as flashlights. I walked with her to her house first, partially so she wouldn't be out at night by herself, and partially so I could say hi to her family. I hadn't seen them in a while.

When we got to her house, Tanya's mom was sitting at the kitchen table, her head buried in a stack of papers and her reading glasses perched on the tip of her nose. She was a professor at Vanderbilt University, and, according to Tanya, she was working most of the time.

Once she saw us, she said, "Caleb! It's so nice to see you. I didn't know you were coming by today?"

"He was just walking me home, Amma," Tanya said, slipping her shoes off at the doorway while I stayed at the threshold.

I nodded. "But it's nice to see you too, Mrs. Gupta."

"How are your parents?" she asked.

"They're . . . all right. We're holding up."

She nodded, a look of understanding passing across her face. One thing I liked about Tanya's mom: When she knew a topic could become uncomfortable, she didn't keep pushing it. She was pretty good about giving people space, and I appreciated that.

"How have you been?" I asked.

She waved a hand toward her stack of papers. "Oh, fine, fine. We're holding up, too. I've just been busy."

Tanya made a face as if to say, *That's an understatement.*

"But I'll let you go," Mrs. Gupta said. "I'm sure you need to get home. Tell your parents I said hello."

Before I left, Tanya pulled me into a hug. "Think about reaching out to Emmett, okay?" she said quietly. "They're pretty cool, you know."

"So you've told me," I said, pulling away. Then I paused. "Actually . . ."

She narrowed her eyes at me. "What?"

"We're doing a project together in songwriting, so I kinda *have* to reach out to them," I admitted.

Her lips turned up in a small, smug smile. "So, Operation Become Emmett's Friend is a go?"

"We can*not* call it that," I said, taking a step toward the door.

She laughed. "Text me when you get home."

The next day, Tanya and I ate in the art room. We had two lunch spots: at a table in the cafeteria with Tanya's friends, or here. She was frequently finishing her art projects at the last minute, so on days when she had work to do, we would eat in there instead.

She was and always had been an artist. For as long as I could remember, she'd painted. Watercolors at first, then acrylics, and now she was learning how to use oils and gouache. Today, she was finishing up a sketch for her next painting—which was based off a photo of her mother from Diwali earlier this month, looking up at fireworks—when Nathan found us.

"Hey, Tanya!" he said, popping his head around the open art studio door. "I thought I'd find you here."

She put down her pencil, sliding her sketchbook to the side. "Hey! What's up?"

Nathan gave me a short nod in acknowledgment. I tried my best to give one back, but I was still mostly out of the loop when it came to "masculine" body language.

That was one of those things that people didn't think about having to relearn when transitioning—how to move your body so that others perceived you as masculine or feminine, which included how to nod at people, how to hug, how to shake hands, how to sit in public . . . the list went on. It seemed ridiculous to me that such small things could be deemed "for boys" or "for girls," but I found myself trying to learn these new codes anyway. I wanted to blend in with cis guys like Nathan, or at least know *how* to.

Nathan glanced around the art room in wonder. The room was messy, with easels and unfinished artwork and tubes of paint left at every station. Each student had their own designated space for each class, and Tanya's area was just as disorganized as everyone else's. Maybe even more so, honestly.

"Whoa," he said, staring at the unfinished paintings. "Which ones are yours?"

She pointed to a painting a few feet away, this one a self-portrait aerial view of her sitting in her bedroom. Its color scheme was made up of only oranges. Her face was obscured, and her hair was long and cascading like a dark waterfall.

"Holy shit," Nathan said, staring at it. "That's really good."

Tanya shifted in her seat, clearly a bit uncomfortable with the praise, but she still smiled. "Thanks."

Nathan moved away from the painting, seemingly satisfied, and came over to our table, leaning an elbow on it. "Sorry to interrupt your lunch. I just wanted to ask you something real quick."

"Oh?" Tanya said. I took a bite of my ham-and-cheese sandwich, trying to pretend I wasn't there.

"Everyone was thinking about going bowling tomorrow night," Nathan said, "so I was wondering if you two wanted to come?"

"Who all's going?"

"The whole crew—me, Dima, Logan, Amy, and Emmett."

Tanya glanced at me as if to get my opinion, but I just shrugged.

"I'll have to ask my parents if they're okay with it," she said, "but if they say yes, then yeah, I'd love to."

Nathan's face broke into a smile, and I could've sworn he was blushing a little. "Okay, great! I'll text y'all the details."

"Sounds good." Tanya smiled back, and for a moment, they

just stood there, grinning at each other. I nudged her side, and she gave me a look like *what?*

Nathan seemed to notice our silent conversation. He started toward the door. "I've gotta go eat, so I'm gonna head back to the cafeteria, but I'll see you two later!"

"See you in chem!" Tanya called after him, waving. He waved back.

Once I was sure he was out of earshot, I turned to Tanya. "What was that?"

"What was what?" She wouldn't look me in the eye.

"You two! Just standing there smiling at each other? And him inviting you to go *bowling*?"

"He invited you, too!"

"Yeah, but just to be polite. And look—you're blushing."

"I am *not*," she said, her cheeks flushing even more.

"He likes you."

She rolled her eyes. "He doesn't *like* me, Caleb. We're friends."

"So? That doesn't mean he can't have a crush on you."

"Can we just drop it, please? He doesn't have a crush on me, I don't have a crush on him, and I don't wanna talk about it."

I frowned and looked down at my sandwich. "Yeah, sure, whatever."

I knew Tanya was somewhat hesitant about romance and crushes; her parents didn't approve of her dating so young, so, last year, when she started talking to this guy she liked, they had to sneak around and hide it from them. But that relationship went up in flames within a few months because he turned out to be a transphobic, racist asshole, and ever since, Tanya had sworn off dating as a whole. According to her, it was too messy, too complicated, and overall not worth the effort.

But I couldn't understand why she refused to even entertain the topic. And a part of me—a part I wasn't going to admit out loud—was jealous. I wanted someone to look at me the way that Nathan looked at her. I wanted someone to invite me out with their friends because they liked me for *me*, not just because I was Tanya's sidekick. And I couldn't understand why she would deny her feelings when Nathan so obviously returned them; if someone *I* liked was falling all over me like that, I'd jump on that chance immediately, even if it *was* complicated and messy and a lot of effort.

But, whatever. If Tanya didn't want to do anything about her obviously requited crush, then I couldn't make her.

"You're going with them tomorrow, right?" I said.

"Yeah, if my parents let me." She gave me a look. "*You're* coming too, right?"

"I don't know. . . ."

"Oh, come on, Caleb, it'll be fun! Plus, Emmett will be there! It's the perfect opportunity to get to know them."

"I have the project."

"I mean *outside* of schoolwork. But, fine, don't go if you don't want to. For what it's worth, I'd love to have you there."

I told her I would think about it, and we finished lunch without any more bowling discussion. But I already knew I was going to give in. That was always how it was with Tanya. I couldn't say no to her.

And, as hesitant about the get-to-know-Emmett plan as I was, I was also curious. I wanted desperately to understand Ghost's recent behavior. Every day that week in songwriting, Ghost had shown up. He wasn't always sitting near Emmett's desk, but he was always around, and that on its own was concern enough.

More than anything, I wanted to know *why*.

Why now? Why Emmett? Why me?

6

"I'M SO BAD AT THIS," Tanya said as she got up to take her turn bowling. It was Saturday night, and Strike and Spare was packed.

"You'll do great," Nathan said, smiling brightly at Tanya.

I looked down at my phone, pretending I hadn't seen the soft look they exchanged. It felt too intimate, like I was somehow invading their privacy or something, even though *they* were the ones making googly eyes at each other in public. It had been like this for most of the night already, with Nathan and Tanya exchanging flirty comments or looks while the rest of us—Emmett; Dima; Logan; Logan's girlfriend, Amy; and myself—pretended we hadn't noticed.

We played like that for another twenty minutes, and at the end of the round, I was shy of winning by only a few points. Amy won, and we decided we wanted to play one more round. While Nathan went about setting up our second game, Emmett stood up.

"I'm gonna go outside and smoke for a few minutes if anyone wants to join?" They flashed a joint and lighter from their pocket, quick enough that strangers wouldn't see.

"I'll pass for now," Tanya said.

Emmett nodded, then looked to everyone else. Dima declined, but Logan and Amy shrugged. "Yeah, I'll join," Amy said.

Then Emmett turned to me, an eyebrow raised. I thought I was going to say no, since Tanya had already said she was staying inside, but when I looked over at her, she was laughing loudly at something Nathan said as he fiddled with the machine, her hand laying gently on his arm.

"Sure," I told Emmett. I kind of wanted a break from the flirting. Plus, I thought that being high might help calm some of my social anxiety, help me feel a little less uptight. I didn't smoke weed often, but the two times I had, they'd been mostly positive experiences.

The sun had just finished setting, so the sky was a dark blue, only a few stars peeking out. The parking lot was empty; we were the only people out here.

We stood near Emmett's car and passed the joint between us for a few minutes. After Amy took a hit, she blew the smoke out gently and handed it to me. "So, how do you know everyone?" she asked.

I hadn't actually met Amy before today, but according to Tanya, she was a sophomore at Brentwood High School. She was Black, with a dyed-green buzz cut and silver braces, and that day, she wore a long, black-and-white striped shirt and ripped skinny jeans.

I took the joint from her. "Um, just, you know, school," I said. When she nodded but didn't say anything, I felt the need to keep talking. "Well, Tanya and I actually know each other because of our parents, so we've been friends since we were really little. But Tanya knows Nathan and the band, and she sort of introduced me, so . . ." I trailed off.

God, I was so anxious. Everyone was nice, but I still felt so intimidated by them. I wanted desperately to be high already. Or maybe just to be somebody else.

I took a bigger hit than I meant to, coughing after I finished, and passed it to Logan.

"Have you seen them play?" Amy asked, seemingly unbothered by my awkwardness.

Logan rubbed the back of his neck. "Aw, come on, Amy. I doubt Caleb wants to spend the whole night talking about that."

"One question isn't the 'whole night,'" she said. "And besides, the band is a huge part of y'all's lives! You should be able to talk about it without feeling embarrassed."

"Yeah, I'm not sure about that." Logan took a hit, then passed it to Emmett, coughing a little as he did so.

"I'm on Logan's side this time," Emmett said. "We're very annoying about it. Sorry about that, Caleb." They grinned at me.

"I don't mind. And to answer your question, Amy, I've seen them, but just once."

She nodded. "Well, you should definitely come to the next show if you can. I mean, no pressure, of course. I just know everyone would love to have you there."

"Um, thanks." I doubted there was a universe were "everyone would love" to have me there, but I was flattered that she said it, anyway. I hoped she couldn't see my cheeks turning pink in the dark.

By the time we reunited with Tanya, Dima, and Nathan back inside, I was definitely high, and my anxiety had begun to noticeably dissipate. I still didn't feel totally in my element, but the tightness in my chest had loosened a bit.

While we started our second game, Tiffany's "I Think We're Alone Now" started playing over the speakers, and Emmett sang along to it as Logan took his turn.

"This song is so creepy when you actually listen to it," Amy said.

Dima nodded. "It would be great for a horror movie."

"I think it's been used in a few, actually," I said. "I'm pretty sure I've seen one that used this song in the trailer, but I don't remember the name."

"Do you watch a lot of horror?" Emmett asked.

"Yeah, I guess so."

"That is an understatement," Tanya said. I flipped her off playfully, and she stuck her tongue out at me, grinning.

Logan returned from taking his turn and clapped Emmett on the shoulder on his way back to his seat. He'd gotten a spare. "Didn't you do a horror movie thing for Halloween recently?"

"Oh, yeah." Emmett turned to me. "I did this thing where I tried to watch all the 'classic' horror movies in October. I only ended up watching a couple before I got busy with school and other stuff, though."

"Which movies did you watch?"

They listed a few I'd expected, like *Halloween* and *A Nightmare on Elm Street*, but then they named *Re-Animator*, and I was sure I visibly perked up.

"Have you seen the sequels?" I asked. *Re-Animator* was a horror movie from the eighties that I loved. It was sort of a cult classic, and it was followed by two sequels. Jack and I watched all three movies together when I was fourteen, the summer before ninth grade.

Back then, Jack had just graduated from high school, and he was in a good place. He went through patterns with his recovery from addiction; he'd seem to be doing well for a few months—once, he even went a whole year clean—before relapsing again, and he'd usually stay in that dark place for another few months before he would try to come out of it again. That summer, he was doing well enough to hang out with me often, and we ended up watching a lot of horror movies.

"No, not yet," Emmett said. "But *Bride of Re-Animator* is on my list."

"You should definitely watch that one," I said. "It's the best out of the three."

"Oh shit, really? I guess I'll get around to it then. Honestly, I was sort of putting it off because I assumed it would suck like most sequels."

"Nah, it's surprisingly fun. It's kind of campy, and the bride just steals the show for the limited screen time she has," I said, and I didn't even care if I was gushing. My body was relaxed and my thoughts were fuzzy, without the usual anxious background chatter. "Plus, unlike the other two movies, there aren't any crude sexual assault scenes you have to suffer through."

"Oh, thank God," Emmett said. "I was *so* uncomfortable with that moment in the first movie."

"It's a million times worse in *Beyond Re-Animator*," I said. "Seriously, I do not recommend watching that one."

Nathan nudged Emmett's side. "Your turn."

They went to take their turn, but not before offering me a smile. *This is good*, I thought. *I'm doing a good job talking to people*. I was feeling all right—relaxed.

"Last time, I was just warming up," Emmett said as they picked up the ball. "But I'm not gonna go easy on y'all anymore. Get ready."

Dima snorted. "Sure, Em, whatever you say."

Emmett hit a total of four pins the first time, then got a spare. They pumped their fist in excitement. "Yes!"

Logan gave them a celebratory high five as they sat back down.

"So, what'd you get up to while you were outside?" Tanya asked me. Her tone was casual, but she spoke quietly enough that the rest of the group couldn't hear her over the bowling alley's loud chatter.

"We just stood around and talked, mostly," I said. "Why?"

"Nothing," she said in a way that very much implied something.

I narrowed my eyes at her. "Well, what did *you* get up to while we were gone? Did you and Nathan get into any shenanigans?"

"No, we didn't, and I think you know that." She huffed. "I mostly talked with Dima, if you *have* to know. We had a nice conversation about our mutual interest in Phoebe Bridgers."

"Oh. Well, I'm glad you had a good time," I said.

"Thank you." She paused, then her expression turned a little more somber. "How have things been with Ghost lately?" she asked, keeping her voice down.

I glanced around. The last time I'd seen Ghost that day was when I picked Tanya up to drive here, but he'd been absent since then. I could sort of feel that he was somewhere around us, though. It wasn't like I could feel him *clearly*; I just got the sense that he wasn't far away.

I wasn't sure yet, but I had a theory that we were connected in some way—spiritually, maybe, or metaphysically. I didn't have any sort of concrete beliefs, but after Ghost came along, my idea of what was possible had expanded a little bit. Now I imagined the feeling as an invisible line between Ghost and me, tying us together.

"Things have been okay," I told Tanya. "I haven't seen him since we got here."

"What do you think that means for our theory?" she asked.

"What do you mean?"

"Well, you know, with Ghost being drawn to Emmett recently," she said, voice so low I had to strain to hear her. "But he didn't seem to follow you tonight. Does that mean maybe he's losing interest?"

"I don't know. I guess it could," I said.

I wasn't sure how I felt about the idea of Ghost losing interest.

It would mean I no longer had a reason to pursue the getting-to-know-Emmett plan unless I just wanted to.

Did I want to?

Without thinking about it, I glanced over at them. They sat with their legs crossed, and they threw their hands around as they passionately explained something to Dima. Dima laughed at whatever they said, and Emmett grinned, clearly pleased with themself.

We kept bowling, and at one point in between turns, I got up to buy a slushie. I'd seen a few people walking by with slushies, and the idea of drinking one seemed so amazing that I felt my mouth start to water just imagining it. Tanya and Nathan both decided to join me, so we headed over to the food counter together.

"I didn't know you were so good at bowling, Caleb," Nathan said while we waited in line.

"I don't know if I'd say *that*," I said. "But thank you."

"Oh, come on; don't be modest," Tanya said.

"Yeah, you almost won against Amy," Nathan agreed. "And she's, like, crazy good."

"Yeah, I picked up on that. Does she go bowling all the time or something?" I asked.

"Her dad's part of a league, so they bowl a lot together," Nathan said as we moved forward in line.

"Oh. That's sweet, actually."

The person in front of us finished getting their food, so I went up to the counter. The cashier looked like she wasn't much older than us, maybe in her twenties, and she really did not seem interested in her job. It didn't help that she spoke softly, so I had to strain to hear her over the loud music and conversation.

As we were leaving—I had my slushie in hand, while Nathan got a slice of pizza and Tanya got some candy—Nathan leaned over to us.

"Did you see the cashier's arms?" he whispered.

Tanya and I both shook our heads. I'd been too focused on interacting with her without letting on that I was high to really notice her appearance.

"They were covered in track marks," he said, a pitying look on his face.

Every nerve in my body reacted to those words, and suddenly, I didn't have that fuzzy, relaxed feeling anymore—just that familiar anxious heat, starting in my stomach but rapidly spreading through the rest of me.

Images of Jack flashed through my head—his slow, heavy steps up the stairs, the needles I saw in his bathroom trash can one time, his hoodies and long-sleeved shirts hiding his forearms.

"I hope she's okay," Tanya said, looking somber.

"Me too," I mumbled, but I was too busy trying to right myself. I took a long sip of my slushie, hoping that would bring me back to now, but all it did was give me a brain freeze. Still, I kept drinking it; the pain was a good distraction.

We sat back down with the others, and I tried to calm myself as everyone kept playing. I wanted to go back to that fun, light feeling, but my thoughts kept returning to that cashier, imagining the scars on her arms, and then I thought about Nathan's reaction, and I wondered what he and his friends thought about drugs. Obviously some of them smoked weed, but I wasn't sure if that was where the interest stopped. I wondered how often they all smoked, and if any of them ever experimented with harder drugs.

I wondered if this was how Jack got started with everything—if it began as that feeling I had earlier, *I want to be high*, just to escape the social pressure, just to escape myself. I wondered if he ever realized that what he was doing wasn't good for him.

A prickle at the back of my neck. There, across the room, was Ghost, sitting in front of a shelf full of bowling balls.

Fuck.

A wave washed over me. Everyone was still talking, but it didn't feel like I was there anymore.

"You doing all right, Caleb?" Logan asked, his eyebrows pinched.

"I'm, uh, fine, yeah. Just didn't realize it was my turn already." I tried to play it off with a laugh, but it probably wasn't very convincing. Logan still looked a little concerned, and Tanya, who had been talking with Amy, now had her attention on me.

You okay? she mouthed to me. I nodded back subtly and picked up the bowling ball, but my legs were a little shaky, and I was definitely still high, and I could feel Ghost behind me, watching. I swung my arm back as hard as I could and rolled the ball.

I got a strike, but as I tried to back up, my legs gave out under me, and I landed hard on my ass.

I heard Tanya call my name, probably seeing if I was okay,

but I didn't respond. I scrambled back up to my feet as quickly as I could.

"Sorry, I'll be right back," I rushed to say, before booking it toward the restroom. I thought I heard Tanya call after me, but I didn't catch what she said.

JACK WAS SIXTEEN WHEN HE started using.

I was eleven and oblivious, hardly paying attention—but even *I* eventually caught on that something was wrong. And that was before Mom and Dad sat me down and explained why Jack had been acting so strange, so distant, so unlike himself.

It started with him staying out later. Wanting more freedom. He was gone so often those days. Then his group of friends changed; slowly, the people he'd been close with our whole lives disappeared, replaced with strangers, people who didn't stay around the house long enough for me to catch their names.

Then—the smoking. He didn't hide it very well. I'd see him pull into the driveway, see him sitting in the car, engine idling, window cracked, a cigarette in his mouth. And even if I hadn't seen it, we could all smell it on him—thick and pungent, following him like a shadow. I started to associate that smell with him. He would come home late, and from the living room, I'd be hit with a wave of cigarette smoke. It didn't take long for our parents to find out, but grounding him didn't change anything. He just kept smoking.

Then his mood started to shift at some point. When he came home late, later than he told us he'd be, and our parents got angry with him, he'd just . . . explode. He was always a little bit confrontational, always a little bit hotheaded, but it had never been like this—huge, blowout fights that ended more often than not with him storming off and driving to a friend's house. Sometimes, he'd be back a few hours later, and I'd hear his footsteps up the creaking staircase. Other times, he'd stay gone an entire weekend, and when the parents called, he'd send them straight to voicemail.

But he always answered me. At eleven, I was given one of our parents' old iPhones, and although it didn't work well, I loved it, if only because it meant I could call Jack on my own and talk to him. Even after a fight with the parents, he'd talk to me. He always skirted around the questions when I'd ask why they were fighting or why he'd been home late or why he wouldn't answer their calls, but we'd talk about other things. What I'd been up to. Something funny he saw online recently. The songs I was writing that week.

He talked with me then more than we ever did at home, where he was always locked in his room, and the message was clear: he wanted to be left alone. Maybe the phone thing was his way of making up for never being available for me when we were together in person. It was like the closer we were physically, the further he was from me, but the moment he had some distance, he was willing to open up.

I didn't know exactly when or how he got into the dangerous stuff. Didn't know when it changed from something he could control to something he couldn't. But by the time I was thirteen, things had gotten really bad. He'd started using heroin.

My parents caught on quickly. It was hard not to: his mood swings got even worse; he lost weight quickly (and, like everyone else in our family, he'd always been on the bigger side, so it was a shock to see him suddenly lose so much); he started skipping more school than he was attending, and his grades reflected it; he stopped telling anyone where he was going or when he'd be back or who he was with; and he was sick almost constantly.

I didn't know what any of these signs really meant. All I knew was that my brother was acting strange, and that, suddenly, it was difficult to be around him. I barely saw him anymore, and when I did, he was always angry, or feeling sick, or freaked out about something. He didn't hang out with me anymore. He didn't ask how school was, didn't talk with me about the latest episodes of the shows we both loved, didn't pick on me across the dinner table. It was like my brother was gone, replaced instead by a stranger.

I missed him.

Even before he died.

At Strike and Spare, I locked myself in a stall in the empty men's restroom and broke down.

I couldn't get the images of Jack out of my head, and as I

sat on the closed toilet lid with my head in my hands, I just kept thinking about how I'd *wanted* to be high tonight, how I wanted to use weed to escape myself the same way that Jack had, and I thought about how he fell into it, wondered how it started, if it started with what I was doing, if I was doing the same things he'd done.

There was panic in that thought, fear that I could end up in that bad place. But there was a guilty kind of comfort, too. I associated cigarettes and weed with Jack so strongly that when I was around either of those things, it was like I felt him there with me.

I could picture him with us tonight, smoking, joking around. And I bet he would've jumped right into that conversation I had with Emmett about movies; he would've had some obscure fact about *Re-Animator*'s production to tell us, something interesting or strange about how it was filmed or what happened on set.

He would've fit right in. And maybe I had felt that—maybe I felt the impression of what could have been, and maybe that was part of why I'd wanted to smoke in the first place. To feel connected to him.

A part of me, a small part that I was ashamed of, wanted to know everything he'd gone through. Wanted to experience everything he did. Because, if I did that, maybe I would understand something about him—about his death, about his addiction—that I'd never understood while he was alive.

Because that was one of the things that, five months after his death, I still didn't understand:

Why?

Why did he start using? Why did he *keep* using? Why didn't rehab ever seem to help? Why didn't he answer my parents' calls? Why did he go out the night that he overdosed?

Why did he have to die? Why him?

I must have sat there in that bathroom, crying, for at least fifteen minutes. It was quiet, the only sound coming from the speakers, Nirvana's "Something In the Way" playing softly.

After a while, the tears stopped and my breathing returned to normal. As I was getting ready to go back out to everyone, the door creaked open, and Emmett stepped inside.

"Oh," they said, surprised. Their eyes flickered between me and the door, as if they weren't sure if they were meant to be here or not. "Is . . . everything okay?"

Heat burned in my cheeks. I didn't want anyone worrying about me, and something about the concern frustrated me.

"Why, did Tanya send you?" I said. I hadn't *meant* it rudely, but even I could hear the bitterness in my voice as it came out.

Emmett frowned. "No. You got up and left out of nowhere, and you've been gone for, like, almost fifteen minutes now. Sorry for worrying, I guess."

Shit. I was being a jerk. I couldn't look them in the eyes when I said, "I'm sorry. I wasn't . . . That didn't come out right."

Emmett was quiet for a moment. A part of me thought they were going to turn around and leave, but instead, they sighed and came to stand next to me at the sink.

"It's fine," they said.

I looked up, and we made brief eye contact through the mirror. It was strange, seeing us next to each other. Emmett wasn't particularly tall, but I looked short next to basically everyone. In the fluorescent lights, the blond in their hair looked almost bright yellow.

"I just assumed no one but Tanya would notice," I admitted finally. "That's why I asked if she sent you. I didn't think you would . . ."

Care about me was the rest of that sentence, but I couldn't finish it. My high had worn off sometime during my breakdown, and now I was back to regular, socially inept, self-conscious Caleb.

"Just because we don't know each other super well doesn't mean I can't care," they said.

I wasn't sure what to say to that, other than a quiet, "I know. You're right. I'm sorry for being a dick."

They shrugged. "It's fine. Everyone can be a dick sometimes."

"I know, but I feel like every time I interact with you, I come off as rude or mean or something," I said, the words coming out in a rush. I knew that if I thought too much about what I was saying, the words would never get out, so I just kept going. "I'm not trying to be a jerk, I swear, I just—I guess I'm not good with people."

They laughed. Even though I felt a flare of embarrassment, I also couldn't deny that the sound was—nice. Kind of cute. "What?" I said.

"Nothing, it's just . . . It's kind of funny to hear someone admit that so easily. Not that I'm laughing *at* you," they rushed to add.

"It's fine. I get what you mean."

We stood there for another moment. Ghost had jumped up onto the bathroom counter, although his presence didn't startle me this time. I'd figured he would be around.

"Sorry I left so suddenly," I said. "To be honest, I . . . I was having a lot of anxiety, and I needed to be alone for a little bit."

"I'm sorry you weren't feeling good. And I get that, hanging out in the bathroom to escape everything. It's basically the only private place to go in public, although I wish there were other options."

"Other options for being alone?"

They nodded. "Yeah because, like, when I'm having a freak-out or something, I want to be able to escape somewhere quiet so I can calm down, but public bathrooms add this whole other layer of anxiety on top of it, too, you know? I mean, I usually just use the men's unless there's a gender-neutral one available, but it's not exactly comfortable for me. I've thankfully only had one bad experience in a public restroom, but . . ."

"It's always scary," I said. I understood that; bathrooms, for us as trans people, were always a risk, but it was especially dangerous in a state like Tennessee.

Thankfully, no one had come in during our conversation, but now I paused to double-check that we were still alone. When I didn't hear any voices or footsteps approaching outside, I asked, "You know I'm trans, right?"

Emmett hesitated before nodding. "Yeah. I wasn't sure if I was supposed to know because Tanya mentioned it once but you've never said anything about it, so I wasn't gonna bring it up first. . . ."

"No, it's okay. I'm fine with people knowing. I'm . . . actually kind of glad Tanya told you."

"Really? Why?"

"It's felt like it's mostly just been me and Tanya as the only trans people at Williams, so when you came out last semester, I wanted you to know I'm trans 'cause it can be nice to have someone else like you around. . . . I hope that isn't, like, weird of me to assume or anything. I mean, I haven't actually *heard* you call yourself trans before and I know that can be kinda personal, but I just thought, you know, it could be nice." I shrugged.

"No worries," they said. "I'm genderfluid, but I also consider myself trans and nonbinary. There are days that I feel a little more masc, a little more femme, sometimes both—but I never feel fully like a 'guy,' you know?"

I nodded. "Gotcha. That's good to know."

"But it's sweet of you to want me to know you're also trans," they said, smiling gently. "I appreciate that."

My cheeks felt hot. "It's—whatever," I sputtered.

In my pocket, my phone buzzed with a text.

Tanya

everything okay?

I sent a quick response—*yeah, omw back*—before looking back up to Emmett. "I guess we should head back now?"

"Are you feeling any better?"

I nodded. "Yeah. I'm good now."

"Good. I'm glad." They smiled again, and for the first time

since I saw them performing at Nathan's house, I thought, *Emmett is . . . kind of hot.*

I immediately tried to ignore it, though. What were the chances that Emmett would ever find *me* attractive back? So, there was no point in dwelling on it.

It was around ten by the time we left the bowling alley, and ten thirty before I got home. My dad was in the dining room with his laptop open.

"Hey, kiddo," Dad said as I entered. "Mom's sleeping, so be quiet going upstairs." I'd assumed that my parents wouldn't be up by the time I got home tonight, since they usually went to bed around nine.

"How was bowling?" he asked, pausing his typing to look up at me.

I started heading toward the stairs. "It was fine."

"Did you get any strikes?"

"A few," I said, taking a slow step up the stairs. "I'm pretty exhausted, though, so I'm gonna go to my room. . . ."

"Caleb," Dad called. "Can we talk for a sec?"

I paused. Took a breath. Then turned around. "Yeah, what's up?"

He took off his glasses, folded them, and set them gently down on the table. That was when I knew that this wasn't going to be a casual conversation.

I hoped I didn't smell like weed. I'd been fully sober for an hour now (I made sure I wasn't high by the time I needed to drive), but since I didn't smoke very often, I wasn't really sure how long the smell hung around. Whenever Jack came home after smoking, my parents always seemed to know and it would turn into a fight—but whether that was because of the smell or some kind of parent intuition, I wasn't sure. Either way, I hoped he didn't know what I'd been up to.

"How has everything been at school?" Dad asked.

"Oh." I shrugged. "Fine."

"Mr. Russak emailed me today," he said. "He told me you're failing songwriting?"

I'd been avoiding telling my parents about the state of my grades. I was sort of hoping that Mr. Russak would let me get my grade up a little before getting my parents involved, but I guessed that was too much to hope for.

"I got behind on some assignments," I said, "but he already talked with me about it."

"So, you're going to make up those assignments? And that will be enough to fix your grade?"

"I have it under control," I said, maybe a little too brusquely.

He gave me a look. "I'm just trying to help, Caleb. This just doesn't seem like you—getting behind in *songwriting* of all classes? And you know colleges—"

"Won't like it if I fail, I know," I interrupted. "Mr. Russak already gave me a lecture about it. I'm gonna keep up with my work from now on and turn in a few missing assignments, and everything will be fine. I'll pass the class, I promise."

He sighed a little. "Okay. If you say you have it under control, I'll trust you. But . . . this just doesn't seem like you. Is Williams not . . . what you thought it would be?"

What you thought it would be. I guessed he meant what I'd been imagining when I decided to audition for WSA instead of going to my public high school, all my gushing about pursuing music at an arts school, my giddy excitement when I was accepted into the program.

"It's—nice," I said. "It's definitely better than a public school. And I really like studying music."

He nodded, then looked down at his computer. "And you're happy there?"

I wasn't sure what to say. How was I supposed to tell him *No, but I'm not really happy* anywhere *right now* without upsetting him? He was already dealing with the loss of one son; I didn't want him to have to worry about me, too.

"Yeah, of course I am," I said.

"All right. Good." He nodded for a few seconds, longer than usual. Then—and this was what I had been dreading—his face fell, and I saw the moment the dam cracked, and then he was sitting there, crying, his head in his hands, and it reminded me so much of how I'd been only two hours earlier in the bowling alley bathroom that I could barely stand it. I didn't want to see my grief mirrored to me. From the corner of my eye, I watched as Ghost entered the dining room, sauntering in as if his presence was invited.

"I'm sorry," I said. "I didn't mean to upset you. . . ." I came over to my dad's side of the table and wrapped my arms around his shoulders in an attempt at a hug. My family wasn't super physically affectionate growing up, but when Jack's addiction first got worse, I noticed that we started hugging more often. I still wasn't quite used to it.

After a moment, my dad brushed me away, reaching instead for a tissue. To my left, Ghost had jumped up into an empty dining chair and was turned toward us.

"It's okay. It's, uh, been a rough couple of days, and I was caught off guard by Mr. Russak's email, so I guess it just all compounded." He sniffed, folding his tissue in half. "And Caleb . . . you know you can talk to me, right? Mom and I both—we're here for you whenever you need. If there's something you're struggling with right now, whether it's school or something else . . ."

I couldn't find the right words to say, so I said nothing. I just nodded.

After a few more moments, he composed himself, sitting up straight and pushing back his hair. "All right, I'm sure you're tired from hanging out with friends, so I'll let you get back to what you were doing," he said, putting his reading glasses back on. "Thanks for talking with me. Good night, kiddo. Love you."

"Love you, too," I said.

And with that, I went up to my room. Ghost followed closely behind.

That night, I did something I didn't normally do: I looked Emmett up online.

Their profile came up on Instagram with only a little bit of snooping. It helped that Emmett and Tanya followed each other, and I scrolled through their feed, taking everything in.

Their most recent post was from the show at Nathan's house. They had uploaded six photos, five of the band playing and one that showed Emmett, Dima, and Logan posing with their instruments at the end of the night, exhausted grins on their faces. The caption read, "thanks so much for everyone who showed up to our anniversary show last night, we had a blast" followed by a rose emoji. I wondered if there was any significance to it, or if Emmett just liked how it looked. Dima, Logan, and Nathan were all tagged in the photo, along with the band's account, @deck_of_fools.

I kept scrolling. More posts—from August, a shot of Dima holding a latte; from July, of Emmett, Logan, and Nathan by a pool; from last May, a mirror selfie of Emmett in a My Chemical Romance tank top, dark red makeup, and black boots; from January, a celebratory New Year's post with photos that looked like they were taken at a party.

I stared at that photo for a while, and I thought, suddenly, about Jack. Somewhere in the same city, at the same time this photo was being taken, there had been Jack, alive and breathing, maybe smiling, maybe happy.

But I didn't want to think about that. So, instead, once I was satisfied with Emmett's Instagram, I went to their band's page. Their bio read:

based in Nashville.
@em_carpenter—vocals + guitar
@dima.khalil—drums
@loganhuang—bass + keyboard

The posts were similar to the ones from Emmett's page—shots of the band playing, close-ups of Logan's hands on his bass, Dima smiling behind her drum set, Emmett at the mic. There were also some photos of them in what appeared to be a recording studio, headphones on, along with posters advertising a few upcoming shows.

I only looked at their Instagram page for a minute before I returned to Google. This time, I looked up "Deck of Fools" and immediately found their Bandcamp, YouTube, Spotify, and Instagram pages. I went to Bandcamp first.

They had only one EP up, titled *I Don't Forgive You*. I listened through it, and I recognized a few of the songs from the show I went to, including the titular one. Most of their music was deceptively upbeat. I hadn't noticed it at the show since I couldn't catch all the lyrics, but now that I was able to read them, I realized a lot of their songs were pretty somber.

And maybe that shouldn't have surprised me; it wasn't like the songs *I* wrote were particularly happy. But I guess I hadn't thought that people like Emmett, Dima, and Logan were interested in writing and playing music like that. Some of the songs sort of had the expected amount of vulnerability for punk rock—themes of "I'm an outcast," "fuck the system," "the world sucks," that sort of thing. But there were others—like this one called "In December," which included the lyrics, "I'd break my fingers / If it'd keep me from talking to you / You apologized / With the last breath you drew." I wondered who the *you* was. The credits said that the vocals, guitar, and songwriting were done by "E. M. Carpenter."

On a whim, I looked up "E. M. Carpenter." Deck of Fools came up first, but a few links down, there was a different Bandcamp page, this one for a group called Limerence.

I clicked on it. There was only one album from the band published two years ago. The cover art showed a photo of a dead, decomposing baby rabbit lying in painfully bright green grass. Other than that, the only identifying information came from the credits, which claimed that "E. M. Carpenter" and someone named "Mallory P." were the songwriters, musicians, vocalists, and producers of the album.

I listened through the self-titled EP, which included six songs. Most of the songs included vocals by both Emmett and this Mallory person, but a few, including "Emotional Affair" and "Slow Down" only featured Emmett. Their voice wasn't unrecognizable, but it was definitely a different style from how they sang with Deck of Fools. In these songs, Emmett sounded—softer. Younger. But somehow more anxious, more self-deprecating, more confused. In "Emotional Affair," they sang the lyrics "I wish that you would stay in bed / I wish you didn't want me dead," and by the time I got to the end of the EP, I was tearing up.

Most of the songs were about love, obsession, and romance, and I felt like I understood Emmett, or, at least, I understood what they were singing about. There was something so hopeless about them, and although all the songs centered on romance, it was never about being *happy* in love. In "Angelic," Emmett and Mallory harmonized during the lyrics "And you know I would kill myself / If you asked me to," and the melodies seemed intentionally discordant.

After I'd listened through the album, I had to close out of the tab. It was too much emotion at once. I just kept thinking about the rabbit on the cover. I thought about Emmett, writing and singing this two years ago, and I hoped, for their sake, the lyrics weren't autobiographical.

From his spot at the foot of my bed, Ghost had seemed to be listening the entire time; he sat with his paws crossed, his ears perked up in the direction of my computer. Now that I'd stopped the music, though, he turned his head toward me and sat up on his haunches. I didn't move for a moment, waiting to see what he would do. I wasn't sure how he would respond to anything after tonight at the bowling alley. He left me alone for so long before finally reappearing, and then he stayed with me for the rest of the night, even following me into the car before I drove home.

And now, here he was, sitting on my bed. I had never seen him really take interest in the things I was watching or listening to before this, and never in such an obvious way. It *had* to be because it was connected to Emmett—right?

I thought about the conversation Emmett and I had after they came to check on me, and I got the urge to text them, to let them know I was here to talk if they wanted to.

I pulled up our last text exchange about the project. I sat there racking my brain for what felt like forever before I finally came up with something to say.

I went to the website I normally used to pirate movies and found a working link for *Bride of Re-Animator.* I copied and pasted that to the message, then added:

Caleb

here's a link to bride of re-animator for when/if you want to watch it

it's also on youtube for like three dollars but i figured you might appreciate a free version

I sent the text before I could convince myself this was a bad idea. After that, I tried to distract myself with homework, but it wasn't long before Emmett responded.

Emmett

thanks! :)

Caleb

no problem, and thanks again for checking on me today

i dont know if it was clear but i really appreciated it

Emmett

yeah of course, dont worry about it

how are you feeling btw?

Caleb

all good now

Emmett

good! im glad!

and im here if you ever need to talk or anything

Caleb

thanks

I thought about Emmett's lyrics, and the dead rabbit on the cover of *Limerence*. I thought about Emmett and that Mallory person writing those songs, and I wondered, then, why I hadn't seen anything about someone named Mallory on their Instagram. I wondered if they were still friends.

I sent a few more texts before I could lose my nerve completely.

Caleb

and same to you

if you need someone to talk to, i mean

im available

Emmett

thanks :) ill keep that in mind

I couldn't think of anything to say after that, but I liked the message so that Emmett wouldn't think I was ignoring them.

I put my phone away and tried to get some homework done, but I couldn't. For the rest of the night, I just kept thinking about those songs and Emmett's laugh and Ghost's perked up ears, listening along with me.

8

SUNDAY MORNING, I WOKE TO the sound of my mom vacuuming. This wasn't unusual; Sundays were our unofficial cleaning days, and Mom always liked to get an early start. What *was* unusual was that she was in Jack's room.

I sat in my bed for a few minutes, staring at the ceiling as I listened to the whir of the vacuum. I could feel Ghost in the room with me, but I didn't move to see where he was. Already a pit was swirling in my stomach, preemptive dread at what I knew was happening.

We were finally emptying out Jack's room.

I knew, logically, that it would have to be done one of these days. It wouldn't make sense to leave his room forever untouched, perfectly preserved. But I wished we could, anyway. I wanted to keep it the way he'd left it—piles of dirty clothes on the floor, soda stains on the carpet, half-empty water bottles strewn around, his bed unmade. I wanted the room to stay *his*, the way he'd used it when he was alive.

I finally pulled myself out of bed and hesitantly joined my mom. She'd finished vacuuming by that time, instead moving on to packing things up in cardboard boxes. When I entered, she was sifting through the things on his dresser and sorting them into two boxes, one labeled Keep and the other Throw Away.

"Good morning," she said, smiling surprisingly brightly, considering the circumstances.

I couldn't find it in me to smile back. "What are you doing?"

She looked down at the box she was holding, Keep. When I peered into it, I could see that she'd only decided to keep a few things so far—a leather watch, a frame that held a picture of Jack and his friends from their high school graduation, a figurine of the character Goku from *Dragon Ball Z* that I'd gotten him as a Christmas present many years ago, a pair of sunglasses. He'd had about a million pairs.

"I'm cleaning his room out," she said.

"Why?"

She put the box down on the bed and sighed gently. "Because . . . it needs to be done. We need to move on, and we can't do that with his room sitting here like this."

I knew she was right—I knew that she was just doing what anyone else would do, *should* do, to cope—but I couldn't help it; I was angry. At her for touching this room. At this room for being a reminder of his life and death. At Jack for dying at all.

"But why do we need to move on *now*?" I demanded. "It hasn't even been six months, for fuck's sake—"

"Language, Caleb."

I barely heard her, though. "And why do we need to move on at all? Why do we need to erase him from our lives and pretend like he wasn't here?"

Mom looked at me, wide-eyed and slack-jawed. Even I didn't know where this was coming from, especially since my parents had done basically nothing *but* acknowledge Jack's life since he died.

If anything, *I* was the one who didn't want to think about him, who wanted to escape the reality that he was dead, who tiptoed around my parents to avoid any conversation that would lead back to this, who'd been trying so desperately for the past five months to make sure I talked about it as little as possible. Who was I to say any of this?

"We're not erasing him," Mom said quietly, and I could feel her disappointment in me. I could feel how I'd hurt her. "We would *never* try to erase him. How could you ever think that?"

I didn't say anything for a moment, trying to compose myself. I was still angry, but I didn't want to turn this into an argument, yelling at Mom the way Jack had.

"I just don't get why we need to throw all his stuff away," I said, measured.

"We're not throwing all his stuff away, honey. We're gonna go through his things and decide what we want to keep and remember him by, and then we'll throw out the things that nobody wants or we can't use anymore." She sat down on the bed next to the Keep box, looking suddenly exhausted.

I thought about how many times I had been held by her while I cried over the past few months. How many times she'd been there while I wept, holding my hand or hugging me or letting me lean my head on her shoulder while the tears streamed—how many times I'd needed her there for me. More than needing her, though, I thought about how many times I'd *wanted* her there—how many times I'd wanted to be held by my mother, rocked and comforted, protected from the world.

And then I thought about her pained sobs, the dreams I'd had about that sound, the way that seeing her grief always overwhelmed me, and I realized that she was the same as me. In pain, missing Jack. Wanting to be comforted. Wanting to be protected.

I tried to imagine what it felt like, having to bury your own child. What it felt like, going through Jack's things, having to choose what parts of him survived and what parts went away.

"I'm sorry," I mumbled. "I'm not trying to be a jerk."

"I know you aren't," she said. "It's okay. I just want you to understand that . . ." She sniffed, a sure sign she would start to cry soon. "We're in this together, you know? You, me, your father. We *all* miss Jack, and we're all just trying to cope with it the only ways we know how."

I nodded. "Yeah. You're right."

She looked down at the Keep box and picked up the Goku figurine, holding it for a moment, turning it over in her hands. "Would you be willing to help me go through his things?"

I took a deep breath. "Yeah. I think . . . I can do that. But . . . not today. I'm just not . . ." *Ready* was the rest of that sentence, but I couldn't quite finish it.

She nodded. "Of course, honey. I understand. Come here."

She held her arms out, and I hugged her tight. "When you feel ready to go through these things with me," she said, "you let me know, okay?"

"I will."

We pulled away, and when I turned around, I saw Ghost sitting in front of Jack's bookshelf, his head facing Mom and me. I figured he'd been in here the whole time. He always seemed to join in on conversations with my parents like this.

Seeing me look at the bookshelf, Mom said, "Do you want to take some of his books?"

I glanced between her and Ghost, whose tail now flicked back and forth as if agitated.

"Maybe," I said, heading over to Ghost. He got up from his spot and made a circle, as if trying to emphasize something, and I frowned. *What do you want?* I thought, and he finally moved out of the way to reveal that he'd been sitting in front of a small box that sat on the very bottom shelf.

I crouched down and took the box. It seemed to be full of miscellaneous things—a few books, a key chain in the shape of a vintage film camera, various scraps of paper that must have been old schoolwork. The books were mostly about film and the art of filmmaking, but there was also a copy of *The Catcher in the Rye*, looking a little beat-up and used. I pulled it out of the box and flipped through it gently.

"You can have that, if you want it," Mom said.

I looked at her, then down at the copy of *The Catcher in the Rye*. I'd read that book last year in English, but I'd just borrowed a copy from the library. When I looked through this version, I saw that a lot of the pages were annotated, with passages highlighted and some scribbled writing in the margins.

Jack's handwriting.

"I guess I'll take it," I said.

Mom nodded. "Whatever you want, you can have."

I left the room after that, bringing the book with me. I wasn't sure why, but seeing Jack's handwriting on those pages, it felt important that I kept this.

On Tuesday, Emmett texted me after school.

Emmett

[the lover.m4a]

here's the first song ive written

i dont know how i feel about it just yet lol, so feel free to tell me if it sucks

also here are the lyrics so u can read them if u want

[the lover lyrics.docx]

I was in my room when I got the texts, lying in bed with Ghost at my feet.

I played the audio file. It started with a few ambient seconds of rustling before an acoustic guitar cut in. Emmett's voice was soft and scratchy, like they hadn't warmed up, and it was obvious that they'd recorded this with their phone's voice memos app. I did that when I was writing music, too.

I pulled up the lyrics, following along as the recording continued. It was about someone who always falls too quickly in love, at the detriment to themself and their relationships, and about how they wish they could protect their heart more. It also included a lot of allusions to storytelling, omens, and how the narrator should've somehow known the outcome.

The audio file ended with more rustling—the sound of Emmett pressing stop on the recording. I sat for a few moments, gathering my thoughts. Ghost didn't move from where he sat at the end of my bed, although his head was turned toward me, clearly paying attention. After a second, I responded.

Caleb

it's good!

Emmett

thanks :)

its just a draft obviously so ya know

is there anything u think i should work on?

Caleb

hmm. cant think of anything at the moment

im interested in all the lines about storytelling and omens and stuff

what made u want to include that?

I watched the gray ellipsis pop up and disappear, and after a moment, a message came through, but it wasn't another text; it was an audio message. I clicked play.

"Okay, so, I didn't want to type this all out," Emmett said

in the recording, "but basically, I thought it would make sense to include stuff about storytelling 'cause this is going to be a collection *about* stories, you know? And one thing I really love is foreshadowing and when stories make it obvious that there's, like, a predetermined end that the audience can see, but the characters can't. Plus, I'm kind of a superstitious person, and I've been writing about omens a lot lately."

I thought back to the songs on *Limerence.* There had been something prophetic about some of the lyrics—like the songs were trying to warn someone of something.

Caleb

ohh i see, that makes more sense

Emmett

wbu? how do u feel about superstitions?

At the foot of my bed, Ghost sat unbothered, and I stared at him while I figured out how to answer. From downstairs, I could hear my mom watching TV, the sounds of the news filtering up through the floor. Our house had obnoxiously thin walls; my bedroom was right above the living room, and sometimes, I could hear full conversations from here without even trying. We'd gotten used to it over the years and started turning on fans or ambient noise machines just to give everyone a little more privacy.

But since Jack died, everything was so quiet that it somehow made every sound even louder. When Jack was home, he'd always have music playing from his room, or he'd have his TV playing some Hitchcock film, and I would hear the muffled sounds of rock music or a monologue from my room. It was comforting, knowing that he was there.

Now, though, the silence from his bedroom made every other sound in the house almost unbearable.

I started to type a response, but I thought about Emmett's audio message. I was kind of flattered that they had sent one; it felt more like a real conversation than texting. I stared at the microphone icon for a moment before tapping it.

"I don't think I'm more superstitious than *most* people," I said, bringing the phone closer to me. "But my family can be, especially my extended family, so I heard a lot of superstitions growing up and believed some of them—you know, stuff like, 'if you leave a rocking chair moving after you get up, someone will die,' or 'if you don't hold your breath while driving past a cemetery, you'll get possessed by a ghost.' I still hold my breath when I pass a cemetery, even though I don't really believe in it anymore."

I sent the recording. A minute later, Emmett called me. I let it ring for a moment, surprised, before answering. "Um, hey."

"Hey! Sorry to call out of nowhere—it just seemed like it would be easier to talk this way," Emmett said. Ghost's ears twitched, as if trying to listen to their voice. "That's so spooky about the cemetery thing, though. I hadn't heard that before."

"Really?"

"Surprisingly, no. But I did believe in Bloody Mary until I was, like, thirteen."

I laughed. "Oh my God, did you ever try to summon her?"

"Absolutely not," Emmett said. "I was *not* about to play around with getting murdered by some lady in a mirror!"

"Tanya and I tried to summon her at a sleepover once when we were in elementary school," I said. "But she chickened out halfway through and I had to finish saying it by myself."

"Wow, very brave of you."

"Thank you, I know."

"So, I guess that means you don't believe in ghosts?" Emmett asked.

I looked at Ghost, still sitting at the foot of my bed, his head turned toward me. Half a year ago, I would've answered differently, but now . . .

"I didn't used to," I said. "But yeah, I believe in them. What about you?"

"I definitely believed in them as a kid, but these days, I go back and forth. Sometimes I'm like, 'yeah, they're not real,' but then I'll hear a noise while alone in my room at night and suddenly I'm a believer. My family isn't into all that, though."

"How come?"

"My parents are über-religious Southern Baptists, and my siblings are more into religion than I am. My parents' stance is that most ghost encounters people describe are actually demons, so they don't like it if I genuinely talk about that kind of stuff."

"I didn't know you had siblings," I said.

"Yep! An older sister and a baby brother," Emmett said. "Braelyn's three years older than me and *really* involved in the church, and my brother Jonathan is six. Do you have any siblings?"

God, I hated that question.

There was no way around Jack's death. If I said, *Yes, I have an older brother*, people started asking me about him, and I could barely handle that. If I said, *No, I don't have any*, that felt like a gross lie and an erasure of Jack's life, and I couldn't stand the thought of acting like he'd never existed. It made me sick just to think about it.

So, the only option left was the whole, shitty, painful truth. Another rehashing of what happened. And I guessed that was another thing about losing someone: you were *always* losing them, over and over.

"An older brother," I said quietly. "But he passed five months ago."

"Holy shit, Caleb. I'm so sorry."

"It's, uh . . ." I started to say, *okay*, but decided against it. I was never really sure how to respond in these situations. In person, I often just smiled or tried to change the subject.

"Can I ask what his name is?" Emmett said, before I could think of something better to say.

Ghost stretched, his nebulous body briefly elongating, before he stood and approached me. He sat down next to me, taking up the rest of the space without either of us touching. My eyes started to burn with tears. I didn't let them fall, though.

"Jack," I said.

I couldn't remember the last time I'd *really* talked about him or his death with anyone but my parents. Tanya and I didn't really address what happened by name—most of the time, if we were talking about how I was doing, it was about Ghost—and I barely talked at Tom's group.

"Jack Stone?" Emmett said.

"Yeah." I wondered how they knew my last name. Had they heard it during class? Had Tanya given my full name to them at one point? Had they found me on social media?

I imagined Emmett looking me up, scrolling through my Instagram feed, the same way I had done to them, and I was surprised by how flattered I felt at the possibility. I didn't post that much on there, so it wasn't like there would be a lot for them to dig through—but I liked the idea of Emmett being interested enough in my life to look me up.

"Thank you for telling me," they said. "I know it can't be fun to talk about."

"Honestly, I'm kind of surprised you didn't know already. I guess I thought it was public knowledge at this point. . . ."

There was the sound of shuffling from their end. "I remember Tanya mentioning something about your family going through a rough time earlier this year, but she said she couldn't go into details. I think she wanted to let you have control over who knows instead of just telling me all your business, and I didn't really know how to ask about it. . . ."

"Ah. That makes sense. . . ." I trailed off.

Neither of us spoke for a moment, and I thought about changing the subject. But something made me want to keep talking to them about this. To tell them what I was actually feeling. I thought about *Limerence* and how connected I'd felt to Emmett, listening to a recording of them from two years ago, the pain in their voice. I thought about Ghost's interest in them, how he always lingered near them.

"Thank you for asking," I said. "About Jack's name, I mean.

Not a lot of people really know how to respond when I tell them he died. . . ."

"Yeah . . . I think most people, especially those who haven't ever lost someone close to them, are kind of uncomfortable talking about death, so most of the time people are well-intentioned and just not sure what to say. . . . But it can definitely feel frustrating and alienating when no one else wants to talk about this person you've lost or when they shut the conversation down."

People who haven't lost someone close to them. Did that mean someone Emmett loved had died?

"Sometimes I get angry when people try to be sympathetic about it," I admitted. "I don't mean to, and I know they're just trying to be nice, but I just can't always handle it."

"I get that. Personally, I get annoyed when people try to make it a Christianity thing without even knowing what the person who died believed in—like, my family will always say stuff like 'they're in heaven now' or 'they're with the angels' even if they know that person doesn't believe in that, and it can really bother me."

"That always sucks. Sometimes I just want to yell: 'You don't know that for sure, and you don't know our lives.'" I took a deep breath. "Maybe that's mean of me."

"I think you're allowed to be a little mean sometimes," Emmett said.

I laughed a little. "Thanks. I appreciate that."

We kept talking after that. The conversation moved away from grief, and we talked instead about the albums we'd started listening to and the movies we watched recently. I didn't ask

Emmett if they had lost anyone or who; I didn't feel like it was the right time.

And besides, Emmett had opened up a lot already. I figured they would tell me when they wanted me to know.

That night, I had a dream about Jack.

I had dreams about him a lot those first few months after he died. Most of them resembled reality—my parents mourning him, the funeral, a constant feeling of overwhelming sadness. Some of them were about our childhood, though, bastardized dream-versions of my strongest memories of him, the home movies we made together, Jack picking me up from Tanya's house, watching him play *Super Mario* on his vintage Nintendo 64 when the parents were away and he was babysitting me. Those weren't horrible in the moment, but waking up—returning to a life where he wasn't around—was always hard.

But this time, I dreamed that he was still alive, that we had been wrong, that the paramedics had been able to resuscitate him, that a miracle had come true. In the dream, we all acknowledged that he had been dead, but we rejoiced in his return, didn't think about what it meant that he had been gone, sighed in relief that our nightmare was finally, *blessedly* over. He was safe. He was alive. He was home.

In the dream, I cried so hard I almost threw up. I ran into his arms, and we sat at the bottom of the staircase, him holding me while I sobbed, promising me it was over, he was here now, it was okay. There were no track marks on his arms, no scars to show what had happened. He smiled a lot, and he looked healthy again—he'd put on weight, and his skin wasn't that sickly pale it usually was, and his blue eyes weren't dull, the life returned to his expression.

"We thought you'd died," I told him in the dream, still hugging him. Dream-me had the thought, *From now on, I am going to hug him every day. I am going to let him know how much I love him every day.*

"I know, but it's okay now," he said.

I felt a wave wash over me, hearing his voice again after so many months without it. It felt like a part of me was put back together, like the piece of me that had died with him was restored. I felt—serene.

"Tell me what I missed while I was gone," he told me once I'd stopped crying, and I filled him in on everything that had happened since that June, our parents' grief, the songs I couldn't write, the people I'd started talking to, Emmett and Nathan and Dima and Logan and Amy, how Tanya's family was doing, the home movies Mom and Dad kept putting on. I didn't tell him about Ghost because, for some reason, dream-me didn't know about him; it was like Ghost had been erased from reality after Jack was brought back.

And after I told him everything, he told me what he planned to do with his second chance—he was going back to college, he said; he was going to focus on studying; he was going to graduate; he was going to get his life together. "I'm gonna come home more often, too," he said. "So I can be here for you. And I'm going to get clean. I'm going to stop using. I'm going to quit smoking."

"Can we watch a movie?" I asked him, and he said of course we could.

As we sat down in front of the TV, though, dream-me felt a prickle at the back of my neck, and I was overcome with dread and despair—there, in the corner, was Ghost, sitting with his head turned toward us. He didn't move, didn't do anything at all, but horror washed over me, and I suddenly remembered him.

"*Get out*," I screamed at him, even as it felt hard to breathe. *"Get out get out get out get out get—"*

And that was when I woke up.

I was covered in sweat, my bedsheets twisted around my legs, my heart racing. From my bedside table, my alarm clock told me it was four a.m.

After a few minutes, I finally sat up in bed. Ghost was sitting at my feet, his head up as if watching me, and seeing him in that moment, I hated him more than I had ever hated anything, anyone. I knew logically that Ghost hadn't caused Jack's death, but I blamed him for it anyway.

"You took him from me," I whispered, staring at him in the dark. It was hard to see him with the lights off—he was more of an outline—but somehow, I knew exactly where he was, what he was doing. I could feel it, even in the darkness.

Ghost began walking toward me, but I scrambled back as far as I could on the bed. He paused at my movement, as if confused by my reaction.

"Don't get near me," I hissed. My heart was still racing, my body overcome with anger and, I realized, fear. I felt delirious. Unlike myself. "Get out of here. Just fucking *get out of here*!"

He kept still for a long moment. Then, finally, he jumped off the bed and sat on the windowsill instead.

Even when he wasn't near me, he was never truly gone. I couldn't escape him.

"Caleb?" My mom's voice at my door. My yelling must have woken her up. "Caleb, honey, is everything all right?"

"I'm fine," I managed, but even I could hear the sob in my throat, and Mom came in a second later.

She sat at the edge of my bed and put an arm around me. I didn't want to do this—I didn't want to be having a breakdown at four a.m.—but I couldn't help it; her hug reminded me of the one Jack had given me in my dream, and I started to cry, and it quickly devolved into sobs, rattling through me so hard I could feel it in my teeth.

"It's okay," she said, rocking me gently.

"He's gone," I kept mumbling.

"I know," Mom whispered, and I felt her own tears drip onto my shoulder. "I know."

We stayed like that for what felt like a long time, but, eventually, like always, the tears stopped coming and we had to put each other back together.

Once she was sure I was okay, Mom tucked me back into bed, kissed my forehead, and left to get some sleep again.

"Sweet dreams," she said as she closed the door behind her, but I hoped I wouldn't have any.

I couldn't fall asleep again after that. Ghost sat on the windowsill for hours, his back to me, and I did my best to pretend he wasn't there.

9

I TRIED TO AVOID MR. Russak's eyes in songwriting for most of the week. I hadn't turned in the song that was due last Friday, let alone made up any of my missing assignments, and I was a little ashamed of myself for letting him down so quickly after our conversation.

It wasn't for lack of trying. At least three separate times over the weekend, I'd sat on my bedroom floor, guitar in hand, computer open to a blank document and RhymeZone.com open on my browser. I'd *tried* to write something. But no matter what I did—no matter how much I thought *I need to do this*—I couldn't come up with anything. I just sat there, feeling like shit, for an hour before I finally gave up.

As class was coming to a close on Tuesday, Mr. Russak made an announcement that at this year's end-of-semester showcase, he hoped for a few students in songwriting to perform some of their original songs. WSA put on showcases every semester, and they were always these huge events; we would get out of classes early and all go to the auditorium, where students performed music, poetry, and dance, accompanied by pieces from the art students, all related to the classes they'd been taking. It was usually counted toward the classes' grades, too.

In my two and a half years at WSA, I hadn't performed at one yet, although there was a part of me that had sort of wanted to. But every time, there were always other students with more passion than me, more drive, better grades, better guitar or vocal skills—and, I figured, if the point was to show off the best and brightest of the school, why choose me? So, I'd never really *tried* to be in one.

But Mr. Russak glanced at me when he said, "I think it would be a really great opportunity for you all to get comfortable sharing your music. We still have a month, so no one has to make a decision right now, but if you're interested in being a part of it, let me know after class, all right?"

We nodded, and it wasn't long before the bell rang. Thankfully, Mr. Russak didn't say anything about my new missing assignment. I was glad for the space.

At lunch on Wednesday, Tanya got up to get a drink, and Nathan offered to go with her. Once they were both out of earshot, Logan leaned in to us and said, "Okay, so, we all know they're totally into each other, right?"

Dima, Emmett, and I all agreed in unison.

"Nathan is never *not* making googly eyes at her," Emmett said.

I snorted a laugh at that, and Emmett gave me a grin across the table. I felt my cheeks starting to burn, and I looked away quickly.

"Yeah, Tanya is definitely into him, too," I said, trying to cover up my own embarrassment. "I don't know why they haven't acted on anything yet, though."

"Unless they have and they just haven't said anything about it," Dima suggested, raising an eyebrow conspiratorially.

Something about that suggestion bothered me. It probably wasn't true, but I didn't like the idea that Tanya would keep something like that from me. Maybe from everyone else, sure—but not from me. We didn't have secrets.

"I doubt that," I said, a little more defensively than I wanted to.

Logan nodded. "Yeah, and Nathan's not good at hiding things. I think we would've known by now if anything serious had actually happened."

Emmett *hmm'd* thoughtfully, putting their chin in their hand. "That reminds me of another couple I know." They wiggled their eyebrows at Logan.

Logan's cheeks turned pink, and he threw his hands in the air. "Okay, but at least Amy and I could admit that we liked each other!"

"It *did* take you a hot minute, though," Dima said.

"How did you two get together?" I asked, turning to Logan.

"Oh my God, it's the cutest story," Emmett said.

Logan rolled his eyes, but he seemed a little flattered. "Well, we were friends for a few years first in middle school, and we kept in touch when I got in here and she went to Brentwood.

One of the things we always bonded over was cosplay, so we would cosplay together and go to anime conventions every summer—"

"Ahh, nerds in love." Emmett sighed dreamily, holding a hand over their chest.

Logan grinned a little. "Anyway, the summer before sophomore year, we went to a con as usual, and this time we went dressed as Winry and Ed from *Fullmetal Alchemist*. Have you seen that show?"

I shook my head. Other than watching *Naruto* and *Dragon Ball Z* in middle school, I wasn't particularly into anime.

"Well, they're the main endgame couple for the show," Logan said. "I felt a little awkward about it, but I just brushed it off because we were such good friends. But then when we got there, people wanted to take our picture, and it was obvious that they wanted us to be couple-y and cute, so Amy would pull me into these couple poses, like hugging or kissing me on the cheek. We kind of laughed it off, but when I was looking at the pictures after I got home, I realized that I liked her as more than a friend."

"And then they spent the next few months pining over each other before Amy finally made a move," Dima finished.

Logan nodded. "That is correct. So, yeah. That's how we got together."

"You were right, Emmett. That *is* a pretty cute story," I said.

Emmett grinned. "Isn't it? Logan and Amy are the only good straight couple I know."

"'Straight' couple," Dima said, using air quotes.

"You're right, neither of them are straight. Sorry 'bout that,

Logan," Emmett said, patting him on the back. "I wasn't trying to be, like, invalidating or anything."

Logan shrugged. "You're all good."

I looked around the table. I hadn't known Logan wasn't straight, but then again, I'd never asked.

"No one has to answer this, obviously," I started, "but . . . is everyone in your friend group queer?"

"Pretty much," Dima said. "I think Nathan might be the only straight one. I'm a lesbian, Logan and Emmett are bi, and Amy's ace and pan."

I nodded. "Cool. I'm queer too, but I don't really use a more specific label than that."

"How come?" Emmett asked.

"I don't really know, honestly. I used to only say I was gay because I'm mostly attracted to guys, but sometimes I think I might be into girls, too. And I've been attracted to nonbinary people who all look and identify really differently, so . . . I don't know," I said. "I just like to say I'm queer and leave it at that. It's not like I have people throwing themselves at me all the time, so I'm not really thinking about it constantly anyway."

"Hey, same!" Dima offered me a fist bump. I returned it.

"Constantly single club," I said, and she laughed.

We moved on to talking about exes and past dating history. Logan said he'd never dated anyone but Amy ("As long as you don't count my girlfriend from kindergarten"), but he told me about Amy's ex-girlfriend, who she was still friends with and who Logan actually thought was pretty cool. Dima, like me, had never dated anyone, but that was partially because she didn't really *want* a relationship for the foreseeable future, anyway.

"I've got too much shit going on already," she said. "I mean, I barely have time for *myself*, let alone another person."

Emmett was strangely quiet. I'd figured that they would've been the kind of person who had a ton of dating experience by now, so I was surprised when they said nothing the entire time. I didn't ask them about it, though. A part of me worried that if I did, it would somehow give away my attraction to them, and then I wouldn't know what to do with myself.

I still wasn't sure how much of it was romantic interest and how much of it was because of the weird things with Ghost. But it didn't matter, I told myself; Emmett wouldn't like me back, so my crush was pointless, anyway.

Tanya and Nathan came back carrying a soda and a few snacks from the vending machines.

"Sorry we were gone so long. I realized I needed to return a book to the library, so we ran and did that really quick," Tanya said, taking her seat again.

"Is that a euphemism for something?" I heard Emmett mumble under their breath, and I stifled a laugh. They locked eyes with me, a small grin in place.

"What are you two giggling about?" Dima said, looking between Emmett and me with a raised eyebrow.

"Nothing, nothing," Emmett said, waving her off.

The conversation shifted to the musical that the theater department was working on. Nathan was a theater kid, preferring to work behind the scenes. He was in charge of lighting.

The musical this year was *Little Shop of Horrors*, and since they only had one more week until opening, he was particularly stressed. They were in the middle of tech week—or "hell week," as he called it—and then the show would open on Friday.

"You guys should come see it. The cast is really good this year," Nathan said, looking between me and Tanya. "I know y'all"—he gestured to Dima, Logan, and Emmett—"were already planning on going, right?"

Emmett nodded. "Yeah. We could all go together."

Tanya smiled. "That'd be fun! And maybe we could hang out afterward."

"For sure," Nathan said.

I didn't say anything. The conversation moved to something else, and while everyone else was talking, Tanya nudged my shoulder. When I looked at her, she gestured toward my phone.

Tanya

do u wanna go with us friday?

I heard Emmett and Dima laugh about something. I pulled my phone out under the table so it wasn't *as* obvious that I was texting.

Caleb

not sure yet

maybe

She "liked" my messages and sent a few hearts in response. I locked my phone.

* * *

Emmett and I decided to meet up after school on Thursday in one of the music rooms, so we could work on the songs together without bothering anyone else. All the classrooms designated for the music conservatory had soundproofing on the walls, and Emmett had gotten permission from Mr. Russak to use one after school as long as we didn't touch any of the equipment. I agreed to meet them there, although I wasn't sure what I was going to tell them about the songs I hadn't written yet.

"Were you *supposed* to have a song written already?" Tanya asked as we walked together to the music room. Ghost trailed quietly next to us, barely visible out of the corner of my eye. He'd been around all day, and in songwriting earlier, he kept pacing between the desks as if bored. Since my conversation with Emmett, Ghost had been following me around even *more* obviously, and he seemed almost impatient, like there was something he was waiting to happen.

"I don't know," I said. "Maybe? It's not like we had a strict deadline for the songs."

"But the project has a deadline, right?"

"Yeah, but it's not due for another, like, month. So, it's not like I don't have time."

She twisted her mouth to the side in thought. "Hmm. Well, are you worried about it at all?"

Yes was the real answer. Not about the project, specifically, or even about my grade—but about not being able to write anything.

And maybe a little bit about disappointing Emmett. I didn't know how to tell them that I couldn't write music the way they could—on demand, quickly, and without having a complete existential breakdown over it.

I didn't say any of that to Tanya, though. Instead, I told her, "Not really."

She seemed skeptical, but didn't call me out on the lie. "Okay, well, if you're not worried about it, then it should be fine, right? It's not like Emmett's super uptight. They're probably not that worried about it, either."

"Right." But I wasn't totally convinced.

When we got to the classroom, Emmett wasn't there yet, but Tanya pulled me into a hug at the entrance.

"I'll be in the art room when you're done," she said. "Then we'll head home."

I nodded.

"Love you, have fun!"

I rolled my eyes. "Okay, Mom, love you, too." But I was still a little sad to see her go.

I made myself comfortable in one of the desks and pulled out Jack's copy of *The Catcher in the Rye.* Since finding it almost two weeks ago, I'd started rereading the book. I was about a third of the way through it, and it was surprising how much I'd forgotten or missed on my first read-through.

Mostly, though, I wanted to see Jack's notes, his thoughts, what he deemed important enough to highlight or underline. When I got to the section where Holden asks the cab driver where the ducks go in the winter, I saw that Jack had highlighted the entire exchange, and next to it was written: *important—being brushed off? trying to reach out to people? childlike curiosity?*

Further in the same chapter, I found what looked like an exchange between Jack and someone else, scribbled in the margins; *u coming tonight?* was written in unfamiliar handwriting. Jack had responded, *no sorry, I can't*, and the other person replied, *boo :(*. I wondered who he'd been passing notes in class to, and I hated that I would probably never know.

Emmett arrived a few minutes later. Today, their hair was braided in two pigtails, and they wore an Against Me! T-shirt. "Sorry I'm late!"

"You're all good," I said, closing the book and putting it back in my bag.

"You're reading *The Catcher in the Rye*?" Emmett said as they sat down in the desk next to me. "I had to read that for class last year."

"Me too. I'm just rereading it for, uh, fun."

They nodded. "Yeah, I remember kind of liking it, even though everyone else in class thought Holden was an annoying asshole. I mean, he kind of is, but I still found the book interesting."

I saw Ghost make himself comfortable under Emmett's chair, folding his paws on top of each other and laying his chin on them as if to doze off to sleep.

I looked back up at Emmett. "Yeah, I get that. Um, so, what should we work on first?"

Emmett pulled out their acoustic guitar, adjusting it in their lap. It was a Fender, the wood a light blond, and from here I could read some of the stickers on it—a tarot card called The Chariot, one that said Punk's Not Dead in bold letters, and a possum with the transgender symbol. The guitar was in good shape, but I could tell that Emmett had owned it for a while; some of the stickers had begun to fade slightly, and there were scratches on the base.

"I started writing another song last night," they said, "so I thought I could show that to you, if you want . . . ?"

"Oh. Yeah, of course." I was surprised by how quickly they had another one ready, although I guess I shouldn't have been; it seemed like Emmett was pretty prolific.

Embarrassment and guilt pricked at me. I wished I could write like they did. I wished I was a better artist, songwriter, student. Person.

"Okay, so, this one is from the point of view of the archetypal villain character," Emmett said, after getting their guitar in tune. "Should I just jump in, or . . . ?"

I nodded. "Go for it."

Emmett smiled, took a deep breath, and started to play. It was a slower song than the last one, more somber. The narrator described how they wished they could be good, but they were designed to be evil, made that way by the author, and no matter how much they tried to do the right thing, they always failed and ended up hurting people.

They let the final chord ring for a moment, and once it had faded out, they gave a sheepish, almost nervous smile. "So . . . how was that?"

"Good," I said, and I meant it. Emmett was a good singer.

Their voice had a unique quality, something different enough that it was intriguing, and there was a rawness to their vocals, a sound that felt honest and real.

What surprised me most, though, was how nervous Emmett seemed while playing. They had looked so confident onstage the last time I saw them, and they never seemed shy about the fact that they were a musician. I was kind of shocked that they hadn't looked me in the eyes at all while playing.

"Thanks," they said, putting their guitar back in its case. "What did you think about the lyrics? I had a bunch of ideas that didn't show up in the final version, so there's some stuff I can move around or change if you think it needs it. . . ."

They passed me a notebook, and I combed through the lyrics.

"Do you think there could be room for a bridge?" I asked. "I mean, you already have three verses and a chorus, and I think those are working well, but it might feel more fleshed out if you added a bridge, and maybe there could be an emotional turn here. . . ."

Emmett scooted their chair forward and looked at the lyrics with me. The space between our chairs was only a few inches, and I was close enough to them to see that an eyelash had fallen onto their cheek. I got the urge to reach up and brush it away.

"Yeah, I see what you mean," they said, moving back again.

I exhaled quietly, thankful for the space between us again.

". . . but maybe I could add something about the villain finally accepting their fate," Emmett was saying when I finally tuned back in. "Like, maybe the bridge is where they sort of go,

'Fine, you want a bad guy? I can give you a bad guy.'"

I nodded. "Yeah. That could be interesting."

Emmett gave a relieved smile. "Awesome! Well, I guess in that case, if there isn't anything else about that one, we could move on. Did you have anything you wanted to show me?"

Shit. Here it goes.

"Um, well . . ." I trained my eyes on Emmett's guitar case. My words came out in a mumble. "I haven't actually written anything yet."

"Oh, okay," Emmett said. Their tone sounded neutral, almost relaxed, instead of the frustration or irritation I was expecting, but I still felt like garbage saying it out loud.

I looked up again, making eye contact now. "I'm sorry. I know it's probably frustrating, since you've already written *half* of the songs we needed, but . . ."

"It's all good," they said with a shrug. "We have four weeks left, and I know not everyone can just—" They made an exploding motion with their hands. "Boom, there's a song. We have time. I'd still like to hear if you have any new thoughts about the songs, if that's okay with you?"

"Yeah, for sure," I said.

I pulled out my laptop and opened the Google Doc I started with some of the song ideas. We looked over my notes, and Emmett came up with a few more ideas I could use. They also said that I could reach out to them whenever if I needed help.

"I love songwriting with other people," they said. "So maybe we could collaborate on something, if that would make it easier?"

I thought about *Limerence*. I wanted to ask them about it, or at least reference that I knew about the EP.

But then I thought about how this Mallory person wasn't in any of Emmett's Instagram posts, and how in all their advertising for Deck of Fools, I had never seen them plug *Limerence* or even make mention of it. I worried that maybe the EP was a secret, or at least something that Emmett didn't want to talk about. Maybe it was best that I didn't bring it up.

Instead, I told them, "That could be fun. Thanks for the offer."

"Yeah, of course!" They smiled, then seemed to pause, like they were debating something, before saying in a rush, "Actually, I was wondering if you were gonna go see the musical tomorrow night? I know Tanya said she was going, but were you interested, too?"

"Oh." I hadn't really expected that question. I was kind of flattered that Emmett thought to ask *me*, and not just assume I was tagging along with Tanya. "Yeah, I can go."

"Cool." Another smile. "We were thinking about hanging out afterward at Nathan's house, kind of as an after-party to celebrate. It would just be the normal group, plus Amy if she can make it."

I hoped my surprise didn't show on my face. "Uh, yeah, sure, that'd be fun."

"Awesome!" Their face lit up in yet another smile. They seemed to be in a good mood now, and I couldn't help thinking it was cute.

We went back to working on our project for a little while,

but it was obvious we'd lost momentum and weren't gonna get much else done today. We'd been there for almost an hour by the time that we decided to head out.

As we were leaving the room, Emmett said, "I'll text you about tomorrow night?"

"Sounds good," I said, closing the music room's door behind us.

We stood there for a second, neither of us moving. It seemed like Emmett wasn't sure what to say, or maybe like they were waiting for me to say something. I shifted my weight from one foot to the other. Ghost had joined us in the hallway, sitting—predictably—near Emmett's feet.

"Thanks for your help, by the way," I finally said. "I mean—with the project and everything."

"Yeah, no problem," they said. "We're working together, after all."

"I know. I just felt bad since I haven't gotten as much work done as you have," I admitted. "I don't want you to think that I'm not trying or that I'm, like, trying to push all the work onto you. . . ."

"Really, Caleb, it's totally okay." They offered a reassuring grin. It hit me that this was maybe the first time I'd heard them say my name, or at least the first time I'd *noticed* them say my name, and something about that . . . it made me all the more aware that I was attracted to them.

My phone buzzed with a text; it was Tanya, letting me know she'd finished with her work in the art room and was in the cafeteria now. We said our goodbyes after that, but as we were walking away, I noticed that Ghost seemed . . . almost agitated. He started to follow Emmett, then stopped and just watched as they walked away.

Later that night, I sat on my bed, guitar in lap, and tried to *finally* write a song.

It was almost eleven. My parents were asleep, and the house was unsettlingly quiet. Usually, I would turn on a show or something to cover up the silence, but I didn't want anything distracting me. I was determined to get this assignment done, even if it was the worst shit I had ever written in my entire life.

I warmed up playing a few songs I'd already learned on guitar—Johnny Cash's cover of "Hurt," AJJ's "Hate, Rain On Me," and Big Joanie's "Fall Asleep." I tried not to think about anything else as I played them, tried to focus on the lyrics, the chord progressions, the familiar melodies. I focused on how it felt to press my fingers into the guitar strings, the pressure against the calluses already built up on my fingertips, the gentle pain. I focused on how it felt to sing—even if it wasn't good, even if my vocals were shaky, even if I was off pitch. I tried to just focus on how *good* it felt to make music.

I hoped that, by focusing on this, it would inspire me. It would remind me why I loved music so much. It would remind me why I even went to Williams School of the Arts in the first place.

And it worked, sort of. After an hour of fiddling with chord progressions and scouring through RhymeZone and writing and rewriting lyrics, I finally had something I felt I could turn in. I recorded myself playing it on my phone, then sent the audio file along with the lyrics in a separate Google Doc to Mr. Russak. When I fell asleep around one a.m., I felt better, fuller. A little bit more like myself.

10

FOR ALL THAT JACK PICKED on me growing up, he was also an intensely supportive brother.

He was the first person in my family that I came out to as trans. Tanya was the very first person I told; we spent a few months bonding over our confusing feelings around gender, and after a while of asking Tanya to use he/him/his pronouns for me, I decided I was certain enough that I wanted to start coming out.

One day, when I was in eighth grade, Jack picked me up from the mall where I had been hanging out with Tanya and a few of our friends. He was doing better during that time. The summer between eighth and ninth grade was the healthiest I remembered seeing Jack since he'd started using, and while the weeks leading up to that summer break weren't the best, we had started hanging out more often, the way we did when we were kids. I'd started feeling like I had my big brother back again.

"Did you get anything cool?" he asked when I got into the passenger seat.

I lifted up my Hot Topic bag. "Just a few new shirts." Lately, none of my clothes had felt right; everything I owned seemed either too feminine or just not "me" enough, so I was trying to slowly rebuild my wardrobe. I pulled the shirts out of the bag to show them off.

"Aw, nice," he said, glancing at the shirts as he backed out of the parking spot. "Does that one have *Naruto* characters on it?"

"Yeah, it's Sasuke," I said.

"Hell yeah." He grinned. "Is he your favorite character?"

"I go back and forth between him and Kakashi."

"Good choice."

We talked for most of the ride about *Naruto* and *Dragon Ball Z*. Jack wasn't a huge anime fan, but he *was* a huge *DBZ* fan; it was and always had been his favorite show of all time, and I would forever associate it with him.

When we were only ten minutes from the house, I steeled myself to tell him. I'd been planning on coming out to him for the past few days, but each time an opportunity came up, I'd decided against it. Now, I was determined. No more putting it off.

We passed the drugstore near our neighborhood, and I took a deep breath.

"Can I talk to you about something?" I asked.

Jack glanced between me and the road. "Sure, what's up?"

Outside, the sun was setting. I tried to remember the speech I had come up with over the past couple of weeks, but the words had evaporated, and all that was left was the feeling that I needed to get this out.

"Have you ever felt like there was something . . . weird about me?" I asked.

He kept his eyes on the road, but I could tell that he was a little confused. "Not any weirder than everyone else in the world," he said. "Why? Do *you* feel like there's something weird about you?"

"Yeah. Well, kinda. I think . . ." I trailed off. I wasn't sure where to go from here, what to say, how to say it. I wasn't sure how to get the words out.

"Whatever it is, you can tell me," Jack said. He said it directly, like he was just stating a fact rather than trying to comfort me, and that was better than if he *had* said it comfortingly. That was the Jack that I knew: direct, straight to the point, but not harsh.

It gave me the strength to finish my thought.

"I think I'm transgender," I said. It was the first time I had said *transgender* aloud to anyone but Tanya.

There was barely even a pause. "Oh . . . Okay. Cool." Jack nodded. After a second of neither of us saying anything, he asked, "So, would that make you my brother, or sibling, or . . . ?"

I wasn't sure why but, hearing that, I just burst out crying.

"Oh, shit," Jack said. He patted my shoulder with one hand, the other still on the steering wheel. "I'm sorry. I didn't mean to make you upset."

"You didn't," I said, wiping tears off my cheeks. "It's just—that just made me happy. And yeah . . . I think I'm a boy, so . . . I guess that means I would be your brother now."

He nodded again, taking his hand off my shoulder. "All right. Thank you for telling me." He started to say my deadname, but then he stopped himself. "Is that what you'd still want to go by, or is there another name I should call you? Not that you *have* to change it, obviously, but . . ."

"I think I'm gonna change it eventually, but that works for now," I said.

"Do the parents know?"

I shook my head. "Not yet. I want to wait a little longer before I tell them. So, you don't have to, like, say 'he' or refer to me as a guy around them or anything until after I come out to them. . . ."

"Sounds like a plan."

We pulled into our driveway and I assumed that was sort of the end of the conversation. But as I was getting unbuckled, Jack paused with the keys still in the ignition.

"For real, though, thank you for telling me," he said. "And I just want you to know that, no matter what happens, I'm always gonna be your big brother. I'm always gonna be there for you. Okay?"

I nodded, and, to my surprise, Jack hugged me. This was one of the few memories I had of me and Jack hugging. When we pulled away, he ruffled my hair and gave me a supportive grin.

After his death, this was a memory I fixated on a lot: his smile, the ease with which he'd accepted me, his pat on my shoulder. We didn't always get along, and he wasn't always a good big brother, but this was how I wanted to remember him—direct, kind, supportive, and, most of all, present.

* * *

Friday night, after WSA's production of *Little Shop of Horrors*, we all went back to Nathan's house. Logan, Amy, and Dima drove there separately, while Nathan drove Tanya, Emmett, and me. I was thankful to not have to be the designated driver for once, since it meant I could drink tonight.

Nathan led us through the sparsely decorated living room down to a basement, which had been converted into a game room. It was complete with a Ping-Pong table, multicolored LED lights that lined the ceiling, three separate consoles with controllers and a stack of video games, and the biggest TV I had ever seen. Once we were settled in, Nathan stood at the Ping-Pong table with an array of drinks spread out. He wiggled his eyebrows and singsonged, "Who wants shots?"

"Me!" Logan said, shooting his hand into the air.

"I'll do *one*," Dima said, "but no more. I don't need to puke tonight."

Nathan looked to the rest of us. Amy and Emmett declined, but Tanya and I, after exchanging a series of looks, said yes.

Nathan wasn't drinking since he'd driven us here, but he seemed to enjoy playing bartender; he poured vodka into tiny shot-size red Solo cups and handed out Diet Coke and sparkling wine as we requested. Tanya, Dima, Logan, and I all circled around him, passing out the shots. I wasn't going to admit it to anyone, but I had never done shots before. I'd only sipped a few beers here and there.

"Okay, on three," Logan said, raising his cup into the air. "One—two—three!"

I tried to copy how I'd seen people throw shots back, but I lost momentum halfway through and ended up spilling some of it on my shirt, coughing all the while. I'd expected it to taste bad, but that still didn't prepare me for the burning as it went down. Tanya patted me on the back sympathetically as I coughed.

Nathan passed out more mixed drinks, and I took my Diet-Coke-and-vodka and sat on the couch. Emmett had turned on *Phineas and Ferb*, and the TV played an episode quietly.

Seeing my expression, Emmett shrugged. "What can I say? It's a good show to put on in the background at parties."

I grinned. "No judgment here. I just wasn't expecting it, that's all."

"Not to change the subject, but Nathan, how is this okay with your parents again?" Amy asked from where she was pressed against Logan, their knees knocking into each other. I wondered how it would feel to sit that close with someone else—how it would feel to be so comfortable with someone that you want to touch all the time, even in small ways.

"My dad and his girlfriend are out on a date tonight," Nathan said, "so they won't be home until eleven at the earliest. And they usually don't bother me if I'm down here, anyway."

"God, I wish I got that much privacy," Dima said. "I would *kill* for Mila to leave me alone for, like, longer than an hour."

"That's your sister?" Tanya asked.

Dima nodded. "And, unfortunately, my roommate. She's eleven."

Emmett winced in sympathy. "Braelyn and I shared a room

until I was fourteen. That shit sucks!"

"*Sucks*," Dima agreed.

We went on like that, sipping our drinks and talking while the TV played quietly as background noise. After a while, the topic returned to the musical, and Dima said, "You did a great job with lighting, Nathan."

He blushed a little. "Aw, you don't have to say that. I know most people don't notice that stuff much. . . ."

"Well, *I* noticed, and I thought it was great. You're good at what you do, dude," she insisted.

"I couldn't imagine having to be in charge of all that," Tanya said, cradling her drink in her hands. "I'd be so worried about missing a cue or something."

"That's the performing arts for you," Logan said. "Just a bunch of worrying about missing cues."

"That sounds exhausting," Tanya said.

"It can be," Emmett agreed.

"I guess there's a reason so many people have stress dreams about performing," Amy said.

Tanya grimaced. "Yeah, I think I'll just stick with my silly little paintings where no one has to watch me make them, thank you very much."

"Your paintings aren't silly. They're amazing," Nathan said, and the way he looked at her was so earnest, it was almost unbearable.

Here we go again, I thought. Another outing where the two of them relentlessly flirted while refusing to admit that's what it was.

"Well, thank you," Tanya said, pushing a strand of hair behind her ear.

"Are you gonna submit anything for the showcase again at the end of the semester?" I asked. Tanya had pieces from her ceramics class presented in the showcase this past spring, and she'd seemed to like it.

"I don't know yet," she said. "I have a few paintings that I might want to submit if I can get 'em done in time, but that's a big *if.*"

"One of them is the self-portrait you're working on, right?" Nathan asked, and Tanya nodded.

I was a little surprised Nathan knew so much about Tanya's current works in progress. Sure, *I* knew about that self-portrait she was working on, but I was Tanya's best friend. It was basically my job to be plugged into her life.

But, whatever, I told myself. It wasn't like Tanya kept her art pieces secret. Other people were allowed to know about the stuff going on in her life. It wasn't a big deal.

I took another sip of my drink. The taste had gotten a little more bearable as I got used to it. I was almost finished with this drink and was officially in "buzzed" territory.

"Well, you still have time to figure it out, right?" Amy said to Tanya. "It's not until, like, what, mid-December?"

Tanya nodded. "Yeah. I should be good on time. It's just . . . you know, hard."

We talked for a little while longer about the showcase, and once I finished my drink, I got up and poured myself another one.

As I took a sip, I felt a prickle at my neck, and I knew before I even turned around that Ghost was sitting in the circle, right near Emmett. Maybe I should've been used to it by now, but it still freaked me out seeing his smudged form in the middle of the group. What did he want from me now?

I poured more vodka into my Diet Coke, just for good measure, before joining everyone again. When I sat down, Ghost got up from his spot near Emmett and came over to me.

"SALINE is doing a show tomorrow night at Gwen and Tommy's place, and I told them I'd be there if anyone wants to join me," Emmett announced to the room.

"Who's SALINE?" I asked, but I was looking at Ghost. He was turned toward me, his tail flicking quickly back and forth as if annoyed, but I wasn't sure why.

"They're a local band," Logan said. "We're kind of friends with a few of the members. They were nice enough to help us figure out how to put on our own shows and stuff when we were first getting together."

"Oh." I nodded. I was having a hard time paying attention when Ghost was still sitting in front of me. I took a large gulp of my drink.

"I'll have to miss it, since we've got another *Little Shop* show tomorrow," Nathan said.

"Damn, that's right." Emmett patted Nathan's back apologetically. "But good luck with the second show. Not that you need it—I'm sure y'all will do awesome."

Nathan shrugged, bringing his cup up to his lips to hide a flattered smile.

"I can probably go," Dima said, and Logan and Amy nodded their agreement.

"I'll have to ask my parents first, but if they say yes, then yeah, it sounds like fun!" Tanya smiled.

Emmett nodded, then looked at me. I realized, after a second, that they were waiting on my answer.

"Uh, yeah, I'll be there," I said, hoping I didn't look as flustered as I felt.

We sat like that for another half hour, just talking and sipping our drinks, and at one point, Amy suggested we put on *Phineas and Ferb the Movie.* About halfway through, Emmett stood up and said, "I'm gonna go outside and smoke if anyone wants to join?"

"I'll join you." I was the only one who followed Emmett outside, and I was kind of glad for it. I'd been hoping for some time to talk, just the two of us, for most of the night.

We made our way to the patio, which was much more spacious without the stage set up. Emmett claimed one of the vinyl chairs, and I sat next to them, crossing my legs. They pulled a joint out of their jacket pocket, along with a lighter with a troll doll case, the flame acting as the doll's hair.

They lit the joint, and, after passing it to me, asked, from seemingly out of nowhere, "What's your favorite horror movie?"

I took a small inhale, but even that little amount was harsh enough on my throat to elicit a cough. "Definitely *Scream*," I managed. "Why?"

They took the joint back from me. "I don't know. I guess I was just curious. I know you're really into horror, and I've been trying to get more into it, but I actually haven't seen *Scream* yet."

"You haven't seen *Scream*?" I repeated, incredulous. "How is that possible?"

"Is this one of those things where it's considered blasphemous in the horror world to not be obsessed with that movie?"

"Not blasphemous. Just bad taste."

They snorted a laugh. The sound was a little bit dorky, but still, I found it almost unbearably cute. "You really love horror?"

"Yeah, of course."

"What do you think you love about it?"

I couldn't help it—I laughed. Maybe it was the weed and vodka, but something about Emmett asking me to talk about something that I liked was so absurd, and embarrassing, and kind of sweet, and it made nerves kick in my stomach.

"What? What's funny?" Emmett asked, fiddling with the lighter in one hand.

"Nothing—it's just—" I suppressed any more nervous, incredulous giggling. "No one's ever asked me that before, and we just got out here, and it's just funny that you want to know that about me 'cause I didn't think anyone cared about that stuff."

"Well, I do," Emmett said, a grin tugging at their lips. "So, what would you say?"

"I don't really know. I guess I like being freaked out by things. I think it can be fun to be scared when you aren't in real danger."

They nodded. "I get that. I like getting freaked out every now and then. But I don't personally love overly gross or shock-value-y stuff. I read the Wikipedia for *Human Centipede* last year and I still have bad dreams about it."

I laughed, then covered my mouth. "Sorry, I'm not laughing *at* you. That movie is just so absurd to me. . . ."

"No, feel free to laugh. I'm a wuss," they said. "You probably have a stomach of steel compared to me."

"Probably," I agreed. "But I'm surprised to hear that. I would've expected you to be into dark, edgy stuff because of the whole punk thing."

"Yeah, that's fair. But, no, I'm more into the anti-establishment, DIY side of things. And the music, obviously. But what about you? What kind of music do you write?"

"Usually folk and rock-ish stuff. But I haven't been able to write since my brother died."

I felt the way the air around us changed, felt the hairs on my arms stand up. Why had I said that?

"I'm sorry," Emmett said after a pause. "That must be really difficult."

There, behind them: Ghost. Keeping a distance, but still undeniably here.

"Yeah," I said. "And it's hard, since, you know, we're supposed to turn a song in every week for songwriting, and I know I need to turn something in to pass, but most of the time, I can't get myself to write anything." I looked down. "And maybe it's stupid of me—"

"It's not stupid," Emmett interrupted. "You're going through something traumatic right now; of course it would affect your creativity. That doesn't mean you're a bad student or a bad musician or something. And it certainly doesn't mean it's stupid."

Going through. Present tense.

Something about that made me feel pierced through—seen. Because that was how it felt: like Jack was still dying. It was still June. The loss was happening over and over, in a million different ways, and each time, the grief was bitter and fresh, raw and new.

"Thank you," I said quietly. "I—I needed to hear that."

In the distance, Ghost lay down, seeming suddenly relaxed.

"And like I said yesterday," Emmett said, "if you ever need help with writing, or if you want to write some more songs together, I'm always here."

"I might take you up on that," I said.

We sat for a few moments, neither of us saying anything. I looked out onto the backyard, the glimmering pool, the swath of trees at the edge of the property, and then at Emmett, who was looking up at the moon, and I had the thought, loud and clear: *I want to kiss them.*

Okay, fuck this, I thought—and before I could stop myself, I blurted out, "Would you wanna come over and watch *Scream* with me sometime?"

They blinked at me. For a long, horrible moment, I thought I'd fucked up, that they were going to grimace and politely decline—

But then their face broke into a smile, and they said, "Yeah, I think that'd be fun."

Logan, Amy, and Dima headed out after the *Phineas and Ferb* movie ended, and Nathan eventually drove Tanya and me home. Emmett was sleeping over at Nathan's, but they chose to ride with us so they wouldn't be alone at the house when Nathan's dad got home.

"He wouldn't mind," Nathan said. "He pretty much adores you."

But Emmett shook their head. "Nah, I'm good. Besides, it means I get more time with you guys." They smiled, and maybe I was making it up, but I swore they glanced at me when they said it.

Before we headed out, Nathan held up the bottle of vodka from earlier, only a fourth of it still there. "Does anyone want this?"

Emmett and Tanya both shook their heads, but I thought about how I'd felt tonight, how relaxed I'd been. . . .

"I can take it," I said.

Tanya whipped her head around to stare at me. "What about your parents?"

"They don't look through my stuff," I said. "As long as I hide it somewhere, it should be fine."

She didn't look convinced, a deep frown etched on her face. I hadn't seen Tanya look this worried about me since I'd decided to jump off the creek's bridge and ended up with a sprained ankle.

"It'll be fine," I said again, but it did nothing to shake her frown.

Nathan shrugged and handed the bottle to me. I slid it into my backpack, careful to hide it at the bottom, Jack's copy of *Catcher* resting gently on top of it.

11

SATURDAY NIGHT, TANYA AND I got to the SALINE show thirty minutes before it was meant to start. The show was being held at Gwen and Tommy's house, which was much more cramped than Nathan's and decorated with industrial-style furniture and dark colors. There was a makeshift bar set up in the kitchen, complete with orange Fanta and Pink Whitney spilled on the dark wood.

I poured myself a drink while Emmett gave Tanya and me the rundown on who everyone in the band was—Walter was the lead guitarist, Gwen was the lead vocalist, her sister Tommy was a guitarist and pianist, and Simon was the drummer.

"So, how do you know them?" I asked Emmett, screwing the cap back on the Grey Goose bottle. I gestured for Tanya to pour herself a drink, but she shook her head. That kind of surprised me, but I didn't question it. Instead, I nudged the bottle in Emmett's direction.

"Gwen graduated from WSA two years ago. She was also in the music conservatory, and we had a class together and a few mutual friends, so we just sort of became friends, too," Emmett said. They poured themself a drink, too, but with only a small splash of vodka. "Then she started SALINE with Tommy, Simon, and Walter after she graduated, so when we were getting started with Deck of Fools, they helped us get gigs and taught us how to host our own shows and stuff like that."

"Cool." I nodded. I didn't remember meeting someone named Gwen during my freshman year, but then again, that was before Tanya joined me at WSA; back then, I kept to myself a lot, so it was likely I'd seen her but just never known who she was.

"That was sweet of them to help you," Tanya said. "I can't even imagine how you get started as a musician."

"Yeah, it can be a lot. It was a little easier for us 'cause we already knew people in the Nashville punk scene, so we had an 'in' for some stuff," Emmett said. "Plus, we had help from Dima's mom's girlfriend, Alicia, 'cause she's done some producing. She helped us out with our first EP."

"That's really cool," I said.

They nodded. "Yeah, Alicia's the best. Ms. Khalil is really cool, too."

Tanya's phone buzzed with an incoming call. "Ah, shit—I'll be right back, my mom's calling." She waved before disappearing out of the kitchen. It wasn't unbearably loud, but the crowd was definitely growing, and with it, the volume.

I took a sip of my drink. I'd had fun yesterday, and I couldn't help but think that was in part because I'd been inebriated, so

I was hoping to get buzzed tonight, too. Maybe then I could finally relax, stop thinking so much.

"I think you and Gwen would get along," Emmett said after a moment.

"Really?" I said, surprised. "Why?"

"She's really into horror like you. I actually convinced her to watch *Re-Animator* recently 'cause of our conversation about it."

"What did she think of it?"

"I think she liked it, but you'll have to ask her yourself." They glanced behind me, then grinned. "Speaking of—hey, Gwen! Come here for a sec!"

I turned to see a girl making her way toward us. She was tall, goth, and butch; her curly black hair was shaved short on the sides, and her dimple piercings wiggled when she smiled at us. I had a faint memory of passing her in the hallways my freshman year.

"Hey, Em! What's up? Who's your friend?" she said, sliding up next to Emmett. Before they could answer, she held a hand out to me. "I'm Gwen. I'm part of the band."

I shook her hand; her grip was tight and confident. "I'm Caleb. I'm part of the audience."

She grinned. "Nice to meet you, Caleb."

"He goes to WSA, too," Emmett said.

"Oh, nice! What conservatory are you in?"

We talked for a while about WSA and the music conservatory and songwriting. When she realized our time at WSA overlapped a little, she apologized for not remembering me, but I waved it off.

Tanya returned after a little while, with Dima and Amy in tow.

"Look who finally made it," Emmett said, before giving both of them hugs.

"Sorry, it took longer to do our makeup than I thought it would," Amy said.

Both she and Dima were dressed up, their makeup bold and heavy. Amy wore a red-and-black dress, with spiked jewelry and platform boots, and her black lipstick matched her eye shadow and star-shaped eyeliner. Dima had similar eye shadow and eyeliner, and just as much silver jewelry, but she wore a graphic T-shirt and baggy, camouflage cargo pants.

I felt underdressed next to them. I thought I'd been doing well to throw on a band T-shirt and jeans.

"It looks *so* good," Tanya said. "I didn't know you were such a makeup artist, Amy."

She waved Tanya off, but I thought she looked a little flattered.

While Tanya and Amy talked some more about makeup, Dima slid up behind Emmett and poured herself some Fanta. Gwen asked her how she'd been, and while Dima, Emmett, and Gwen talked, I looked out to the living room, sipping my drink. The crowd had only gotten bigger as we stood around, and people moved in and out of the kitchen, pushing past us to get to the bar.

A cloud of smoke had started forming in the living room, and I realized a group of people had begun passing a bowl around. I glanced around the crowd, looking for Ghost.

Then there was a flash out of the corner of my eye—a boy pushing past me in the crowd—and for a second, I thought it was—

But—no. He joined the group smoking, and I got a better look at his face.

Of course *it's not Jack*, I thought. *How the fuck would it be Jack? Why would I even think that? I'm so stupid, so stupid—*

"All right, y'all, looks like it's time for me to head down and get the show going," Gwen said. "It was nice talking, though, and thanks for coming!"

She disappeared downstairs to the basement where the show was happening. I saw other people starting to head that way, too, and Dima suggested we go. I hadn't completely finished my drink yet, but I refilled it anyway before we made our way downstairs.

As we walked, Tanya bumped my shoulder gently. "Hey, is everything okay?"

"Yeah, definitely," I said, maybe a little too quickly. "Why?"

She bit her lip. "Well, it's just . . . you drank a lot yesterday, and you're drinking tonight, too. It just doesn't seem like you. Plus, when we were all hanging out earlier, it seemed for a second like . . ."

I tried to fill in the blank. Like I was checked out of the conversation? Like I was looking for Ghost? Like I was imagining seeing my dead brother walking around?

"What's wrong with me drinking?" I asked instead.

"I don't know, it's just not what you usually do. . . ."

"Well, things change," I said. "And besides, it's not like I'm overdoing it or anything. I'll eat some food after the show and be sober by the time we need to drive."

I couldn't help the prickle of annoyance I felt. I didn't want her to worry about me—and there wasn't anything to worry about, anyway.

"It's fine," I assured Tanya. "*I'm* fine. Let's just have fun tonight, okay?"

She nodded, but she still didn't look convinced.

The basement was as big as the living room and kitchen combined, with a small stage at the back of the room and all the equipment already set up. There was a sizable crowd claiming the best spots, so we stayed a little farther back. We made sure to avoid where the mosh pit would be, which I was kind of thankful for.

The show started a few minutes later, and the drummer counted them off. They jumped straight into it. The first song was loud, frantic, and cacophonous in the best way, and although I couldn't make out all the lyrics, it seemed like it was about trying to have fun in the face of adversity.

Next to me, Emmett moved to the music, singing along to the chorus with a wide, almost goofy grin. During the bridge, there was a call-and-response section, and Gwen held her microphone out to us as we sang on her cue. Emmett belted the words, their hands in the air, jumping in place to the beat.

The second song was a little slower paced. It was a duet, with the lead guitarist, Walter, joining Gwen at the microphones. Walter was white, a little shorter than Gwen, with curly red hair and a bigger build.

It wasn't until he spoke into the mic, telling us how they wrote this next song, that it hit me: I knew him.

"Do you know where Walter went to school?" I asked Emmett, leaning in to them so they could hear me over the crowd.

"He's at Belmont," Emmett yelled back.

"What about for high school?"

They paused, thinking. "I think Brentwood High?"

Shit. I couldn't believe it took me so long to recognize him. He had been one of Jack's friends from high school. One of the friends that had slowly stopped hanging around the house as Jack got further into his addiction.

A prickle at the back of my neck. I didn't even bother looking for him—I knew Ghost would be making his way toward me.

It suddenly felt like everything was too much. The music was too loud—people were too close to me—the world was closing in.

I couldn't be here right now.

"I'll be right back," I said to Emmett, but I didn't wait for their response before making my way back upstairs.

With the show going on, there were less people on the ground floor, allowing a little more room for me to move. In the living room, the people smoking had disappeared, but two people were bent over a glass coffee table, and it took me a moment to realize they were snorting something. I ran past them and up to the second level, searching for someplace to be alone. I found a bathroom and escaped to it.

I sat on the closed toilet, set my drink down on the floor, and held my head in my hands. Images of those people downstairs flashed behind my eyelids, and against my will, my brain supplied the image of Jack in their position.

I thought about him at parties like this. Laughing, joking, enjoying the music. Drinking. Smoking.

I thought about him trying not to think—*don't think, if you slow down for a moment the thoughts catch up, don't think, stay high, don't think*—until suddenly it wasn't a choice, and it wasn't even about not thinking anymore, it was about surviving, it was about getting his body what it needed to keep going.

I thought about when I went bowling with Emmett's group—about how I'd wanted to be high. I'd wanted to not be *me* anymore. I'd wanted to think differently; I'd wanted a break from myself.

And I got it, sort of. I kind of understood how someone could start out not knowing what they were getting into, how Jack could have thought, *I'm in control, this is just what I need.* How someone could think *I don't care if this hurts me*, or even *I* want *this to hurt me.*

Sitting in that stranger's bathroom, I wanted, suddenly and intensely, to go home. But not just back to my house—I wanted to run into my parents' arms. I wanted to be held and rocked. I wanted to cry hard.

I wanted to hear Jack's laugh. To see him in my doorway, a stupid, smug grin on his face as he poked fun at me for something. I wanted to hear him come home at night, his footsteps creaking up the stairs. I wanted to hug him and smell the cigarette smoke on his jacket.

I wanted my big brother back.

Someone knocked on the bathroom door. "Occupied," I called, my voice cracking, and after a second, I heard footsteps retreating. When I knew they were gone, the tears started falling.

I just kept thinking about how badly I wanted Jack here, and how he would never be here, he would never be alive again, and I thought about how unfair that was, how fucking unfair it all was, how he would never get to graduate college, he would never get to make his films, he would never watch another horror movie with me again, never talk about *Dragon Ball Z* with me again. Never eat another of Mom's casseroles. Never buy any new clothes. Never meet anyone else. I had all these new friends at Williams, and they would never get to meet Jack, and Jack would never get to meet them.

And it was all so *fucking unfair.*

I sat crying for what must have been a while, and when I finally stopped, I felt Ghost staring at me. I looked up and saw that he was in the tub next to me, pacing back and forth. He seemed agitated.

"What's wrong?" I asked him, but he just kept pacing, turning his head between me and the floor, as if to look at me. I got the urge to reach out for him, to comfort him. Slowly, I held my hand out.

He paused his pacing. Seemed to think about it for a moment.

Then he moved toward me until, finally, my hand was hovering above his head.

When I touched him, he wasn't solid—not really. I could feel him, his dark fur, but it wasn't like anything I'd ever experienced before.

It was like touching a dream.

Chills ran up my spine, and warmth washed over me.

He calmed down after a moment and sat back on his haunches. I thought I could hear the faintest purring—the only noise I'd ever heard from him so far—but it was possible that was just my imagination.

When I pulled away from petting him, I felt lightheaded, fuzzy, like the world was returning to me, like I was coming out of a stupor. My head was spinning; I wanted to lie down.

I climbed into the tub, reclining like I was taking a bath. I lay in there for what felt like a long time, trying to steady my breathing, the porcelain cool against my skin.

My phone buzzed in my pocket.

Emmett

hey, whered u go?

is everything ok?

I stared at the messages for a moment. When I looked up from my phone, Ghost was perched on the side of the tub, his head turned toward me. He didn't seem as upset anymore.

Caleb

second floor bathroom

It didn't take long for Emmett to find me. There was a knock at the door, and Emmett's voice: "Caleb?"

I hadn't locked it, so without getting up, I said, "Come in."

Emmett didn't seem shocked to see me in the bathtub. They just closed the door behind them and took a seat on the closed toilet lid.

"What's going on?" they said, after a moment of neither of us speaking.

I figured there was no use in pretending I was fine. I was drunk, lying in a stranger's bathtub, and looking very obviously like I'd been crying—there was no way to brush that off as emotionally stable behavior.

"I just . . . needed to be alone for a while," I said.

Emmett nodded. I glanced at Ghost, who hadn't gotten off the side of the tub, and I thought about his interest in them. Even now, he had turned toward Emmett the moment they entered the room, as if drawn to them.

I thought about how I felt connected to Ghost—about how there was something pulling us together, something that meant he was always with me. I imagined that line connecting us, pulled taut, then loosened again, the distance between us shrinking and expanding.

I thought about Jack, and grief, and about how Emmett had seemed to understand. I thought about *The Catcher in the Rye* and those scribbled notes. I shut my eyes tight.

"Have you ever lost someone?" I asked Emmett.

They didn't pause. "Yeah. I have."

There was a tightness in my chest, and I felt my eyes start to burn with tears again. I squeezed them shut even harder.

"Do you ever feel like no one else in the world understands what you're going through? Like no one else is grieving the way you are?"

"All the time," they said.

I opened my eyes. Emmett was staring at me, their expression gentle, and somehow, I managed to hold their gaze. I could faintly hear the music leaking in from downstairs, mostly just the bass, and the muffled sounds of people talking and laughing.

"I'm sorry I'm talking about this," I said, finally looking away. "I know it's not exactly fun."

They shook their head. "No, it's fine. I get it. I . . ." They took a breath. "I haven't really talked about it in . . . a while."

"Why?"

"It just hasn't come up, I guess. I don't know. I don't mean that I don't think about her all the time, but most of the people I see every day didn't know her. At least not the way I did. So, no one brings it up unless I do."

I nodded. "I get that."

We were quiet for a few moments. I sat up and pulled my knees up to my chest. Ghost jumped off the side of the tub and sat at Emmett's feet, curling up into a loaf, his paws tucked under him.

"My ex-girlfriend killed herself a year ago," Emmett said.

I looked at them. Their eyes were trained on the ground, but their expression was almost neutral, their voice even.

I recognized that look, that sound: it was the numbness. The horrible feeling of something unthinkable becoming a part of your reality, and then you just had to accept it. You just had to tell that story over and over again, never able to change the outcome.

"I'm so sorry," I said quietly. After a moment, I asked, "What was her name?"

"Mallory. Mallory Patton."

Oh.

Shit.

I tried to keep my expression neutral, but Emmett seemed to catch my surprise.

"What?" they asked.

"Nothing, it's just . . ." I shifted a little. I knew there was no point in hiding it, but I still felt a little uncomfortable admitting that I'd looked them up online. "I found your Bandcamp page a while ago, and I saw that you'd written some songs with . . ."

"With Mallory." They sighed. "Yeah. She was a musician, too."

"You don't have to talk about it if you don't want to," I said quickly.

"No, it's okay. I . . . I haven't really talked about her in a long time. Dima and Logan didn't really know her that well, and they didn't like her very much, either. Gwen and Walter knew her, but I'm not that close with them. We really only see each other at events like this." They gestured around us. "And this isn't exactly the *best* place to have emotional conversations."

"Unless you can find a bathtub to sit in," I said.

They smiled a little. "Yeah."

There was a pause while Emmett seemed to gather themself. Then they pulled their knees up to their chest, resting their heels on the toilet lid.

"We met in one of our music classes," they started. "She was this cool, charismatic, talented senior with a lot of friends and a music career obviously on the horizon, and I was a freshman with absolutely no clue how anything worked and no friends at school except Nathan, so of course I was flattered when she started talking to me. I didn't realize it was maybe a little weird that an eighteen-year-old would want to date someone who had been in high school for only a few weeks. I thought I was mature for my age, probably because she always told me that. She would say things like, 'you're so much more mature than I was at fourteen, you know that?'"

"Did anyone else ever say anything about that?" I asked gently.

"Yeah. Dima and Logan thought it was kind of a red flag, but I'd only known them for a few months at that point, so I didn't really listen to them. I thought they were just being judgmental. . . . And Nathan was trying to be supportive, so he didn't push back against it much. And my parents—they didn't know about me and Mallory."

"Why didn't you tell them?"

They shrugged. "I don't know. Maybe because I knew deep down, they wouldn't have been cool with it. Mallory had become my world before I'd realized it, so the idea of someone keeping us apart was, like, my worst nightmare."

I nodded.

"Anyway . . . we dated for almost a year, and we wrote a bunch of music together during that time. She'd already recorded a few of her own projects by that point, so she sort of showed me the process, and we put together an EP that we named *Limerence*." They glanced at me, then down at the floor. "Have you . . . I mean, you said you found it online. Did you listen to it?"

"Yeah," I admitted.

"Well, then I guess you understand, uh, the things I was going through were *not* healthy," they said with a humorless laugh.

"I got that feeling, yeah."

I remembered some of the lyrics from the EP, and thought about freshman Emmett writing that—"And you know I would kill myself / If you asked me to." What did Mallory do or say to them? How did she convince them that was love?

"Was she . . . I mean, was the relationship . . . good?" I asked quietly.

Emmett snorted a laugh. "God, no. She was abusive and manipulative in pretty much all of the ways you can imagine.

"She was . . . I don't know if she was naturally a bad person," they continued. "She was doing really, really bad mentally at the time and in need of a *lot* of help. She had severe depression, and her parents had been abusive to her for most of her life. . . ." They took a deep breath. "She did some shitty things to me, but there's a part of me that believes she could've gotten better, could've gotten help and realized how she was behaving, you know? Sometimes, I don't even think she knew what she was doing. . . . I think she thought it was normal. Maybe she didn't know how to love me any other way."

Emmett's voice broke at the end. I laid a hand on the side of the tub, my palm facing up, and, after a moment, they took it. Their hand was warm in mine, and I squeezed it gently.

"After almost a year of that, I realized what was happening. I started hanging out with Dima, Logan, and Nathan more and making my own friends who *weren't* Mallory's friends first, and eventually, I decided to end things. It was the summer after she'd graduated, and she was going away to UTC soon anyway, so I broke up with her. . . . Well, actually, I broke up with her about three times before it finally stuck. The first time, she threatened to kill herself if I left her, and the second time, she just straight up pretended like I'd never said anything and kept texting me and showing up at my house like nothing happened."

They paused. Took another deep breath.

"But the third time," they continued, "I blocked her on everything and told Gwen not to let her know where I was. That was the last time I talked to her. She went away to UTC after that, and . . . a few months later, she was dead."

I sucked in a sharp breath. Emmett's eyes looked wet with unshed tears, and they squeezed my hand.

"I'm so sorry," I said softly.

They shook their head. "Yeah, me too. It was just—everything's so fucked, you know? I mean, I try not to blame myself. I try to just have compassion for the younger version of me who was taken advantage of by someone they thought they could trust. I try to remind myself that I did the right thing by leaving her. And realistically, what could I have actually done to stop it, you know? She was in a really bad place, even *before* we met. She needed help that I couldn't give her. It was just a fucked-up situation."

"It wasn't your fault," I agreed.

That was when their tears started coming. "But how am I supposed to feel about it, you know? Should I be *happy*? She raped me, Caleb—I shouldn't care that she's dead. But I *do* care. I care that I lost her, that she's gone, even though I was the one who left *her* in the first place. Isn't that just so fucked up?"

I got out of the tub and came over to Emmett's side. We were hugging before I could think about what I was doing, and then I was holding them while they cried, their face buried in my shoulder. I rubbed their back as they shook.

"You deserve so much better," I said quietly. "I'm so sorry that happened to you. I'm so sorry, Emmett."

We stayed hugging until their tears eventually stopped. When we finally pulled away, I started to move back, but Emmett grabbed my hand to keep me there. I sat on the edge of the tub, close enough to them that our hands were still locked and our knees bumped into each other.

We were both silent for a moment. I rubbed my thumb across Emmett's knuckles.

"Jack was a drug addict," I said finally. "He died of a heroin overdose."

"I'm sorry," Emmett said quietly.

"It's—" I started to say, *It's okay*, but stopped myself. "Yeah," I said. "It fucking sucks, and it's fucking unfair, and I miss him every fucking day. I haven't . . . I haven't really figured out how to be a person again since he died. It just seems so pointless most of the time. Like, what's the use in going to class when my brother is dead, you know?"

They nodded. "I feel that way sometimes, too."

"Does it get easier?" I asked. I hadn't meant to say that; the question just sort of—slipped out.

Emmett smiled sadly. "Most of the time. Other times, it's just as bad as those first few days after she died."

I nodded.

Silence again. I focused on the feeling of Emmett's hand in mine, focused on just being here with them. I could feel Ghost sitting near us, but he seemed to be way calmer than he was earlier. He seemed . . . content.

"I'm sorry to bring all this up tonight," I said. "I know you probably didn't wanna talk about this out of nowhere."

Emmett shook their head. "No, it's okay. It can be hard to talk about, but . . . I think it's good for me. I don't like pretending it didn't happen."

I thought about that. Was talking about Jack's death "good" for me? It certainly didn't *feel* good—it felt like there was a part of me missing. It was the worst pain I'd ever experienced, and I had to experience it every day. Could it be good for me—to think about it more, to draw out the pain?

I thought about Tom's support group, all of us sitting in a circle with Ghost at my feet, bouncing our griefs between us. I thought about how it felt, hearing other kids talk about the pain of missing their loved ones. I wondered if any of them felt like talking about it helped, or if they were all also going just to appease their parents.

"Do you wanna go back down?" Emmett asked. "They should be starting the second half of the show soon."

I took a breath. Nodded. "Yeah. Let's go."

We left the bathroom and headed back downstairs. I finished the rest of my drink and quickly grabbed a refill in the kitchen. When we passed the living room, I noticed that the people I'd seen bent over the coffee table weren't there anymore. I was quietly grateful.

The rest of the night was a little better. I was still drunk for the second half of the show, and I felt myself give in to the music in a way I hadn't in a long time. I'd missed going out—having fun. Dancing in a room full of people, none of them even noticing me. SALINE's music was harsh and hectic, and I lost myself in it, the room becoming a blur, the people around me just heat and flashes of color.

At one point, I felt the ground coming up to meet me, and then Emmett was there, hands on my shoulders to keep me from falling down, and I couldn't help but laugh, beaming at them all the while.

They were so sweet—perfect—and my chest ached with how badly I wanted to kiss them—but I didn't. That was a step too far. But I looked at them, only half-illuminated by the lights shining from the stage, and I already knew—I was in deep.

12

Caleb

tanya im so sorry about last night

i really thought i was going to sober up in time to drive :(

it was stupid of me and it wont happen again i swear!!

I stared at my string of texts, reading *delivered*, and waited to see if a bubble would pop up to let me know Tanya was typing. It was Sunday, and I was lying on my bedroom floor. Last night after the show ended, we had to stay an extra hour and a half so I could sober up enough to drive home safely, meaning she and I were late getting home. My parents hadn't cared that much—I'd texted them to let them know I would be a little late, and although my mom wasn't thrilled about it, she didn't seem too mad when I got home. But Mr. and Mrs. Gupta were apparently super pissed about it, and they'd grounded Tanya for the week.

Tanya

yeah it was pretty stupid

but i know u didnt do it on purpose . . .

so i guess i can find it in my heart to forgive you

but seriously though, dont do that again!!!

if you want to drink you have to at least PLAN so this kind of thing doesnt happen!!

Caleb

i know and ur 100% right, i shouldve thought ahead :(

There was a pause. I watched her bubble pop up and disappear again three times before she sent a response.

Tanya

at least its just a week

i think my parents went easier on me when i said i was with u the whole time

they still adore u and think the sun shines out of ur ass

Caleb

are u implying it doesnt? :P

Tanya

oh haha

The conversation petered out after that. I could still tell Tanya was upset with me—which was fair, but I hated when we fought or got upset with each other. Our friendship had never been littered with arguments, and we rarely stepped on each other's toes or did something seriously wrong.

It didn't help that it was *me* who'd so fully fucked up, either. I was embarrassed, ashamed I hadn't known my own limits, and I felt guilty for getting her in trouble with her parents. Especially because this upcoming week, we got out of school after Tuesday for Thanksgiving break, and Tanya and I usually liked to go Black Friday shopping. She'd have to stay home this time, though.

I lay on the floor, staring up at my ceiling fan, My Chemical Romance playing from my phone speakers. I'd woken up this morning feeling like absolute shit—in part because of the alcohol, but mostly because I couldn't stop thinking about everything that had happened yesterday, seeing Walter and that strange moment with Ghost and telling Emmett about Jack—it was a lot to take in. I wanted to clear my head.

My parents were downstairs, which I was thankful for because it meant that when I got up and headed to Jack's room, they didn't know I was in there. I hadn't gotten around to helping them clean his room out yet; I wanted to go through his things alone. I knew I would get even *more* emotional if Mom or Dad were there with me, and that was the last thing I needed.

Half the room was boxed up already. Cardboard box after cardboard box sat stacked on top of each other in every corner, and the room felt both messy and, somehow, upsettingly empty. Unlived in. Mom had gone through his dresser, and the drawers sat empty on the floor, gutted.

Mom and Dad must have realized they needed multiple Keep boxes, because I found about five of them lying around. I peered into one that hadn't been closed yet and started slowly taking the items out, staring at each one before placing them gently back in.

I found a picture frame with a photo of Jack and Brooke, his ex-girlfriend from high school. I wondered where my parents found it—under his bed? In his drawer? It hadn't been on display since they broke up a few years ago.

I wanted to ask him what it was like, when he and Brooke broke up. How it felt when they first got together. I wanted to ask him for advice about Emmett, to talk about the stuff with Tanya and Nathan—about my writer's block and my grade in songwriting—about the show I went to yesterday—about Walter.

Why had he and Walter stopped being friends? What had made Walter stop coming around the house? Did they have a fight? A falling out? Did they just grow apart?

Did Walter know about Jack's addiction? Did he see it early on, did he recognize the signs, did he distance himself because of it? Or was it a coincidence that Jack stopped hanging out with Walter around the same time that he started using?

What was I missing?

How much was I missing?

I didn't know. And I *hated* that I didn't know.

Ghost sat near the windowsill, watching as I went through box after box, scouring for something, anything—I wasn't even sure what I was looking for, exactly. All I knew was that I wanted answers, and I thought maybe I could find them here.

I spent a long time digging through Keep boxes, meticulously putting everything back so that it wasn't obvious I had been here. I started going through the Throw Away boxes, too, hoping there would be something there.

At the end of my search, I kept two items: a pack of cigarettes and a thumb drive.

I kept the cigarettes because they had been opened, but it seemed like Jack had only smoked one or two. I thought that, maybe, very possibly, this was the last pack he had ever bought, ever opened, ever touched. And although my parents had obviously wanted to get rid of it since it was in a Throw Away box, I couldn't. I slid them in my pajama pants' pocket.

The thumb drive I found buried at the bottom of a Keep box. I was more than a little curious to know what was on it. I pocketed that, too.

From downstairs, I heard my mom say that she was going to get something, and then I heard her footsteps on the stairs. I left Jack's room as quietly as I could, slipping back into my own just before Mom made it upstairs.

Ghost followed, of course, but he seemed hesitant, almost upset, to leave Jack's room.

"You can stay in there if you want, you know," I said to him, once I was back in my room with the door closed. "You don't have to follow me *everywhere*."

He jumped onto the bed, the mattress dipping just barely under his semi-real weight, and curled up on my blanket, ignoring what I said.

I sighed. "Yeah. I don't know what I expected."

I opened up my laptop and plugged in the thumb drive. It pulled up a dozen files, most of which were titled things like "desktop 04/19" and "video project 3." I scrolled through the folders, filled with script documents and iMovie files, but I didn't click on anything yet. I didn't want to see videos of Jack right now; I didn't know if I could handle seeing him laughing, talking . . . alive. And I didn't think I could read his scripts either—I couldn't face all the art he'd never make, all the films that could've said *written and directed by Jack Stone* now gone, buried with him.

But there was one folder that caught my eye— "Eng2 Catcher in the Rye Project FINAL—Jack S, Walter Y, Brooke E."

I opened it and was met with a video file that seemed to be the finished film project, as well as another folder that led to "project outtakes."

I still didn't watch any of the videos, but I thought about Jack's copy of *Catcher*, and all his underlining and highlighting and annotating. I assumed that was for the same class as this project, and I wondered what he thought of the book—he seemed to like it, from the annotations I'd seen. I wondered what his favorite part was, which characters he sympathized with, what lines stuck with him.

I wondered if he saw himself in Holden Caulfield, if he ever thought about running away, the way that Holden did. I wondered if he ever struggled to connect to people—if he ever reached out, over and over again, in the only way he knew how, only to be shot down every time. I wondered if he ever wanted, just on his own, without my parents pushing him, to get help.

I remembered the few times he had talked about mental health with me. It was a couple of months after I'd come out as trans, and I wasn't doing great emotionally.

There's something that can happen right after a trans person comes out, where their gender dysphoria gets even worse before it can get better, and for me, it was as if acknowledging that I was trans opened the dysphoria Pandora's box, and suddenly it was debilitating. I started locking myself in my room, withdrawing from our parents, avoiding social interaction—now that I thought about it, it was a lot like how I acted after Jack died. I didn't want to get out of bed. I didn't want to write or play music. I mostly just wanted to sleep and cry. My parents noticed the change, and they were worried about it.

One night, at the beginning of summer break, Jack came home earlier than usual. He knocked on my door, and I told him to come in, expecting it to be one of the parents. When I saw it was him, I sat up in bed.

"I thought you weren't gonna be home tonight," I said.

He sat down at the edge of my bed and shrugged. "Me too. But I heard you've had some stuff going on lately, so I wanted to, you know, check up on you. See how you're doing."

I looked down at my comforter. "I guess Mom told you how I've been doing, then," I mumbled.

"Yeah. She filled me in." He shifted a little. "How're you feeling?"

I was quiet. I didn't know what to tell him—how to get the words out. There was so much running through my head. I didn't know how to say that everything felt grating, painful, wrong—that I couldn't look in the mirror without wanting to escape from my skin, that I couldn't walk out in public without comparing myself to everyone around me, that every accidental *she* and *her* was a stab in the gut.

Jack waited, patiently, for me to say something.

When it became clear that I wasn't going to, he said, his voice gentle, "You can tell me. I know how you're feeling right now—I've been through it, too."

I finally looked at him. "You have?"

He nodded. "Maybe not the *exact* same thing, but I've gone through a lot, and if I had to guess, it's probably similar to some of 'em. Depression, anxiety, mania, intrusive and suicidal thoughts . . ." He paused. "And you know that I . . . I'm . . ."

He struggled to find the words, but I thought I knew what he was trying to say. He never addressed his addiction by name. I always wondered why—was it too big, too much, to talk about it directly? Or was he so ashamed that he couldn't even say it?

I wasn't sure. And I never asked.

"Well, let's just say I've been through some shit," he said with a small, ironic smile. "And I hope you never, ever, ever have to go through that. I know it sucks when you're in it. I know how horrible it feels, how isolating . . . how it can take over who you are. . . ."

His voice cracked, and I realized he was tearing up. I barely ever saw Jack get emotional.

"But don't keep it in, okay? Don't just sit in all these feelings. You're not alone. Talk to someone—the parents, Tanya, me. We're here for you, Caleb. You're *not* alone. And things are gonna get better. Trust me. Okay?"

I nodded. A tear slipped down my cheek, but I wiped it away quickly, hoping he hadn't seen.

"Can we hang out sometime soon?" I asked quietly.

"Yeah." He smiled again. "Of course we can."

I kept thinking about that as I looked at the thumb drive—about that one moment, his tenderness, his care for me. We hung out and watched a movie together later that week, and it was the catalyst for our routine of watching movies together that summer.

But then ninth grade started, Jack went off to college, and things got bad again.

And that was one of the last times I had a moment like that with him.

That Monday during lunch, I checked my grade for songwriting on the school's portal. My overall grade was still abysmal—it sat at forty-two, a good thirty points below where it needed to be so I could pass—but when I went to the assignment I turned in most recently, I saw that Mr. Russak had given feedback.

Caleb–
Good job on this one! Your creative voice really shows in the lyrics. I would suggest singing higher, however, in future songs; you're singing so low here that it sounds like you're straining.
–Mr. Russak

Underneath that, I saw that I'd gotten a ninety-one. I let out a relieved sigh.

"What're you looking at?" Tanya asked, leaning over to glance at my phone. After what happened on Saturday, she and I had been somewhat normal around each other, although I could still tell that there was something a little off. She didn't seem *mad* at me, per se, but it didn't seem like things were 100 percent all right, either.

"Just my grade for songwriting." I put my phone away.

"How are things going with that?" Emmett asked, taking a bite of their burger.

"All right, I guess. I'm not passing yet, but I got a ninety-one on my last assignment, so I'm hoping I can catch up. . . ."

"Oh, nice! I'm proud of you!" Emmett smiled and held up their hand across the table for a high five. I accepted, and it was so cliché of me, so annoyingly predictable, but I swore I felt a little jolt when we touched, and I looked away, hoping it wasn't visible on my face.

My crush had seemed to grow exponentially since Saturday, and it was a strange feeling, liking someone I was friends with.

It was also weird, having these light, bubbly feelings in between everything else going on in my life. It almost felt wrong having a crush, having *good* feelings, when Jack hadn't even been gone half a year.

But I tried not to think like that. I tried, for the most part, to just be friends with Emmett, to not get too caught up in my attraction.

Halfway through lunch, Tanya got up. "I'm going to the

vending machines. Anyone want anything?"

"A Diet Coke, please?" Logan said.

Tanya nodded. "Anyone else?"

We all shook our heads, so she left for the vending machines. To Logan, Dima said, "I don't get how you can drink that garbage. It tastes like battery acid."

"Yeah, but *delicious* battery acid," Logan said.

On the table next to me, Tanya's phone buzzed. She'd left it face up on the table, and without thinking too much about it, I glanced over at the notification. It was a text message.

Nat♥

i miss you today :(

I frowned. Nathan hadn't been at school today—a dentist appointment or something, I thought he said.

But the heart emoji next to his name was a little strange. That didn't seem entirely platonic to me.

Another message came through, and I couldn't help seeing it as it flashed across the screen.

Nat♥

i know you're grounded this week, but maybe we could video call and watch something together?

It was followed by several heart emojis. Maybe I was reading too much into it, but that definitely seemed at least a *little* romantic.

Had Tanya and Nathan confessed their feelings for each other? And did Tanya forget to tell me?

Or . . . had she not mentioned it on purpose?

"Everything good, Caleb?" Emmett asked as Tanya returned with food and a Diet Coke.

She sat back down next to me, and I avoided her eyes. "Yeah, all good," I said.

After lunch, as we were walking to our next classes, Emmett slid up next to me.

"Hey," they said. "So, I was thinking . . . maybe we should get together after school soon to work on the project some more? And maybe we could also watch *Scream*, if you were still interested in doing that . . . ?"

"Yeah, that'd be fun," I said, trying to control my enthusiasm.

"Cool." They smiled. "What day would you wanna . . . ?"

"Tomorrow," I blurted, before I could even really register what I was saying. "My place?"

Their smile only grew. God, they were so cute. "Sounds like a plan."

13

EMMETT CAME OVER TO MY house on Tuesday, and since my parents were still at work when we got home, it was just the two of us. I wasn't sure if I was thankful that we were alone, since it meant I wouldn't have to worry about feeling weird with my parents around, or if I wished for the company, since now we were *alone*.

Well, except for Ghost. Predictably, he was following Emmett around like a shadow.

We went up to my room to work and sat on the floor, my guitar in my lap. I pulled up a Google Doc on my computer with recent song ideas and lyric snippets that I could maybe use for our project. Ghost sat near us—far enough away to not be right in our space, but close enough that I couldn't forget he was there.

"So, what've you got so far?" Emmett asked.

I tilted the computer screen so they could see it better. "It's not much. . . . Just a few ideas, and some melodies I started messing around with."

"What's this?" They pointed to a verse I'd started writing.

"Oh, that's not really anything. Just a song I started about *Catcher in the Rye* since I've been rereading it lately. . . ."

"Can you play it for me?"

I blinked at them, but they seemed serious. "Um, sure. . . . Let me just tune real quick."

I tried to not feel self-conscious as Emmett watched me tune my guitar. To make up for the silence, I said, "Don't get too excited. This is probably garbage—"

"Hey, no shit talking," Emmett interrupted, giving me a stern look. "That's my friend you're talking about."

I couldn't help smiling a little. "Yeah, well, you haven't heard it yet."

I played what I had for them before I could lose my nerve. The song was meant to be slow, each word drawn out, and I picked the chords, making up a pattern as I went along. I'd wanted the song to sound eerie, ghostly, uncomfortable. I wasn't sure if I'd achieved that, but when I was done singing the verse and a half I'd written, Emmett was looking at me thoughtfully, their chin in their hand.

"So . . . yeah. That's all I have so far," I said.

"I love it."

I scoffed. "Oh, come on, it's barely anything."

"No, I'm serious!" they insisted. "It wasn't what I was expecting, but that's what I liked—the surprise. We should definitely use that for the project."

"But it doesn't fit the 'character archetypes' theme we were doing."

"We can change it."

I stared at them. "Emmett, you've already written *two* of our songs. Why would we start over? And what would we even change it to, anyway?"

"I can write some more; I don't mind. And we could change it to be about *Catcher in the Rye*—don't give me that look, I'm serious! I read it last year, too, and I'm into the idea of writing a collection of songs based off a book."

I wasn't sure what to say. I didn't want to make Emmett start over, and I didn't know if I liked the idea of changing our project just to accommodate me . . . but this *was* the only good material I'd been able to write so far, and Emmett seemed genuinely excited about the idea. . . .

"I don't know yet," I said finally. "Maybe I should actually finish *this* song first before we decide to pivot completely. The problem is, this is as far as I got."

Emmett nodded. "Well, what part are you struggling with?"

I sighed, taking my guitar out of my lap and laying it gently on the floor next to me. "Everything. I don't know where to go from here, and I don't know how I feel about what I've written."

They thought about it, then turned to the computer. I watched as they reread the verse, their eyes skimming over the page.

"I was thinking about the scene where Holden watches his friend James jump out a window, and the fact that he was wearing James's sweater when it happened," I said. "I was trying to write something from Holden's point of view, which is where I was going with the 'blood on the floor' line, but then I introduced a 'you' in the song, and now I'm not sure if it's supposed to be James or . . ."

"Or Allie?" Emmett finished, looking at me now.

Allie: Holden Caulfield's dead younger brother. In the book, Holden writes an essay about a baseball mitt that Allie scribbled poems on in green ink. "There's this scene at the very end, as Holden is getting ready to run away, that really stuck with me when I first read it," I said. "He's walking down a street, and he starts feeling that if he comes to the end of the sidewalk, he'll fall off, so he starts talking out loud to Allie, begging him for help."

"'Allie, don't let me disappear,'" Emmett quoted.

I nodded. "Exactly! So, I started out writing about James's death, but I guess it's kind of hard to write about grief in *Catcher in the Rye* without mentioning Allie. He just sort of bled into the song, I guess." That happened a lot with my songwriting; things seemed to sneak in without me noticing.

"Well, then let's lean into it," Emmett said. "Let's make it about James *and* Allie."

"But I don't know where else to go with the lyrics."

Emmett and I talked about the song for a while, working through the lyrics, bouncing ideas around. They gave me a bunch of suggestions, and I started warming up to the process, revising lines as we went.

We worked on the song for almost an hour. The final version

was melancholic and circular, as if Holden was singing to himself, and when we decided it was finished, I let out a heavy sigh. Even though all we'd done was write one song, I was exhausted, but also a little bit happy. Proud of myself, maybe, for getting through that. It had been a long time since I'd actually felt *proud* about something I'd written.

"Thank you for your help," I said.

They shrugged. "Don't mention it. And besides, I like writing with other people. It's nice getting to do it with a friend." They smiled gently, and I knew we were both thinking about Mallory and *Limerence.*

I offered a small smile back. "It *is* nice," I agreed.

We didn't say anything for a moment, and there was a somberness to Emmett's expression. I felt it—their past, their grief, lingering in the space around us. Was this what it was like to other people, when it was clear that Jack was on my mind?

I wondered if that was what Ghost felt like to other people—if I was really the only person who sensed him, or if there was a hint, a shadow of his presence, laid around me as he followed me.

I wondered if Emmett could feel him now, sitting on the floor with us, listening as we wrote.

We took a snack break after that. I made us pizza bagels, and while we were waiting for them to cook, Emmett leaned against the kitchen counter, their arms crossed loosely over their chest, and said, "So, what was going on during lunch yesterday?"

I looked at them. "What do you mean?"

"When Tanya left for the vending machines, you seemed bothered by something. I didn't ask 'cause I didn't want to be rude or anything, but . . ."

"It wasn't a big deal. I just saw some texts Nathan sent Tanya," I said.

Emmett raised an eyebrow. "Were they . . . bad?"

"No, they were fine. It's just . . ." I turned back around, looking at the pizza bagels cooking in the oven. "I don't know. I saw that Nathan's contact in her phone had a heart next to it, and he was sending her stuff like 'I miss you' and 'we should video call this week' and I just thought . . . doesn't that seem kind of romantic?"

"Yeah. But we already know that they like each other, right? So, what's the issue?"

"I mean, yeah, but . . ." I wasn't sure how to put this. "But if something happened between them—if they confessed their feelings, or whatever—then why hasn't Tanya said anything about it to me?"

Emmett looked at me for a moment, and then something seemed to click in their brain. "Are you worried she's keeping something from you?"

The timer went off, cutting through our conversation. "Sorry, one sec." I silenced the alarm and took the bagels out, setting them on the stove to cool and turning the oven off. I always associated pizza bagels with Jack. It was our go-to snack when we got home from school before our parents, or when he was babysitting me.

I turned back to Emmett. Ghost had reappeared, although

he only sat in the threshold of the kitchen.

"I don't know. I guess . . . maybe," I finally admitted. "It's just . . . I upset her last weekend at the show 'cause she had to wait for me to sober up before we could get home, and she ended up getting in trouble with her parents for coming home so late. She said it was fine, but things still seem kind of off between us, and now it feels like she didn't tell me about whatever this thing is with Nathan, if something *did* happen. . . . I don't know. It just feels weird that she wouldn't have said anything by now. We don't keep secrets from each other."

"I get that," Emmett said. "But she probably just needs a little more time to get over it. I doubt she's keeping a secret from you. Maybe nothing's changed, and they've just always texted like that, or maybe something *did* change, but they're not ready to say anything about it to anyone. Who knows?"

I nodded. "Yeah . . . you're right. I guess I was just . . . getting in my head about it."

"If it makes you feel any better," Emmett said, "I haven't heard anything from Nathan's end, and he's usually an open book when it comes to stuff like this."

"Yeah. That's a good point."

We dropped the subject, but I was frustrated with myself for getting upset over something so small, and a part of me was embarrassed for showing that to Emmett. But I was thankful, too, that they were here to give me a reality check.

I tried to let go of my anxiety about Tanya and Nathan as we grabbed our snacks and went to the living room. We were getting *Scream* up on the TV when my dad got home from work.

"Oh, hey, kids," he said, poking his head into the living room. Before I left for school, I'd told my parents that I was having a friend over to work on a project, but Dad still seemed surprised by Emmett's presence.

"Hi, Dad." I waved. "This is Emmett. We were working on a project earlier, and now we were just gonna watch a movie. . . ."

"Nice to meet you." Dad nodded at Emmett, and they waved politely. Ghost came out from under the coffee table and sat at my feet.

Emmett somehow managed to hold the conversation with my dad for a few more moments, before Dad finally said, "All right, well, good luck on your work, you two. Let me know when you're hungry for dinner and I can fix us something. Mom'll be home a little later tonight."

He went upstairs after that, and once it was just the two of us again, I turned to Emmett. "Do you wanna watch *Scream* now?"

I tried not to be too distracting during the movie since I didn't want Emmett to miss anything, but I couldn't help making a few comments every now and then.

"Apparently the composer, Marco Beltrami, had never even *seen* a horror movie before Wes Craven hired him, so he had to learn the horror soundtrack conventions as he went," I said in between plot-heavy moments. "He also used excerpts from the original *Halloween* score."

"That's pretty cool," Emmett said. When we'd started the movie, we had sat on opposite sides of the couch, leaving a good distance between us. But I could've sworn that we were inching closer—although if it was them or me doing it, I wasn't totally sure.

By the time we'd gotten to the beginning of the house party scene that sets off the film's climax, there were only a few inches between us, and when I shifted, our arms brushed. I felt another jolt at the contact; I was so hyperaware of every touch, as small as they were, and my arm felt hot.

"It took them twenty-one days to film the finale," I told them, trying to distract myself from my nerves.

Their eyebrows shot up. "Really? Jesus Christ."

"Yeah, it was apparently really exhausting. The crew had T-shirts made that said I Survived Scene 118 when they finally wrapped."

I'd still been looking at the screen when I said it, but I could feel Emmett's eyes on me, and I glanced at them. A small smile was tugging at the corners of their lips, almost like they were watching *me* watch the movie.

"What?" The word coming out a little more defensively than I meant it to.

"You know a lot about this movie," they said, that smile still there.

I shrugged, my cheeks starting to warm, and I looked back to the screen. "I guess I do."

"It's cute."

If I wasn't blushing before, I definitely was now. "It's—I mean—shut up," I said in a rush.

Emmett laughed. "I'm serious," they said. "I like how much you love it."

I wasn't sure what to say, but thankfully, I didn't have to; Ghostface entered the scene, and then Emmett's attention was pulled back to the TV. We didn't say anything else for a while, but when I found a moment that wouldn't distract Emmett too much from the movie, I said quietly, "Thanks."

They bumped their shoulder into mine, and there it was again—that heat.

We watched the rest of the movie in relative silence, but I couldn't concentrate on it.

Was Emmett into me? Had they been flirting when they said that, or was that something they said to lots of people? And if they *were* flirting, did that mean that they thought this was a date?

Was this a date?

But maybe a better question was: Did I *want* it to be one?

Yes. That much was immediately clear to me: I wanted this to be a date. Because I liked them.

It was almost seven by the time we finished the movie. Mom had gotten home during it, but she'd only popped in briefly to say hello before disappearing upstairs. I knew that my parents could hear the film from their room, but I wondered if they could hear our conversations—if they had heard Emmett call me cute. I desperately hoped they hadn't.

Since I drove Emmett here from school, I had to drive them home. We were still discussing the movie as we got into my car.

"I get why that changed the slasher genre now," they said as they got buckled into the passenger seat. I put directions to their house in my GPS.

"And then it got a million sequels and unfortunately became a part of the horror-franchises-that-are-milked-for-all-their-worth club," I said as I started to pull out of the driveway.

"That sucks," Emmett said. "Although, I kind of see why they would do that. I mean, I probably would've stopped after just one or two sequels, but I guess if your main priority is making a profit, then money is money."

"Money is money," I agreed. "Speaking of sequels, did you ever get a chance to watch *Bride of Re-Animator*?"

"Not yet, but it's still on my to-do list," they said. After a moment, they added, somewhat hesitantly, "Maybe we could watch it together sometime."

I glanced at them. They were looking at the road ahead, but I could tell—they were a little nervous, too.

Was Emmett asking for us to hang out again? Or were they asking for a date? Or, I guessed, maybe *another* date, depending on what they considered today?

"I'd like that," I said, and there was something comforting about the relieved smile on their face, like they'd been worried I would say no. It made me feel a little less embarrassed, to think that maybe Emmett was in a similar boat as me. We rode for a few minutes in silence.

"Does your family have any plans for Thanksgiving?" I asked.

"Nothing exciting. We'll do the regular Thanksgiving things, and then my mom and Braelyn will go Black Friday shopping, and if I'm lucky, I'll get to interact with my sister as little as possible."

"I guess that means you two don't have a great relationship?"

They snorted. "You could put it that way, yeah. We already weren't very close, and then when I came out, she told me in no uncertain terms that she doesn't 'approve' of my transness, and she uses Jesus as the excuse."

"I'm sorry," I said. "That's so fucked up."

"It could be worse, I guess. My parents are slightly better than Braelyn. I've only heard them use my correct pronouns a few times in the entire nine months I've been out to them, but they're trying, I think, and . . . I guess that's all I can really hope for."

"Still," I said. "That doesn't make it suck any less."

"Yeah. You're right." They smiled a little. "But what about you? When did you come out to your family? If you're okay with talking about it, I mean."

"In middle school, Tanya and I both came out as trans within a few months of each other," I said. "My parents struggled with it a little at first, but they came around. When I turned sixteen and said I wanted to start testosterone, they were supportive and willing to go out of state with me to get HRT, so we drive up to Illinois every six months for that, and I'm really glad for it, even though it's ridiculous that we have to go out of state at all. . . ."

Emmett nodded. "The HRT bans are so horrifying. . . . I think I'd want to get on hormones in the future, but it would have to be after I'm eighteen since my parents would never be on board with it. But I'm really glad yours are supportive, and that you and Tanya got to be there for each other when you transitioned. So, you two have been friends for a long time?"

"Yeah. We've known each other our whole lives."

"I've always wanted a friend like that. The oldest friend I have is Nathan 'cause we met in middle school, but I've sort of grown apart from my other childhood friends."

I tried to imagine what it would feel like to grow apart from Tanya—to wake up one day and realize she wasn't in my life any longer. "Do you ever miss them?" I asked.

"I guess sometimes," they said. "Not as much these days, though. I've got pretty great company." They grinned.

I smiled back.

We spent the rest of the ride talking about our friends. Emmett told me about how they became close with Nathan during a chaotic sixth-grade field trip to the zoo that had ended with the bus almost leaving both of them behind; about how they met Logan in Music Theory their freshman year, and then met Dima through Logan; and about how they'd realized that Dima and Logan were both incredibly talented musicians with similar tastes as them, and how all three of them decided to create Deck of Fools almost on a whim.

I told them about Tanya's pet hamster from third grade, which she'd gotten against her parents' wishes and which I'd helped her hide; about how I'd inherited my dad's love for bluegrass and classic-folk-slash-country music, and how that inspired me to learn to play banjo; and I told them about Jack—how he'd always loved filmmaking, how my horror movie obsession originated with him, and how the summer before ninth grade, we watched more movies together than I could count.

The drive from my house to Emmett's was thirty minutes, but by the time I parked on the road near their mailbox, I wished it had been longer. I didn't want them to leave.

"Thanks for tonight," they said, but didn't get out of the car just yet.

"Yeah, of course. Thanks for hanging out with me," I said.

The car engine hummed in our silence. Then, Emmett looked at me, and, their voice shaking a little, said, "I kind of want to kiss you."

I felt like the air had been knocked out of me.

"Oh," I managed. Then, when my brain had caught up enough: "I—Yes."

They cracked a grin. "'Yes'?"

"I mean—I would—I'd like that, too." I stumbled over the words, but they were out—finally, blissfully, terrifyingly.

Emmett leaned toward me. "So, does that mean we should kiss now?" they asked, their voice low and gentle.

I answered them by leaning over and pressing my lips to theirs.

It was more forceful than I'd meant for it to be, but I didn't care—*we were kissing*—and Emmett's hand was resting on my shoulder, and I moved mine up, just hovering there for a moment, not sure what to do, before I brought my hand to their cheek and cupped it gently.

Everything about them was soft and warm and wonderful.

By the time we pulled away, we were both out of breath, and I was sure that I was bright red. I didn't feel too embarrassed about it, though, because Emmett's cheeks were tinted pink, their pupils dilated. Their hair was disheveled from where I'd run my hands through it. We just looked at each other for a moment, both catching our breaths. I couldn't remember the last time I'd kept eye contact with someone for this long.

"You're cute," they said, and I couldn't help it—I laughed. I was so happy, it felt like it was bubbling out of me.

"You're cute, too," I said.

Emmett glanced at their phone, checking the time. "I wish I could stay," they said. "But I should probably go inside for dinner. . . ."

"That's okay," I said. "I should probably get home, too."

They looked out the window toward their house, then back to me, then leaned over and gave me one more lingering kiss. When they pulled away, I felt just as stunned as the first time.

"Can I tell you something?" they asked quietly.

Their seriousness surprised me, and I nodded, a part of me worried there was something wrong.

But they just smiled, wide and genuine and so earnest it almost killed me, and said, "I like you."

"I like you, too," I admitted.

With that, they got out of the car. Before shutting the door, they said, "I'll see you later, Caleb."

"See you, Em." I hadn't meant to call them that—the nickname had just sort of snuck out—but from their smile, I had a feeling that they didn't mind.

"Text me when you get home safe."

And with that, they walked up their driveway.

14

"DOES ANYONE HAVE PLANS FOR Thanksgiving?" Tom asked.

It was Wednesday evening, and I was back at group therapy in Tom's office at our bimonthly meeting, sitting next to Raúl and Garrett. We didn't usually have meetings this close to a holiday, and we were actually supposed to meet last week, but Tom had to reschedule for personal reasons. Because of that, Katherine couldn't make it, but Jewel and Candi sat across from me, while Ghost sat curled up at my feet.

For a moment, no one said anything, and Tom looked around the room, making patient eye contact with all of us. Jewel shifted in their seat.

"Um, I guess I can go first," they said. "Well . . . my mom and I are going to go to my grandparents' place this year. We used to always do these big Thanksgiving dinners at home, but, um, you know, without my dad there, I don't think it would feel . . ."

"The same?" Candi offered. Jewel nodded.

"But I'm glad we're going to my grandparents'," they added. "I think it might make things easier."

"It might," Tom agreed. "The holidays can be a particularly rough time for grief."

"Which is doubly frustrating," Garrett said, crossing his arms over his chest, "'cause it's supposed to be about being happy and with family and all of that shit. It's not meant to be so . . . depressing."

Tom nodded. When no one else added anything, he turned to me. "What about you, Caleb?"

I shrugged. "I guess we're just gonna do something at home like normal."

In truth, I hadn't thought much about it, maybe in part because I didn't want to, but mostly because I hadn't thought about much else but Emmett since yesterday. I kept replaying the night in my head, their voice when they said *I kind of want to kiss you*, the moment when our lips touched. It felt almost too good to be true.

I sat through the rest of the meeting without saying much else. At one point, Ghost came over and turned his head between Tom and me, as if to ask if I wanted to speak, but I didn't have much to contribute to the conversation.

After the meeting ended, we walked out to the parking lot as a group like usual, Ghost trotting alongside me. I felt my phone buzz in my pocket.

Emmett

hey :) hows ur night going?

I couldn't help smiling at the screen as I typed out a reply.

Caleb

fine so far

just got finished with a group therapy thing and im heading home now

wbu? :)

I looked up from my texts when I heard a *thunk* on the pavement. Lying on the ground was a pink iPhone, but Candi must not have noticed she'd dropped it because she kept walking, saying something to who I assumed was her dad. I rushed to pick it up.

"Uh, excuse me, you dropped this," I said, jogging to catch up to her. She turned around, surprise on her face.

"Oh my God, I didn't even realize!" She took it from me, checking for damage. "Thank you so much! Caleb, right?"

I nodded.

"I'm Candi," she said. "It was nice seeing you at the meeting today."

I blinked. "Yeah, uh, it was nice being there."

"Tom's such a great therapist," she said. "And it's so cool there are groups like this where we can get together and talk, you know?"

"Yeah," I said, although I wasn't sure I totally agreed. Maybe it was because I didn't say much, but I didn't feel like group had really *helped* me yet. I felt a prickle at my neck; when I glanced behind me, Ghost was sitting a few feet away, turned toward us.

There was an uncomfortable pause as I tried to think of something else to say, but Candi didn't let the silence stand for too long. "Well, thanks again," she said, a polite smile on her face. "Have a good Thanksgiving!"

"You too."

She and her dad got into their car, and I walked to mine. Ghost sat at Candi's car for a moment longer, as if wanting something else, before he finally followed me.

I got into the car, but I didn't start driving just yet. I thought about what Candi said, how genuine she'd sounded. Did she really feel like talking helped? I remembered Emmett had said something similar at the SALINE show.

My phone buzzed, pulling my thoughts away.

Emmett

pretty good!

ive been watching a youtube video essay about the scream tv show and it reminded me of u :) <3

Butterflies kicked in my stomach, and I couldn't help grinning as I replied. I sent the message before turning my phone off and starting the engine. Ghost sat in the passenger seat, but I ignored him.

I didn't think about Candi or the meeting or Ghost the whole drive home, my mind still filled with Emmett, Emmett, Emmett.

"Caleb, can you help with dishes, please?" Mom said, poking her head into my room.

It was Thanksgiving morning, and I was trying to make up some of the assignments I'd missed for songwriting. I'd turned in two late songs over the past few days, and now I was working on a third one. But I was thankful for a distraction; I hadn't written more than a chord progression and one shitty verse, and I was ready to take a break.

In the kitchen, Mom was in the middle of cooking Thanksgiving dinner. It was more of a "Thanksgiving late lunch" because we always ate around three p.m. and then spent the rest of the day watching Christmas movies and decorating the tree. She'd already made sweet tea—you would be hard-pressed to find a meal my mother made that didn't include sweet tea—and she was currently working on the mashed potato casserole. It had been Jack's favorite.

I started unloading dishes from the washer. I'd gotten my short height from Mom, and we had to keep a step stool in the kitchen so we could reach the highest cabinets. I used it now as I started to put the clean plates away.

We worked in silence next to each other. I could feel that she wanted to say something, that there was something on her mind, but I wasn't sure how to ask about it. The *clink* of dishes and the sound of the kitchen fan washed over us.

"I ran into Brooke at Publix the other day," Mom said suddenly.

"Really?" I said, surprised. Jack and Brooke got together not long before Jack started using, and they dated for a few years before things eventually imploded. The last time I'd seen her, she was leaving the house late at night after visiting Jack, her eyes bloodshot and her expression hollow. She and Jack had been in all their mess together; a part of me wondered if he had turned her on to drugs, or if she was already using when they got together.

I didn't remember seeing her at his funeral, but whether that was because she didn't know about it or because she just didn't want to go, I had no clue.

"I didn't realize she was still living around here," I said.

Mom nodded. She'd finished peeling the potatoes and now went to work cubing them; the sound of the knife as it hit the wooden cutting board was loud. "She goes to school out in Knoxville, I think, but I guess she was back in Nashville for Thanksgiving."

"How's she doing?"

"Okay, I think. She looked . . . healthier than the last time I saw her. And she seemed to be happy at school," Mom said. "She's studying to be a veterinarian."

"Oh." I wasn't sure how to feel about that. Most of me wanted to be happy that she had been able to get her life back on track. She hadn't been doing well when she and Jack were together; she stayed at our place a lot of the time because her parents periodically kicked her out, and she dropped out of high school during her and Jack's senior year for health reasons.

But a part of me couldn't help feeling like it was unfair that *she* got a second chance—*she* got to keep living—*she* got to get her life together—when Jack didn't.

I couldn't understand why *Jack* died when Brooke had been doing the same things, making the same choices, getting just as sick as he had. How come she escaped that life when he didn't?

It all felt so unfair.

"Did she know about Jack?" I asked quietly.

Mom paused the rhythm of her chopping. "Yeah. She said she found out from Facebook."

Facebook. The messenger of my brother's death. I hated it all so much, I wanted to puke.

From the corner of my eye, I saw Ghost slink into the kitchen. I watched him walk toward the fridge, and he seemed to flicker for a moment, his body disappearing from my sight. The next thing I knew, he was sitting at my feet. I looked down at him, and he sat completely still, clearly planning to stick around for a while.

Maybe I should've been annoyed that he was here, but a part of me was kind of glad. It seemed . . . right. If he *hadn't* shown up, that probably would've bothered me more.

I finished putting the clean utensils away and started loading the dirty dishes. Mom was silent again for a moment. She'd finished cubing the potatoes, and now she put them in a large stockpot, placing that on the stove.

"I don't get it, either," she said, her voice thick. When I didn't say anything, she continued: "I have a feeling that I know what you're thinking—why does Brooke get to have Thanksgiving with her family when Jack doesn't? Why does she get to keep going when he's gone?"

Shame flooded through me. I hated Mom revealing that nasty part of me, hated that someone else could recognize those horrible thoughts. I didn't want to be the kind of person who thought things like that, but, well . . . here I was.

And here Mom was, too, I supposed. That was a bit of comfort, at least—knowing that I wasn't the only one.

"I ask myself that question all the time. Why him? Why *our* family? Why now?" She took a deep, shaky breath. Her back was to me as she stood at the stove, and I could see the way her shoulders hunched up, the tension in her body. "Why couldn't he survive?"

When she turned to me, her eyes were wet with tears, but they hadn't escaped yet.

"Do you remember the time that Brooke overdosed in Jack's bedroom?"

I did. It was something I'd always tried not to think about.

Once, several years ago, in the middle of the night, I woke up to an ambulance in our driveway, and when I got up to see what was going on, the paramedics were taking Brooke away. Mom was sitting on the stairs, her head in her hands. Jack and Dad rode in the ambulance to the hospital, so it was just Mom and me, sitting there, not speaking.

Brooke survived that night, but it had stayed with all of us ever since.

"I saved her life," Mom said, so quiet it was almost a whisper. "I resuscitated her before the ambulance arrived. I got her heart beating again. Did you know that?"

I shook my head. No one had really said much about the details of what happened, and I hadn't felt like I could ask. I was probably thirteen or fourteen then, so all I really knew was that Brooke had OD'd but managed to survive.

"Sometimes . . ." Mom shut her eyes tight, as if to erase the image in her head. "Sometimes I think that I used a miracle on her. And sometimes I think—what if I could have done that for Jack instead?"

She was crying now. Almost unnoticeable tears.

"I'm sorry," she said, turning back toward the stove. "I didn't mean to dump this all on you now, honey. I don't know where this is all coming from."

"It's okay," I said, and I meant it.

At my feet, Ghost twitched, and I felt him brush against my leg. A shock went through me, but not a painful one—it was like I was filled, briefly, with images of Jack, memories, feelings I'd had when he was still around. It was weird and disorienting, but . . . a little bit comforting, too.

Mom returned to cooking, and I went back to the dirty dishes. It was only when I'd loaded the last dish that I spoke again.

"The biggest thing for me," I said, "is that I can't figure out *why* any of it happened."

She sniffed, wiping a tear off her cheek. "What do you mean?"

"I mean—I don't even really understand why Jack started using in the first place," I said. "I don't understand why he *kept* using, why he went to rehab so many times and yet it never seemed to work, why he had to take so much that night—why he died. I don't *understand*."

Mom was quiet, and for a second, I worried that I had upset her or made her angry. I was ashamed of myself, my feelings.

Ashamed that a part of me was angry at Jack for doing the things he did, even when I knew, logically, that his addiction was an illness, a sickness, a disease—something that he couldn't just *stop*.

After a long moment, she asked, "Did Jack ever talk to you about what life was like at the old house?"

"No," I said. I knew that we'd lived in another house before this one. It was an hour away, and I had no memories of it because I was only two when we moved, but Jack spent the first seven years of his life there, and Mom and Dad had lived there for at least a decade.

She nodded. "I guess that makes sense. Jack was never very . . . open about those things."

"What things?"

She took a long breath in. I felt a pit form in my stomach, and I knew Mom was about to tell me something important, something heavy.

Ghost swished his tail back and forth on the tile floor.

"Jack had a . . . difficult childhood," Mom said. "Your dad and I were young parents, trying to juggle childcare and our jobs, and we weren't . . ." Another deep breath. "I don't know. Maybe we were naive. Maybe we trusted too much. Maybe . . ."

"Why? What happened?" I could feel panic building the longer she took, and I wanted her to just get it out, get it over with.

"Jack . . . Jack was sexually abused."

It was like I'd been punched in the gut. Like the air was knocked out of me.

"What?" I managed.

Mom shook her head. "He—he didn't tell us or anyone for *years*. Not until he was in high school. For so long, your father and I had no idea what had gone on in that house."

"Who . . . ?" I whispered.

"A . . . a former friend of mine."

I couldn't breathe. I felt sick. I had to sit down, but I could barely move.

"Caleb, honey? Are you okay?" I heard Mom saying distantly.

She put a hand on my shoulder and led me gently toward the kitchen table, where she pulled out a chair for me and helped me sit down. She brought me a cup of water without me asking.

"How long did it go on for?" I asked.

Mom kept a hand on my back, and I appreciated the contact.

"I don't know exactly," she said. "He never told me a specific timeline. It's possible that he couldn't even remember, he was so young. . . . But we moved when you were two and he was seven, and as far as I know, Jack never had any contact with that man again. Thank God."

"He never told me," I said. "I never . . ."

I never knew.

How had I missed something like this? How had I never known? All those times Jack and I hung out . . . And that time when we talked about our mental health, when he opened up about his experiences . . . I thought back to when he said, *I've been through some shit. And I hope you never, ever, ever have to go through that.*

Had he been trying to tell me then?

And I never asked what he meant by that.

What kind of brother *was* I?

Ghost moved closer to me, his tail brushing against my leg again, but I didn't find it comforting this time.

"He didn't talk about it much," Mom said, her voice low. "I'm not surprised he didn't tell you. It was . . . something he kept very private. I think the drugs . . . I think they were a way to cope with it all. I can't imagine how painful it must have been, dealing with that on his own from such a young age, never knowing how to reach out for help. . . ."

I stared at the glass of water Mom had brought me. For some reason, I thought about all those home movies Jack and I made as kids, and about Jack's interest in film, how he always told me that one day he was going to be a filmmaker. I thought about Jack as a child, so young, and when I imagined him being hurt like that—

I couldn't. It was too much. Everything was too much.

"I think . . . I think I need to be alone for a little while," I said.

Mom sniffed. She was trying to keep her tears in, I knew. I wondered if she would fall apart when I left the room, the same way I knew that I would, and I pictured us both on opposite sides of the house, crying over the same thing, feeling that same pain, that same ache.

"I understand, honey," she said. "I'll call you when dinner's ready, okay?"

I nodded. I stood to go back upstairs, my chest heavy, and on the way, I gave Mom a hug. It was meant to be quick, but when I felt her arms around me, I wished I could stay there forever.

After Thanksgiving dinner, my dad got the Christmas tree and boxes of ornaments out of the garage, and Mom put on *Santa Claus Is Comin' to Town*, a stop-motion Christmas special from the seventies that we watched every year.

Ghost had not left me alone since my conversation with Mom. When, at dinner, we went around to say one thing we were thankful for like we did every year, all I could think about was what I'd learned about Jack's childhood, and I was hyper-aware of how quickly our circle ended, of the piece that was missing, the empty chair to my left, and I felt Ghost sitting at my feet under the table.

This was the first Thanksgiving we'd had without Jack. There would never be another Thanksgiving *with* Jack. From now on, it would always be this, always an absence, and I couldn't stop re-realizing it—every time I thought about it again, it pierced through me, just as painful as the first time.

Dad put up the tree, and after I helped him wrap red-and-white lights around it, Mom and I got to work hanging the ornaments, each taking a side. The movie was halfway over now, but we already had another one queued, *A Miser Brothers' Christmas*. That one was Jack's favorite, and even though I was pretty sure Mom and Dad knew that, too, none of us acknowledged it.

I thought about the thumb drive I'd found in his room. I thought about Jack keeping the secret of his abuse until high school.

"How old was Jack when he told you about what happened to him?" I asked abruptly.

I didn't look up from the tree as I fiddled with an ornament's placement, but I felt my parents' stares, and there was a heavy silence, filled only by the sounds of the movie. I wondered if Mom told Dad about the conversation we had.

"I think it was his sophomore year of high school," Mom said quietly. "He was probably fifteen, maybe sixteen then. . . ."

"So, a year younger than me," I said, more to myself than anyone.

Dad was silent from his place on the couch. I looked up from the ornament I was messing with to see him staring down at his hands, laced in his lap.

"Why didn't you tell me earlier?" I asked, although I knew the answer.

"It didn't seem like our place," Mom said.

And I'd expected that. But for some reason, it didn't stop it from hurting any less.

The question I didn't ask out loud, though—the one I kept repeating to myself—was what I really wanted an answer to. Why didn't *he* tell me? Was he planning on it, eventually?

"I didn't want to dump this on you right after his death," Mom continued. "I worried it would be . . . too much."

Too much. All of this—Jack's death, his addiction, my parents' grief, Ghost—everything that had happened in the past five and a half months—it was all *too much.*

But that didn't make it any less real. I still had to face it. I still had to keep waking up every day and live with this.

I fucking hated it.

"It's okay. I get it," I said to Mom.

She nodded, then picked up a ballerina ornament and placed it on her side. It was a gift given to me when I was a kid; I did ballet in kindergarten for exactly one year, but I was so obsessed with it at the time that we still had some ballet-related memorabilia.

I was five when I did ballet, which meant Jack would've been ten. Some number of years before that, he was sexually abused by one of Mom's friends. Eight or nine years after that, he told our parents. I tried to move my mind off it, but I couldn't stop recontextualizing everything, every moment of our shared childhood cast under this new shadow.

"What did you do when he told you?" I asked.

Mom and Dad shared a look I couldn't decipher.

"We . . . wanted to press charges," Mom said, "but Jack asked us not to. I think he was afraid of what could happen to our family, and to him. He didn't want it to become this huge thing . . . and I think he didn't want to have to relive it."

A part of me felt sick, thinking about the man who did that to Jack just walking around, unpunished, getting away with what he did to my brother. But I knew it wasn't as easy as filing a police report. And I knew how rape survivors could be treated when they came forward publicly; I knew how often they were called liars, deceivers, just looking for attention. I couldn't blame Jack for wanting to avoid that. For wanting to try to move on.

But it still felt wrong—knowing that my brother was dead, while the person who'd abused him was probably walking around, living his life as if nothing happened.

None of us spoke for a while.

Dad got up from the couch. "I think I'm gonna go make some hot chocolate," he said. "Anyone want some?"

"I'll take some," Mom said.

Dad looked to me, waiting for an answer.

"Uh, yeah, I'll have some," I said quietly. I was still trying to wrap my head around everything I'd learned.

He nodded and disappeared into the kitchen. Mom and I worked in silence, the movie still playing in the background. We were coming up on the end of *A Miser Brothers' Christmas*, with *The Year Without a Santa Claus* in the queue, when my phone buzzed.

Emmett

i hope ur having a good time with ur family :)

I paused my decorating to respond.

Caleb

thanks!

i hope things r all good with u?

Emmett

about as good as they can be

braelyn hasnt said anything weird to me all night (which is especially surprising b/c im wearing feminine clothes and she usually comments on it) and my parents are only picking small(er) fights with each other

so things could definitely be worse!

and on the bright side, i look cute! :)

They attached a mirror selfie, showing that they were wearing a black skirt and red sweater, their hair pulled back into a ponytail.

Caleb

im glad things havent been as bad as they could be, even though i hate that u have to deal with that stuff at all

and u look very cute <3

They sent a horde of heart emojis in response.

"What's got you smiling like that?" Mom asked.

I sent a heart in reply, then locked my phone and slid it back in my pocket. "Nothing. Just texting someone."

Dad came back into the living room with three mugs of hot chocolate balanced in his arms. He set them down on the coffee table and took his seat on the couch.

"Thanks, Dad," I said, grabbing one of the mugs.

"Be careful; it's hot," he warned. "Anyway, who were we talking about?"

"I was just texting a friend," I said.

"Anyone we would know?" Mom asked, sipping from her mug. She took a seat on the couch next to Dad, taking a break from decorating.

"Emmett," I said.

Dad nodded. "Oh, yeah. I liked talking with him the other day."

"Emmett uses 'they,'" I said gently. I'd told my parents Emmett's pronouns before they came over the other day, but I knew they could be forgetful about it sometimes, especially if they didn't know the person well yet.

"I liked talking with *them* the other day," Dad corrected. "They seem like a nice young . . . person."

I snorted in a laugh. "Yeah, they are."

"I'm sad I didn't get to speak with them very much," Mom said. "I would've liked to get to know them."

"Well, they'll be around the house again sometime," I said.

She nodded, and I thought about Emmett talking with my parents, getting to know my family. I thought about how Emmett would never get to meet or know Jack, about how, for however long we were in each other's lives, they would only ever know about Jack through stories.

I gave in and joined my parents on the couch, too, watching the movie as we sipped our drinks, and we didn't talk about Jack or the past again for the rest of the night. I had more questions, more things I could've said, but I didn't want to push the subject. I just wanted to decorate the tree and drink hot chocolate and look *away*. From the truth. From Jack's death.

And from Ghost. Although he never left my side during the night, I avoided looking at him as best as I could, trying to pretend he wasn't there.

15

THE NEXT DAY, WHILE MOM was out Black Friday shopping, I told Dad I was going over to Tanya's house for a little while.

Instead, I drove to the creek. In the playground's parking lot, I rolled the windows down and sat with the engine running, my music playing from the speakers and heat blasting to make up for the chill in the air. Before leaving my house, I'd grabbed the pack of Jack's cigarettes from where I'd hidden them in my dresser, along with a lighter I used for candles, and Jack's copy of *The Catcher in the Rye*. Now I pulled the cigarettes out and stared at the logo.

He'd touched these. He'd smoked some of these.

I took a cigarette out and lit it.

I'd never smoked cigarettes before. Most of the people I knew at school got hooked on nicotine through vaping, so other than Jack, I wasn't around them much. I knew they were bad for you; I'd had that drilled into me from basically the day I was born, and I knew, from when Jack first started smoking, that our parents were vehemently against it.

But this felt like one of the only ways left to connect to him. The smell reminded me so much of him, it was almost like he was there.

I put the driver's seat back and lay down, staring up at my car's ceiling as I smoked. I'd put a playlist on shuffle, and now it played Nirvana's "Something In the Way." I thought about the night I went bowling with everyone, how this song had been playing as I sat in the bathroom, trying to breathe.

I thought about the cashier with track marks on her arms, and about the people I saw snorting something at the SALINE show. I thought about how it had felt, getting drunk and high, and about how I'd used it to feel better, to feel a little less like myself. I thought about getting drunk at Nathan's, and at the show, and about the almost-empty bottle I'd hidden in my room.

I thought about Jack in his sophomore year, telling our parents about what happened to him as a child. I wondered what he said when he finally told them—how it came out, if he planned it in advance, or if it just slipped out of him one day. I tried to imagine what it would feel like, having to come up with the words to describe such a pain after keeping it hidden for so long, and my chest ached for him.

I thought about what I would do to escape a pain like that. What lengths I'd go to.

When I was done with that cigarette, I lit another one. I didn't even care much for how it tasted, how it felt in my lungs, the rush—all I could think about was how these had been

Jack's. He'd done this, too. The knowledge was comforting. I imagined him also in his car, the windows down, music on, the two of us connected through this, and I felt—for the first time all day—a little bit better.

I looked at the passenger seat. Ghost was sitting there, and the smoke seemed to move through the air around his body. He turned his head toward me.

"Let me be alone," I whispered. That was as loud as I could force my voice to get. "Please, Ghost. Please just let me be alone."

I closed my eyes. I knew he wouldn't leave, but I just needed to pretend, even if only for a moment.

I sat in my car like that for an hour. When I was done with the second cigarette, I resisted the urge to smoke another. I wanted to save them for as long as I could.

* * *

Emmett

hey! what are you doing tomorrow afternoon?

I'd let my dad know that I got home before I went to my room, hoping he wouldn't smell the cigarettes on me. Before coming inside, I'd taken off the jacket I'd worn while smoking and left it in my car, trying to mitigate the smell. He didn't say anything, so I assumed he hadn't noticed.

In my room, I sat on my bed and responded to Emmett.

Caleb

as of right now, nothing

Emmett

wanna go out with me?

theres a new coffee shop that just opened up near my house

i was thinking it could be a nice spot for our first official date

Since our kiss three days ago, we'd been texting (and flirting) regularly, but with Thanksgiving, neither of us had brought up anything date-related. I'd assumed—or hoped, at least—that it would come up soon, but I wasn't expecting today.

Caleb

does that mean the homework/scream hang out is our un-official first date?

Emmett

if we want it to be

we get to make the rules! >:)

Caleb

lol

then in that case, yes, id love to go out with you

They sent the coffee shop's address, and I agreed to meet them there at three. We texted for a little while longer. Once the conversation died out, I locked my phone and looked up to see Ghost sitting at the foot of the bed.

Everything that happened yesterday came rushing back to me. I felt suddenly ashamed for my date with Emmett. It wasn't even six months since Jack's death, and barely even twenty-four hours since I learned that Jack was assaulted as a child—how could I be sitting here, planning a date?

I thought about what Mom had said, about how Jack didn't want to press charges. I thought about how he was fifteen or sixteen when he told our parents. A sophomore. The same year he read *The Catcher in the Rye.* I grabbed his copy from my backpack, and I started flipping through it, scanning each page for Jack's notes. I wasn't sure what I was looking for, but it felt important that I see everything he'd written, every scribbled comment and underlined paragraph. A part of me knew it was silly, but I thought maybe there would be answers here, embedded in the pages he touched.

At the very end of the book, I found a phone number written on the last, blank page. It was signed *B.*

Brooke. It had to be. But why had she written her phone number down here? A scene solidified in my mind of Jack and Brooke in English class their sophomore year, sitting next to each other, maybe flirting. I imagined Brooke leaning over and writing her phone number in his book. In my head, Jack tried to hide a grin.

Did he ever tell her what happened to him as a kid? Did he ever tell any of his friends?

I got out my laptop and googled Brooke's name. It took a while of digging, but eventually, I found her Facebook and Instagram. I looked through her Facebook profile first; it was sparse, with the most recent post from almost a year ago. I scrolled through old birthday wishes and reposted memes, but I couldn't find images of Jack on her page. I wondered if she'd scrubbed it clean of any mention of him after they broke up, or if she'd never posted pictures of him in the first place.

Then I went to her Instagram, which she seemed to use a little more. The last post was from May. I scrolled through photo after photo, and eventually, I found a few pictures of Jack. They seemed to be from their sophomore and junior years. In one, they were on a park bench, beaming up at the camera and squinting against the sun.

Next to the blue Follow button, it said Message. My thumb hovered over it.

I thought about what I would write to her. *Hey Brooke, it's Caleb, Jack Stone's brother.* But that was as far as I could imagine; I wasn't sure how to ask what I really wanted to know, or if it would be fair to her to ask it at all. I thought about how she was studying to be a veterinarian, about how Mom said she'd gotten her life together. I thought about how she'd almost died like Jack, overdosing in someone else's house.

I doubted that she wanted a reminder of that time in her life again. I knew I couldn't message her.

Instead, I went to her list of followers. After a while of aimlessly scrolling and looking through accounts, I came across Walter's. His bio read: *1/4 of @salinetheband. Nashville born and raised.* Underneath *Follow*, Instagram alerted me that Emmett, Dima, Logan, and Nathan all followed him. I thought about when I saw him at the show, how it felt when I realized who he was.

Did Jack ever tell Walter about his past? Had he ever confided in Walter about how he was feeling—how he was hurting? Or had that stayed a secret, even from his closest friends?

Hey Walter, I thought about typing, *this is Caleb Stone, Jack Stone's brother. I saw you at the SALINE show on the 23rd. Can I ask you something about Jack? Why did you two stop being friends?*

But when I imagined sending the message, anxiety twisted in my stomach. I closed out of his profile and turned my phone off, putting it on my bedside table.

Ghost got up from his spot and walked over to me. I was still feeling hesitant around him after what happened when he touched me yesterday, but I didn't move away. He turned his head between me and the bedside table, as if gesturing to it.

I narrowed my eyes at him. "What?"

His tail flicked, as if annoyed.

"I don't have the energy to decipher your weird codes right now," I huffed, but he didn't react. That black tail just kept flicking.

I sighed and rolled over, facing away from him.

"How was your week?" I asked, taking a sip of my latte.

It was Saturday, and I sat in a booth across from Emmett, a coffee and pumpkin muffin in front of me. I'd spent almost an hour trying to decide what outfit to wear; I eventually decided on a short-sleeved button-up shirt and my nicest pair of jeans.

"It was all right," Emmett said. It also seemed like they put thought into their outfit; they wore a green sweater and sharp eyeliner, and their grown-out blond hair sat in waves on their shoulders, like they'd styled it. "Braelyn and my mom went shopping for most of yesterday, so at least I didn't have to hang out with her for very long."

"You *really* don't get along with her, huh?" I said.

They snorted in a laugh. "It's sort of always been like that, honestly. We spent a lot of our childhood fighting."

"How come?"

"Well, I guess 'cause Braelyn was—*is*—the golden child. She's smart, charismatic, involved in the church, and she's currently studying to be a lawyer. Meanwhile, I'm . . . well, I'm *me*. My parents are kind of okay with the band stuff, even though I don't think they expect me to make a career out of it, but they're not thrilled about everything else I've got going on. . . . I think they've always secretly hoped I would become more like Braelyn. Or, at least, that's how it's always felt."

I frowned. "I'm sorry. That's so shitty."

They shrugged and took a sip of their strawberry-and-banana smoothie.

"Well, for what it's worth, *I* don't think you should be more like Braelyn," I said. "I think you're amazing just the way you are."

They smiled a little. "Thanks, Caleb. I think you're pretty cool, too."

My cheeks heated, and I waved the compliment off.

"So that was my week," Emmett finished. "What about you?"

Images from the past few days flashed through my mind—my mom and me in the kitchen, Dad staring down at his hands, the cigarettes, the ornaments, the truth.

"It was okay," I said, spearing a bite of pumpkin muffin with a fork. I looked down at the piece as I spoke. "It was just . . . kind of hard, doing Thanksgiving and putting up the Christmas tree and everything, without . . ."

Emmett's hand, palm up, slid into view, and I looked up at them. They kept eye contact as they said, "I'm sorry. . . . I know how hard that must be."

I took their hand. There was a jolt when we touched, but I soon relaxed into holding their hand. I liked the feeling of our palms pressed together.

"Thank you," I said. "It was . . . a lot. But . . . I'm glad I get a break from it. I'm glad you invited me here."

They squeezed my hand. "I'm glad you agreed to come."

I squeezed their hand back.

We sat there for a moment, still touching but neither of us saying anything, and I thought about our kiss, how I moved my lips against theirs, how they touched my shoulders. I wanted to lean over the table and kiss them again—but it was all still too new, and we were too out in the open.

Instead, I said, "I haven't told Tanya about us yet. She hasn't really texted me since break started, and since she's grounded, we can't hang out in person . . . but I was kind of wanting to tell her soon, if . . . that was okay."

Emmett smiled and laced their fingers with mine. "I'm okay with you telling whoever you want. And I haven't told anyone about us, either; I was waiting until we talked about it."

"What would you tell people, if you did?" I asked. "Like . . . about us?"

They looked at me for a moment, head tilted gently. "Well," they said slowly, as if testing the waters, "I'd like to tell people that you're my boyfriend."

I couldn't help it—I was grinning from ear to ear before I'd even really processed what they'd said.

"I'd like that, too," I said. "And you would be my . . . ?"

"Partner," they said. They were grinning, too, their cheeks pink. "Or we can come up with a better term. I just don't feel great about 'boyfriend' or 'girlfriend.' . . ."

"Partner works," I said.

We sat there looking at each other, our hands entwined, for a few moments longer. *Boyfriend*, I kept thinking to myself. I was officially *Emmett's boyfriend*. We were dating. We *liked* each other. It was almost surreal.

We stayed at the coffee shop for another half hour before Emmett said there was a place they wanted to show me. We took their car and left mine in the parking lot.

On the drive over, Emmett turned on the Mountain Goats's newest album and left it playing quietly underneath our conversation. I asked, "Where are we going?"

"You'll see," they said with a grin.

It was only a ten-minute drive. The sun had started to set, and the sky was blooming red, giving everything a pink overcast, by the time Emmett parked.

"Here we are," they said.

I followed them up a hill, located in the middle of a neighborhood. They'd brought a blanket, and now they laid it on the ground at the top of the hill. It wasn't until I turned around and saw the view of Nashville, with that red and pink saturating everything, the city lights beginning to sparkle, that I realized why Emmett would take us here.

"How'd you find this place?" I asked, sitting down next to them. The blanket they'd brought was black and covered in constellation patterns.

"It's called Love Circle," they said. "Logan found out about it and introduced me to it last year. It's, like, a semi-popular place for dates and stuff, even though it's kind of hidden. I've been here a few times with Logan and Dima, but not as a romantic thing, obviously. So, I figured it would be a cute place to take you, now that we're officially dating. . . ." They looked down at our hands on the blanket and asked hesitantly, "What do you think?"

"It's beautiful," I said.

I wasn't sure how to tell them how much this touched me—how my chest was filled with warmth, how everything with them felt bubbly and good and safe.

All I could do was lean over and kiss them.

We spent a long time out there, kissing on the blanket, the sun setting in front of us. We didn't say much, just alternating between making out and lying there, looking at the sky.

"How did you guys decide on Deck of Fools as the band name?" I asked after a while. We were on the blanket, our shoulders pressed together and our hands entwined. I was staring up at the sky, but I could see Emmett looking at me in my periphery.

"Dima and I are into tarot," Emmett said, "and one time, she, Logan, and I were hanging out, and somehow we came up with this idea of a tarot deck only made up of The Fool card, and it sort of became an inside joke. So, when we were coming up with a band name, we landed on that."

"That's fun," I said. "I didn't realize you were that into tarot."

"Yeah, I wouldn't consider myself an expert on it or anything," Emmett said, "but I think it's interesting to learn about, and Dima and I like to do readings for each other every now and then. Maybe I could do a reading for you sometime."

"Maybe you could." I smiled and squeezed their hand. "And . . . how did you come up with 'Limerence'?" I asked gently.

They were quiet for a moment.

"I wrote a lot of sad songs about bad relationships back then," they finally said. "Some of them were based on how she'd started making me feel, but most of it was about other people's stories or characters I'd made up. Mallory really liked them, so we decided to record an EP about a 'fictional' toxic relationship. 'Limerence' basically means obsessive infatuation, so it was about the dysfunctional way that these thinly veiled self-insert characters loved each other."

"Wow." I turned on my side so I was facing them.

"Yeah. It's . . . hard for me to listen to those songs anymore, which kind of sucks, since I was really proud of some of them. But I've made a lot of stuff with Deck of Fools that I'm proud of too, so . . ." They shrugged.

"You're really talented, you know that, right?" I said. "Like, you're a great lyricist and storyteller, and your voice is so good at making people feel things, and I almost cried listening to your music the other day! Do you know how rare that is?"

They laughed. "Sorry, I'm not laughing *at* you. You just sound so angry about the fact that it almost made you cry—"

"Because I am!" I said, and they buried their head in my chest, shoulders shaking with giggles. I wrapped an arm around them. I didn't think I'd ever get tired of hearing them laugh.

"But I'm serious," I said. "You're an *amazing* musician, and I want to make sure you know that because you deserve to."

"Thank you," they said. "And sorry for almost making you cry."

"You're forgiven." I kissed the top of their head.

It got dark before long. We spent another thirty minutes there, wrapped around each other and talking, before we headed back to Emmett's car. In the passenger seat, I held the constellation blanket folded in my lap.

"Thank you for opening up about stuff with Braelyn, by the way," I said, once we were on the road. "I know that can be hard to talk about."

"It feels easy, talking with you about that stuff," they said, glancing away from the road long enough to offer me a smile. I smiled back.

We drove back to the coffee shop, and Emmett parked their car next to mine in the now mostly empty lot. We both got out, and they came over to my side before I could get into my car, pulling me into a long, hard kiss, their hands cupping my cheeks.

We were both out of breath when we pulled away, and Emmett's cheeks were red, their pupils dilated and hair disheveled. I wondered if I looked the same way.

"I am never going to get tired of that," they said.

I laughed. "Me neither. But I should probably get going, unfortunately. . . ."

"Ugh, you're right." They pouted, but I couldn't resist getting on my tiptoes and stealing one last peck.

"Text me when you get home!" they said, before heading back to their car. I waved goodbye and turned to open my driver's side door.

I was giddy from the date, drunk off my time with Emmett, my mind only on *us* and Emmett's lips and their smile when they called me their boyfriend—so, I wasn't expecting the strong smell of cigarettes when I opened my car door, and it was a hard crash back to reality, the world outside us slamming into me in one hard swing: Jack's book. Jack's thumb drive. Jack's cigarettes. Jack's childhood. Jack's addiction. Jack's death.

The hair on my arms stood up. When I glanced in my rearview mirror, I saw Ghost's outline.

He stayed there like that for the rest of the drive home.

December

16

I PICKED TANYA UP FOR school on Monday. "So . . . how'd your weekend go?"

She took a sip from her orange thermos, probably filled with tea; she always drank tea in the morning before school.

"About as normal as staying home can get," she said.

I winced. "I'm sorry again about . . ."

"Really, Caleb, it's fine," she said, waving a manicured hand. "Besides, I needed to spend the time working on my paintings for class, anyway. I still have two more that I need to finish."

"How's that going?"

"Surprisingly okay," she said. "I'm making good progress, and I'm kind of proud of the ones I've already completed."

"The portrait? Or the one of your mom?"

"Both. I think I'm gonna submit those for the showcase, if my teacher is okay with it."

We talked for a little while longer about her paintings, and

I updated her about the project with Emmett, and how we'd pivoted to writing songs about *The Catcher in the Rye*.

"And, uh, speaking of Emmett," I said, trying to push down my nerves, "there was actually something else I wanted to tell you. . . ."

"Ominous," she said. "But continue."

"Emmett and I, um, went on a date this weekend."

The words were barely out of my mouth when Tanya all but screeched. "WHAT?! That's amazing! You two like each other?! How long has this been going on?! Did you kiss?! Are you dating now?! I *told* you, you two would get along!"

I laughed, and by the time I was done filling her in on everything that had happened over the past week, we were pulling into the school's parking lot.

As we started to get out, I said, "But what about you? Have you had any—you know, romantic developments?"

Tanya raised an eyebrow. "Like always, nope. Why do you ask?"

I shrugged in what I hoped was a nonchalant way. "Just, you know, while we were on the subject . . ."

She gave me a confused look but didn't ask anything else, and I changed the subject as we walked into the building. On our way to the cafeteria for breakfast, we bumped into Nathan and Logan, who seemed to be intently discussing something.

". . . don't make a decision yet," I heard Logan say, right before he turned to us and grinned, any note of seriousness already gone. "Hey! How were y'all's Thanksgivings?"

"As good as it could be, I guess," Tanya said. Nathan and

Logan both fell into step with us as we walked. "What about you?"

"Fine. My family doesn't do much for it." Logan shrugged. "Mostly I just like it for the few days off we get."

"I wish it could've been longer," Nathan said.

"God, tell me about it," Logan said. "I can't *wait* for winter break."

"I'm so ready for this semester to be over," I agreed.

The conversation continued, but Tanya was unusually quiet. When I looked at her, she was staring at the floor, her eyes glazed over. I pulled my phone out.

Caleb

everything ok?

But she didn't check her texts for the rest of breakfast, so it wasn't until later in the day, when I was in songwriting, that I got a response.

Tanya

sorry! just saw this. yeah i'm fine, just tired today.

thanks for checking on me!

No heart emoji this time? That wasn't like her. I frowned at the screen.

"Caleb, Emmett?" Mr. Russak said.

I rushed to put my phone away. "Uh, yes, sir?"

Emmett and I were sitting next to each other; it was nearing the end of class, and we were given fifteen minutes to work on our projects, although neither of us were being particularly productive today.

"Can I speak to you two after class?" he asked.

Emmett and I glanced at each other.

"Don't worry. It's nothing bad," Mr. Russak chuckled. "And I'll write you both notes for your next period if you need it."

"Yeah, no problem," Emmett said. Mr. Russak nodded and left our table to check on other people. When Emmett glanced at me, I just shrugged.

After the bell rang, we went up to Mr. Russak's desk. "How are you two doing on your project?" he asked.

"Fine," Emmett said. "We're . . . well, we *were* halfway through writing the songs, but we recently decided to pivot to something else, so . . ."

"Why?"

"We were originally writing songs based on classic character archetypes," I explained, "but then I wrote something about *Catcher in the Rye* and, uh, we kind of decided we liked that direction better."

He nodded. "I see. So, you've decided to have a cohesive theme tying all the songs together?"

"That's the idea," Emmett said. "They're gonna all be about characters or scenes from the book."

"Interesting. I've noticed a few other groups took that direction, too." He glanced down at something on his desk. "Well, I was hoping to see if you two would perform at the showcase on December twentieth."

I blinked. "Really?"

"I know I haven't seen what you've written yet, but, well, it would be a great extra-credit opportunity." He looked very pointedly at me. "And, Emmett, I know from other conversations we've had that you're always looking for more performance experience. I figured this would be good for both of you, assuming you're interested?"

"Wow." Emmett looked between Mr. Russak and me, a wide smile on their face. "Thanks, Mr. Russak, this is awesome. We'd love to."

I wasn't sure I agreed. I knew this would help me pass the class, but I hadn't performed in public since my audition for Williams. I'd fantasized about being up on that stage again, guitar or banjo in hand—but now that the opportunity was in front of me, it was kind of terrifying.

But I didn't protest. I just nodded and said, "Thank you."

As we were leaving the classroom, Emmett nudged me. "What's up? Are you not excited to be in the showcase?"

"I just . . . don't perform in front of crowds very often," I said.

They raised an eyebrow. "Stage fright?"

"I mean, it's not *severe*, but I guess you could call it that."

"Well, the best way I've found to get used to performing is just to do it a bunch." They grinned. "It's gonna be fun; trust me. Plus, we get to do it together!"

I smiled, too. "Good point."

We went to our separate classes after that, notes from Mr. Russak in hand, but I still couldn't help feeling uneasy. It wasn't just the idea of performing in the showcase weighing on me—it was the conversations I'd had with my parents, and Tanya's uncharacteristic quietness this morning, which didn't get better as the day went on. During lunch, she said she was going to eat in the art room today, instead of in the cafeteria with us.

"I need to get work on this painting done," she said, smiling apologetically.

We all nodded. Nathan asked, "Do you want company?"

She waved him off, and I could've sworn she was avoiding his eyes, her gaze landing somewhere to his left. "It's fine. I need to focus on getting this done, and I know I'll just wanna hang out and talk if someone else is there. . . ."

Nathan nodded, and I watched Tanya walk away, frowning. I knew she was busy, but it wasn't like her to turn down company; I hung out with her while she painted all the time. So why did she turn down Nathan's offer? And, more selfishly, why didn't she ask me? She said everything was fine this morning, but it still felt like there was something between us taking up space.

Emmett noticed my concern and bumped their shoulder into mine gently.

"Everything all right?" they asked quietly. Logan was typing something on his phone, and Dima and Nathan seemed to be in the middle of a discussion about novelizations of musicals.

I tried to give Emmett a reassuring smile. "Yeah, it's no big deal. I'll tell you about it later."

They nodded. "Speaking of later, do you want to come over to my place tomorrow?"

I noticed they didn't say it was for the project, and when I looked at them, there was a glint in their eyes.

I fought a giddy grin at the thought. This was really happening—*Emmett and I are dating!*—and it filled me with warmth. I wanted to live in this good feeling forever.

"Yeah, I'd love that," I said.

After school on Tuesday, I went over to Emmett's house. Although I'd technically been here once before, it had been dark, so this was my first time getting a good look at its white shutters and long gravel driveway. When I got to the door, I saw that their welcome mat proclaimed a Bible verse in curly letters.

Emmett let me in a moment later, and when I stepped inside, I took in the big leather couches, Jesus-themed decor, and family photos filling every wall. Emmett's mom came out from the living room to greet me; she was a short white woman with the most voluminous blond pixie cut I'd ever seen, and she smiled widely when she saw us.

"You must be Caleb!" she said, already hugging me. "I'm Emmett's mom, but you can call me Susan."

"It's nice to meet you, ma'am," I said, stepping back.

"Emmett tells me you're also studying to be a musician," she said. "What do you play?"

"Oh, uh." I glanced between her and Emmett. "Mostly guitar, but also some banjo, and I write songs. . . ."

"Oh, wow!" She nodded appreciatively. "I think banjo is one of the few instruments that Emmett *hasn't* tried yet. But then, I'm sure you know that about him already, since I hear you're working on a project together."

Him rang out loud and clear, and I wondered if I should

correct her, or if she'd see that as disrespectful. I glanced at Emmett, but I couldn't read their expression.

"Speaking of that project," Emmett said, "we were actually gonna go work on that upstairs. . . ."

"All right, all right, have fun! And if you want to stay for dinner, Caleb, you're more than welcome!" She smiled one last time before heading back to the living room, and Emmett led me to their room.

"Your mom seems nice," I said as I followed them up the stairs.

They made a face that I couldn't quite interpret. "She . . . is, yeah." And when they didn't offer anything else, I didn't push it.

Their room was small, in part because half of it was being used for a makeshift, in-room recording studio. Several microphones stood in the corner, surrounded by monitors and cables, and two guitars sat on stands, hooked up to amps—the acoustic Fender they brought to school, and the black electric guitar they played at their Deck of Fools show. They also had a small keyboard pressed against the farther wall, along with a mandolin and a ukulele in the corner.

"This is where you record all your songs?" I asked, setting my backpack and guitar case down on the floor. Emmett closed the door before sitting down on their bed.

"My solo stuff, yeah. But we have to go to Dima's house when we record Deck of Fools. I bring most of my equipment, and Ms. Khalil's girlfriend helps us out sometimes."

"That's so cool that you can just do this whenever you want,"

I said, getting a closer look at their microphone.

"It's pretty nice," they agreed. "And, on that note, I was thinking we could record the first song today, if you feel up to it?"

I turned back to Emmett, surprised. "Oh—uh, yeah, we could do that. I just . . . I'm not the best at playing in front of other people, so it might not be that good. . . ."

"You'll do great," they said, and the smile they gave me was soft and earnest. "It'll be good practice for the showcase. And it'll be fun, getting to play together. I liked singing with you the other week."

"It *was* fun," I agreed. I took a seat on the edge of their bed, letting out a breath. It was full-size, and their plaid green duvet was soft. Emmett shifted so they were closer to me, the mattress dipping under them as they moved.

"Hey," they said, and when I turned to look at them, we were so close, I could count their eyelashes. Their hand sat pointedly between us.

I took it, lacing our fingers together. "Hi. What's up?"

"Can I kiss you?"

I surged forward and kissed them hard in answer, our teeth clattering together. Emmett laughed against my mouth, and warmth flooded me at the sound, my pulse fast in my ears.

They leaned back and I followed with the kiss, until suddenly we were lying back, tangled on their bed, Emmett's fingertips running along the hem of my shirt and our kisses feverish.

It was still so surreal to me, the idea that someone could like me back, could want to kiss me. Yet here Emmett was: their mouth against mine, our torsos pressed together and our legs tangled up, my hands in their hair and their hands on my hips. We kissed until our lips were raw, until we were both out of breath, until we got to the brink of something more—

And then it hit me what we were doing, and I thought, *oh my God, this is actually happening right now*, and suddenly it was too much.

"I—Sorry," I managed, breathless, pulling away from them. "I think—I think I need a break."

Emmett nodded. "Yeah, for sure. No need to apologize."

We both sat up, and I looked away, wiping my sweaty palms on my jeans. I felt pulled in two directions. I was *really* into Emmett, and *really* into making out with them, and a part of me wanted to keep making out—but I was also terrified and insecure and ashamed of myself. It was hard not to compare our bodies when we touched, my round belly against their flat stomach, our differing anatomies, and my gender dysphoria reared its ugly head. Then shame joined the chorus: How could I be thinking about romance and sex and relationships right *now* of all times? What was I thinking?

"I'm sorry," I said again.

Emmett shook their head. "Don't be. I was gonna, uh, ask to take a break, too, and anyway, we should probably get started on recording soon. . . ."

"Right." I cleared my throat and got up from the bed. "So, um, should we practice for a while first, or . . . ?"

"Yeah! Let me get everything set up."

Emmett went to their desk with their recording equipment,

hooking their laptop up to their audio interface and monitors. They messed around with it for a while before passing me a pair of headphones.

We got the microphones set up for both of us, and I adjusted my guitar in my lap. We'd decided I would play guitar for this song, and we'd both sing, alternating verses and harmonizing at the end. I pulled the lyrics up on my phone, balanced on my knee.

"All right, I'm good whenever you're ready," Emmett said.

I took a breath and started plucking out the chords. I was shaky when I sang the first verse, but I tried to relax into the song. Emmett joined in, their voice gravelly and low, and we got almost all the way through the song before I messed up for the first time, fumbling a chord and tripping over the lyrics. I stopped playing.

"Sorry about that," I said.

"It's all good. We're just practicing." They smiled. "Wanna run through it again?"

I let out a breath, trying to relax my shoulders. "Sure."

We played through the song again. From the corner of my eye, I saw that Ghost had joined us and was sitting on the carpeted floor across the room, but I tried to not let him distract me. I focused on the lyrics as we sang them—*the blood on the floor / I float up to shore*—and tried to stay in the song. Emmett and I both messed up once, but on the third try, there weren't any mistakes, and we both felt sufficiently warmed up.

The actual recording didn't take that long; we only had to record it twice before we both agreed to keep the take. Emmett said they would work on the actual mixing of the song later, and we decided to work on writing the second song.

Emmett had already started another one, told again from Holden's point of view but directed toward his younger sister, Phoebe, and we worked on it together. It was about how Holden thought Phoebe was a better, more honest person than anyone else—about how she was the only one who he could trust and speak honestly with. We named it "The Only One," while the song we'd recorded earlier was titled "Ducks on the Pond."

By the time I needed to head home, we'd pretty much finished the Phoebe song. Emmett seemed really happy about all the progress we'd made, and I was, too. We were chipping away at this project, slowly but surely.

As Emmett walked me out to my car, they said, "SALINE's performing again this weekend, along with a few other bands, and I was planning to go. Wanna go with me?"

I thought about it for a moment. If you didn't count the breakdown I had or the fact that I got too drunk to drive us home, last time had been fun.

And it was SALINE performing. I thought about when I'd looked at Walter's profile, how I'd thought about messaging him. Maybe if I went to this show, I would get the chance to talk to him.

Maybe I could ask him about his friendship with Jack. Maybe I could get some answers.

"Yeah, that'd be fun," I said.

We kissed goodbye after that—the newness of being able to *kiss Emmett goodbye* made me embarrassingly happy—and they waved as I backed out of the driveway.

Dad was sitting at the dining room table, typing on his laptop, when I got home.

"I'm home," I called, taking my shoes off at the entrance.

"Hey." Dad paused his typing, looking up from his computer. "How was your study session with Emmett?"

"It wasn't a study session; we were working on a project," I said. "But, uh, it was good. We recorded one song and started writing another one."

He nodded. "This is the project based off of a book, right? *Catcher in the Rye*?"

"Mm-hmm." I started heading toward the stairs, hoping to exit the conversation soon.

Since Thanksgiving break, I hadn't been in the mood for long conversations with my parents. There was this cloud hanging over us that made every interaction feel fragile, brittle, and I wanted to avoid it as much as I could.

And—like I knew he would—Dad tilted the conversation toward Jack.

"I could've sworn Jack did a project on that book when he was in school, too," he continued. "I think I remember him telling me about it. . . ."

I paused at the bottom of the staircase. "Yeah, you're right," I said. "I found it on one of his old thumb drives."

"Really? I guess that means you've been in his room, then?"

"Just . . . for a few minutes."

Dad was quiet for a moment, looking down at his computer. "You know, Caleb, I was thinking that this weekend . . . maybe you, me, and Mom could watch some home videos again. We haven't done that in a while, and it might be nice to go through old memories, right?"

"I can't," I said. "I have plans already."

"Oh." He blinked.

"Yeah, um, Emmett invited me to a show on Friday night."

He frowned. "Well . . . is this something you have to go to? I mean, you've been out a lot lately. . . . Couldn't you just stay home?"

I wasn't sure why, but irritation flared at the suggestion. "I already committed to this thing, Dad. I can't just drop it now." I huffed.

"Well . . . what about Saturday or Sunday?"

"I can't do that, either."

"Why?"

I racked my brain for an excuse. "I—I was gonna try to catch up on my songwriting homework this weekend."

"You won't be doing that *all* day, though, right? I mean, couldn't you just take thirty minutes or an hour out of your day to—"

"Dad, I don't *want* to!"

I hadn't meant to raise my voice. Dad stared at me, shock written across his face.

We heard Mom's footsteps down the hallway, and she greeted us with furrowed eyebrows and hands already on her hips. "Is everything okay?"

I looked between her and Dad, and suddenly I couldn't stand it—this family, this house, this life. I couldn't stand that Dad wanted to rewatch home videos of Jack, and that he was sitting here, staring at me like he didn't recognize me, and I couldn't stand that Jack had been so much like Dad—that, when I looked at Dad now, I still recognized the reflection of my brother, the origin of his blue eyes and pointed nose.

Jack was dead, but he wasn't gone—he was everywhere, the fact of his death permeating everything, his absence a constant.

And I just couldn't stand it.

"Everything is fine," I mumbled, and before anyone could say anything else to me, I turned and sped up the stairs, slamming my bedroom door.

Ghost was waiting for me, curled up on my bed. My anger only grew at the sight of him—I could never get a break.

Friday couldn't come fast enough.

I WAS IN A BAD mood for the rest of the week—irritable and tense, everything pissing me off. It felt like everyone laughed too loudly or walked too slowly or talked too much, and I slid into anger at the smallest things.

My conversation with Dad had set me on edge; something about his insistence on watching home videos together bothered me, frustrated me. Why couldn't he see that I didn't *want* to relive old memories—I didn't *want* to see Jack alive, smiling, walking around and talking, before he became that pale corpse now buried in a cemetery fifteen minutes from our house?

A part of me knew my irritation wasn't fair to him. This was how he wanted to grieve, how he was trying to remember Jack. But no matter how much I tried, I couldn't get out of this mood. And I couldn't hide it well, either.

On Wednesday, when I got to the cafeteria for lunch,

Emmett was already sitting at our table, and they frowned at me when I sat down.

"Everything okay?" they asked.

I set my tray down in front of me. "Yeah," I said. "Just . . . kind of in a bad mood."

"I can tell." They cracked a grin, and I nudged their foot under the table, not unkindly.

"I'm a pretty bad actor," I agreed.

After I went to my room last night, I'd thought about texting Emmett, telling them what happened. But when I wrote out the conversation between Dad and me, I couldn't really explain why I was so upset. It only made me feel worse, and I ended up deleting the text.

"I'm sorry you're in a bad mood," Emmett said. They held out a french fry from their tray. "Would this help?"

"Well . . ." I took it from them. "It certainly wouldn't *hurt*."

Tanya and Dima showed up a moment later, already in a heated conversation.

". . . isn't that some bullshit?" Dima said as she sat down. Tanya sat down next to me, putting her backpack in the empty seat next to her.

"What's bullshit?" Emmett asked.

"A poem I wrote was up for workshop today," she said.

"And it seems like it didn't go well," Tanya added.

Emmett winced sympathetically. "Ugh, that always sucks. Was it Brent again?"

"Of course it was Brent." Dima huffed. "That guy's been nothing but an asshole during workshop the whole semester."

"Fuck Brent," I agreed. This had been an ongoing theme in her Advanced Poetry class this semester, so this wasn't the first time she'd come to the lunch table with a story like this.

She gestured to me. "*Thank* you. And it's especially annoying because I was thinking about reading this poem for the showcase, but now I'm worried it's garbage, and I don't know what I would replace it with."

"Aw, don't take Brent's comments to heart! He's bitter and jealous and doesn't know what he's talking about," Tanya said.

In the distance, I spotted Logan and Nathan heading to our table, talking as they walked together. Tanya seemed to notice them, too, because the next thing I knew, she was grabbing her backpack and standing up.

"Speaking of the showcase, I should get some work done in the art room again," she said, right as Nathan and Logan got here. "I'll see y'all later."

She turned around and left before we could say much of anything other than "bye."

I glanced at Nathan as he sat down. He watched Tanya walk away, a small frown etched on his face. Something *had* to have happened between them for her to get up and leave so abruptly.

A pang of hurt accompanied the thought. Once again, it felt like I was missing something, like she was keeping a secret from me, and all the frustration and anger that I'd been able to push down bubbled up again.

I didn't say much for the rest of lunch.

In songwriting on Thursday, we were given time to work on our project again, so Emmett and I got to work on our third song. Emmett had decided they wanted to write a song based off the character Jane Gallagher, an old friend of Holden's who he thinks about calling in the book, and we brainstormed lyrics for a while. Mr. Russak came over to our desks at one point, looking way too chipper for my perpetual bad mood.

"How's everything going?" he said.

"Pretty good," Emmett said. "We're working on the third song today."

Mr. Russak nodded. "And where are you on your recordings?"

I groaned internally. Why did he have to choose to interrogate us *today*?

"We have one recorded," Emmett said, "so we just need to write two more songs, and we'll spend next week recording everything, and then we should be all set."

"All right," Mr. Russak said. "And remember—if you're going to be presenting one of these songs at the showcase, you'll need to get it ready to perform. We really only have two weeks left before the showcase, and you wanna make sure you're ready in time."

"Okay, we got it," I snapped, and I didn't realize it came out as forcefully as it did until Emmett and Mr. Russak both looked at me, eyebrows raised.

Shit. I looked down, my face warm. "Um, we'll be ready by then," I said quietly.

Mr. Russak hesitated, and for a moment, I thought he was going to call me out on it, but he just nodded. "Okay, keep it up. I can't wait to hear 'em."

When he was out of earshot, Emmett turned to me. "What

was *that* about? Is everything okay?"

"Yeah." I rubbed my temples. "I just don't feel good, I guess."

Emmett angled themself so they could offer their hand to me on the desk without others seeing, their laptop and open notebooks blocking the view. I took it surreptitiously.

"If there's something going on, you know you can talk to me about it, right? And . . ." They looked down at our joined hands. "And if the way you've been feeling has to do with *us*—"

"It doesn't," I rushed to assure them. "Emmett—you're, like, the only *good* thing going on in my life now."

They let out a breath, squeezing my hand. "Okay, cool, cool. But what *is* going on, then?"

I sighed. I didn't think rehashing it would do anything but upset me more. And when I thought about trying to put into words everything that had happened over the past week, it felt like my insides were cracking open a little.

"It has to do with my parents," I decided on saying. "I don't really want to get into it during class, though. . . ."

"Yeah, of course. But I'm here if you wanna talk about it later, okay?"

"Thank you." I smiled. "You're the best."

"Well, I don't know if I'd say *that*, but you're welcome." They squeezed my hand once again before dropping it. "Now, I guess we should get back to work?"

I agreed and turned back to my computer, but I couldn't help the shame that had gathered in my stomach—shame that I'd snapped at Mr. Russak, that I had been so irritable all week that people had noticed, that I was feeling this way at all.

I didn't like myself when I got like this. I doubted anyone else did, either.

On Friday, Emmett drove us to the SALINE show.

It was at the same house, and I was kind of thankful for the familiarity. The first thing I did when I got there was head to the makeshift bar and pour myself a vodka and Dr Pepper. Emmett grabbed a can of Coke, since they were driving us tonight.

"Whoa, hey, maybe let's slow down there," they said, watching as I downed the cup in a few gulps.

I wiped my mouth with the back of my hand. "Sorry, I'm just—excited to be here, I guess."

I was restless. I felt this fire in my blood, raging through me, and I was itching for *something* to happen. I needed answers—I needed to talk to Walter tonight, but I didn't want to be myself when it happened.

And, I thought, I sort of *needed* to not be myself. I remembered how much smoother social interactions seemed, how much more I came out of my shell when I wasn't sober, wasn't me. And tonight, I needed all the help I could get.

"I noticed." Emmett snorted. I started to pour myself another drink, but they stepped in closer to me, placing a hand on my arm.

"Thank you for inviting me to this," I said quietly. Standing this close, it only felt right. "It's nice, going out together."

They grinned. "Yeah, it is. Thank you for agreeing to come."

I stood on my tiptoes to kiss them, and they met me halfway.

As cliché as it sounded, it was electric, getting to kiss Emmett so freely. When we pulled away, I was smiling, and some of that fiery feeling had started to fade.

Emmett and I walked around the house until we eventually found some empty chairs in the living room to claim. The show was in the basement again, but the bands weren't playing for a little while. There were less people here this time, but still more than I was used to. No one was openly snorting anything this time, thankfully, but the smoke and smell of weed and cigarettes hung thick in the air.

"Hey, Emmett!" A girl who looked a lot like Gwen approached us. I recognized her as Tommy; she wasn't as goth or butch as her sister, but from what I'd seen at the last show, she was just as friendly and talented. "I didn't know you were coming tonight?"

Emmett nodded. "Yeah, I saw your post on Instagram earlier this week, and I figured I could come out."

"Aww, you're *so* sweet," she cooed, then held her arms out in a hug, which Emmett accepted. She was very clearly drunk, her words coming out a little slurred, and I wondered how she was going to play like this—if she planned on being able to sober up by the time the show started, or if she was going to just go out and perform like this.

But, then again, maybe it was different when you went to shows like this every week, when you drank and smoked on the regular, when this was a huge part of your life.

I wasn't sure why, but thinking about that, I wanted to be like Tommy. I wanted to be swaying, slurring my words, with that carefree grin. I didn't want to give a shit about anything.

I downed my second drink, and the alcohol started to catch up to me; it was suddenly hotter in here, and I took off my hoodie, draping it over my arm.

Emmett and Tommy talked for a little while, something about Gwen, and the new album SALINE was working on, and Deck of Fools's plans for after high school. I didn't mean to, but I sort of tuned out. I was too busy looking around the room, trying to catch a glimpse of Walter.

I wondered if he would remember me . . . or Jack.

I wondered if he even knew that Jack was dead.

"I'm going to get another drink," I said to Emmett, once there was a lull in the conversation. They nodded, and I left them and Tommy alone to talk.

In the kitchen, a girl and boy I didn't recognize stood in the entrance, positioned to perfectly take up the walking space, so I had to squeeze past them to get to the bar.

"Excuse me," I said. They didn't seem to hear me, though, because the guy backed up and bumped into me, pushing me into the fridge. "Ex*cuse* me," I repeated, louder this time.

"Oh, uh, yeah, sorry." But I saw him roll his eyes to the girl after they finally moved out of the way.

"Asshole," I mumbled, twisting the cap off the bottle of Burnett's and pouring a generous amount into my cup. I added a splash of Dr Pepper to make it bearable, then took a long gulp of my drink. God, that tasted like shit.

"Is there a problem?" the girl said, her lips pursed.

"Yeah, you two are taking up all the space," I said. Distantly,

I thought, *Why am I doing this? Why am I bothering with them? It doesn't matter. This isn't going to help anything.* But my mouth didn't seem to be on the same page as my brain.

The guy scoffed. "Well, you still managed to squeeze your fat ass past us, so I don't see the problem—"

"Man, fuck you!" I snapped.

Emmett was suddenly by my side, their hand on my shoulder. I hadn't even realized they'd followed me.

"C'mon, Caleb, it's not worth it," they said, tugging me away. I let them lead me back to the living room, where Tommy was still sitting on the couch, doing dabs with someone.

"What was that about?" they asked, their eyebrows furrowed, once we were finally out of earshot of that guy and girl.

"They were being assholes," I said. I heard how my words were already slurring. I hadn't thought I'd drunk *that* much already, but maybe I'd put more vodka in my drinks than I'd realized. Or maybe I was just a lightweight.

"I know," they said, "but it's not worth starting a fight over it. What was your next move gonna be? What if it had gotten physical?"

"I could've taken him," I said, and in the moment, I really thought I could've. I had this energy, this anger, like I was ready to tear something to shreds. Maybe it would've felt good, fighting that guy. Maybe it would've helped. In the moment, I was looking for something—*anything*—to make me feel better.

Emmett sighed heavily. "Let's just go home—"

"No!" I put my hands on their shoulders, trying to keep them here. "We can't yet!"

"Caleb, you're already drunk enough that you're trying to

start fights with strangers. I don't think we need to be here anymore."

"But we *have* to stay—I haven't even talked to Walter yet!"

They raised an eyebrow. "Walter? Why do you need to talk to him?"

Ah, shit. I hadn't told Emmett about this part. I hadn't wanted to get into it yet, not unless Walter *actually* had answers for me.

But there was no way around it now. "He used to be friends with Jack, and I wanna know why they stopped hanging out."

I watched the understanding flicker on Emmett's face, then watched as it turned to worry.

I took their hands in mine. "*Please*, Em, let's stay for a little bit longer. At least until I can talk to him, and then we can leave if you still want to. Please?"

They sighed again, looking down at our hands. "Okay. . . . Yeah. But you need to promise me you won't do anything stupid, okay?"

I nodded. "I promise I won't do anything stupid."

"All right. Well, let's go see if we can find Walter, in that case."

They started to turn away, but I pulled them back to me and into a kiss. They kissed back hesitantly, and when we pulled away, they looked only a little bit less worried.

"Hey, guess what?" I said.

"What?"

"I like you a lot."

They smiled softly. "I like you a lot, too."

"Like, a *lot* a lot," I continued. "And I like that we're dating, even though I feel guilty about it sometimes because I probably shouldn't be allowed to be happy right now, but you make me happy, anyway, and I think you're very cool and talented and kind and hot."

"You're drunk," they said quietly.

I nodded. "Yeah, I think I am."

And then—I wasn't sure why, because I'd said all that to them to make them happy, not upset—their face twisted into a grimace, and they looked like they were gonna be sick.

"What's wrong?" I asked.

"Nothing. Everything's fine," they said. "Let's go find Walter."

I let them drag me by the hand through the house and downstairs.

On our way down, I saw Ghost in the living room, pacing back and forth among the crowd, looking distressed.

Downstairs, Walter was talking with Gwen and Simon. Some people I didn't recognize, and who I assumed were members of the other bands, were tuning their instruments and adjusting the microphones.

"Oh, hey, Emmett!" Walter said as we approached. "Thanks for making it out."

They did the same song and dance that Emmett did with Tommy, talking for a minute about the show tonight and SALINE's projects and whatever else, before Emmett grabbed my hand and said, "By the way—this is my boyfriend, Caleb."

Even in my drunken state, I felt butterflies, hearing them introduce me like that.

"How've you been, Caleb?" Gwen asked me, before taking a drag from her cigarette. She blew the smoke to the side, and I watched it float and disappear into the air.

"Uh, all right," I said. "You?"

She grinned. "Living the life as always."

Walter was looking at me, and I met his gaze. "Um, Walter, right?" I said, as if I didn't know exactly who he was.

He nodded, then tilted his head to the side. "Sorry if this is weird, but—have we met before?"

"I'm Caleb Stone," I said. "Jack Stone's brother."

Recognition flashed across his face, and he threw his hands in the air. "*Oh!* I *knew* you looked familiar! How's Jack doing?"

The question washed over me in an icy shock. Emmett still held my hand, and they laced our fingers comfortingly, but I barely registered the touch.

"I guess you don't know," I said, but the words sounded far away. Walter frowned, and before he could ask, I said, as calmly as I could manage, "He died last June."

It was strange, watching someone else receive that news. I saw myself in the way his face fell, in the look behind his eyes. He blinked, looking down at the floor.

"Oh my God," he said quietly. "I'm so sorry to hear that. . . ."

No one said anything for a moment. Gwen and Simon both looked down solemnly, shifting in their seats uncomfortably.

"How . . . ?" He didn't finish the question, but he didn't need to.

"Overdose," I said.

"Oh my God," Gwen said. "That's horrible."

Maybe it was because I was drunk—maybe it was because of everything that had happened this week—but I barked out a laugh, cruel and acerbic.

"Tell me about it," I said. "It fucking sucks."

"I'm so sorry," Gwen said, but I wasn't sure if she was apologizing for my loss or for her response or for something else entirely.

"Were you friends with him when he was using?" I asked Walter. I felt my filter disappearing, felt myself getting to the point where it didn't matter what other people were thinking; I was going to say what I needed to say.

Walter looked between Emmett and me. "Kind of," he admitted. "We sort of grew apart right when he was getting into . . . everything."

"Why?"

His eyebrows went up. "Why did we grow apart?"

I nodded. I felt Emmett tighten their grip on my hand, but I didn't look at them. Nothing mattered right now except getting answers from Walter.

"I don't know," he said. "I guess we just stopped being as close as we used to. Jack . . . started hanging out with other people, getting involved in—"

"Heroin," I finished for him. If I sounded bitter, I didn't care.

He nodded slowly. "Yeah. . . . It wasn't one thing, really. And we didn't stop hanging out on bad terms. Stuff just . . .

changed. He had different priorities from me. And I could tell that he was . . ." He pressed his lips together. "Well, I've seen enough people go down that road that I knew that's where he was headed."

When I heard that, all I felt was that anger surging through me, demanding to be let out.

"So you *knew*?!" I said. "You knew what he was doing to himself and you didn't do *anything*—"

"Caleb." But I ignored Emmett.

"You just left him alone to do that?! You didn't try to—to help him, or stop him or—"

"Hey, hey, hey!" Gwen stepped forward, putting her hands out. Walter just stood there, slack-jawed and wide-eyed. "Listen, Caleb, I can see that you're going through a lot right now, but you can't blame Walter for what happened. It wasn't his fault."

"Then whose fucking fault was it?!" I didn't even realize I was crying until now. "Why did it have to happen like this?! Why didn't anyone do *anything*?!"

Silence again. When Gwen looked at me, it was with so much pity that I thought I might puke.

I turned around, and before anyone could say anything else, I was sprinting back upstairs.

Ghost followed me through the house.

"Leave me alone," I said to him, not caring that other people could hear me. "Leave me alone."

I headed to the kitchen and poured myself another drink,

but this time, I left out the Dr Pepper. I slammed back more vodka than I'd ever had, gagging on the taste.

I didn't care about that, though. I wanted to be out of my mind. I wanted to be someone else. I wanted to be dead.

I stumbled out the front door, trying to find my way to Emmett's car. I couldn't remember where we'd parked, but I just started walking. Ghost walked next to me, but then he started weaving between my feet. When he almost tripped me, I stopped.

"Just *leave me the fuck alone*!" I yelled at him, my words slurred, my head hurting. I was on the ground now. When had I fallen? I sat with my head in my hands, trying to make the dizziness bearable.

Ghost brushed up against my leg, and I felt what I'd felt the other day—that rush of memories—but I didn't want it, I couldn't stand it, it was too much—

"Caleb!" I heard Emmett call for me somewhere in the distance.

Emmett.

Emmett was still here. Emmett, who was my partner, who I liked and who liked me back, who'd put up with so much from me already, who knew about Jack but not about everything—

Emmett, who had taken me here tonight, to whom I had promised I wouldn't do anything stupid.

Too fucking late for that, I guessed.

Then they were there with me, their hands on my shoulders, helping me up off the ground.

Where was I? I was outside. I was on the road, in a neighborhood I didn't know, in the dark.

"I can't take this anymore," I slurred to them as we walked. My legs could barely move, my weight all pressed into Emmett. "I can't, I can't, I can't, I can't. . . ."

"We're going home now," they said gently.

The rest of the night was a blur. All I remembered was looking out the passenger window as Emmett drove, watching as the stars blinked at me, the haze of the dark, and, in the side-view mirror, Ghost's form in the back seat.

18

I HAD ANOTHER DREAM ABOUT Jack.

In this one, we were at a house show, not unlike Deck of Fools's. Emmett was at the microphone, singing about love, but there were no instruments. Jack sat with me and Tanya, watching the show with a grin on his face. Dima, Logan, Nathan, and Amy were swimming in the pool, singing along with Emmett. No one else was there.

Halfway through the show, I remembered Jack was supposed to be dead.

"How are you alive again?" I asked him. "You died last June."

He looked at me, that smile still in place. When he spoke, it was Walter's voice. "How did I die?"

And then the dream shifted, and we were kids again, taping a sheet to the wall as a backdrop for Jack's latest movie. We were holding my Barbie dolls, looking as new as the day I got them.

"In this scene," Jack told me, "Barbie is telling Kelly that she's going away for a while, so Kelly needs to be really upset."

"Why do *I* have to play Kelly?" I said.

"Because you're younger," he said. "And I'm going to leave you one day."

"No, you're not," I scoffed.

"It's true," he insisted. "One day I'm going to grow up and I won't be around anymore, and you'll have to be ready for it. So, you have to play Kelly, and make sure you play her *really* realistically, okay? Three, two, one, and action!" He mimed a clapboard and gestured for me to begin.

I stared at the doll in my hand, and somehow, I knew the lines I was meant to say, but I couldn't get my mouth to move. I just kept looking at her, at her plastic skin and painted-on eyes, and suddenly, I remembered the coffin—Jack's pale body, the suit he was buried in—and I screamed.

I woke up in a cold sweat.

I felt like I'd been hit by a truck. My head was pounding, and I was nauseous. I stayed in bed for a long time, the dream still playing in my head. Everything that happened last night came back to me in pieces—yelling at Walter, drinking too much, stumbling down the road until Emmett found me. I remembered Emmett driving me home, and I remembered leaning against them as they helped me up the stairs, trying to be as quiet as possible so we wouldn't wake my parents.

Shame filled every crevice of my body—not only for what I'd said to Walter, but for the position I'd put Emmett in. I wouldn't blame them if they never wanted to talk to me again.

On my bedside table was a glass of water, a bottle of ibuprofen, and a napkin. I recognized Emmett's handwriting on it.

TEXT ME WHEN YOU WAKE UP.
♥ - Em

I took two pills and drank the water slowly. Once it kicked in, it would help, but only a little. I had a feeling that the rest of the pain wouldn't be fixed that easily.

I checked my phone. Emmett had sent me a few texts, all from last night and presumably after they dropped me off.

Emmett

let me know how ur feeling when u wake up

im not mad at u, btw. i just want to know that ur alright

i care about u a lot, caleb

I started to text them back, but everything I typed felt so inadequate. I didn't feel like I even recognized myself anymore. What was I supposed to tell them?

After a long time of typing and deleting and retyping, I finally settled on a message.

Caleb

Hey, im up now, and im ok. thank u for getting me home safe last night, and im really, really sorry for everything. i swear i dont usually get like that. i dont know what happened. i understand if u dont want to talk to me for a while. im sorry again.

I watched as the gray ellipsis bubble popped up, letting me know Emmett was typing, but I turned my phone off before I could see their message. I didn't want to know what they would say just yet.

I stayed in my room almost all day, avoiding my parents. Even if my parents hadn't known I was drinking last night, I couldn't talk to them. We hadn't spoken much since my conversation with Dad earlier in the week, and I still wasn't sure what to say to them.

It wasn't until that evening that I left my room. I got a text from Dad, just reading *Dinner's ready*, and when I got downstairs, Mom was setting the table, a homemade lasagna ready to be served.

"Who wants sweet tea?" Dad asked, and Mom and I both asked for some.

Once we were all sitting down, three glasses of sweet tea in front of us, Mom said, "So, what did everyone do today?"

I didn't say anything, just looked down at my lasagna. I poked the sauce around, revealing a piece of spinach inside and dragging it out onto my plate. Right as I had the thought that I was surprised Ghost wasn't here, I felt a chill, and I knew he'd joined us even before I saw his frame gliding into the dining room.

Dad shifted in his seat. "Well, uh, I went and got my car's headlight fixed."

"Oh, good! Did you get both bulbs replaced?"

Mom and Dad talked about their days for a while, but their voices faded to background chatter as my mind wandered. I kept returning to what happened last night—the warm glow of the streetlights, Walter's wide eyes when I started yelling at him, Emmett's grimace when they said *you're drunk* and I agreed. I thought about what Walter said, about how he could tell that Jack was headed down a bad road.

I remembered one of the last times I saw Jack before he died. It was last May, right after we'd both gotten out of school for summer break. It was the end of his sophomore year of college, and my sophomore year of high school. I'd turned sixteen only a few weeks before.

At that point, Jack was two months out of a rehabilitation program, and doing okay, I thought. He seemed more . . . levelheaded. Clearer. He moved back into the house for summer break, although I knew his part-time job as a waiter would keep him occupied most of the time. It was like that with Jack. Even when he was living at home, he usually wasn't around.

But that day, his shift was called off due to the restaurant having to close early, so when I came downstairs for lunch, Dad was making a sandwich at the kitchen counter while Jack sat at the table, eating a bowl of chips.

"All I'm saying is that they should float when the ship loses power," Dad was saying to Jack, and when they heard me enter, Jack glanced up at me.

"Oh, hey, Caleb," he said.

"What are y'all talking about?" I asked, sliding past Dad to get to the fridge. I pulled out leftovers from the day before, and then used the step stool to get down a plate.

"The physics of *Star Trek*," Jack said.

"The characters never float because they're supposed to have some kind of gravity generator, but even when the ship stops working, they're still walking around," Dad explained. "It's not realistic."

"I don't think you're supposed to watch *Star Trek* for its realism," I said, scooping rice onto my plate.

"You know what sci-fi movie deals with artificial gravity well?" Jack said, popping a chip into his mouth. "*2001: A Space Odyssey*. Also, a phenomenal movie in general."

"I've never seen it," Dad said.

"You *need* to," Jack said, and he went on for a while about Stanley Kubrick and the cultural impact that movie had and how they managed to achieve their visual effects without CGI, while I finished heating up my lunch.

As Dad, Jack, and I sat around the kitchen table, talking about films, I realized that I hadn't heard Jack gush like this in a long time—not since before he went to rehab, at least.

Last winter, his addiction had gotten bad again, and I didn't see him for weeks, only hearing from my parents how he was doing. After New Year's, he checked himself into a ninety-day rehab program—the third one since he started using at sixteen.

I had the thought: *maybe this is the one*. Maybe he would stay sober this time. Maybe the cycle of recovery and relapse would end here.

Maybe my brother would be okay.

But I was wrong. After that, he got busy with work, and I was out with Tanya most days, and we didn't see each other much. Two weeks later, I was at Tanya's house for a sleepover when my mom called saying that Jack had overdosed and he was in the hospital, and I stayed with the Guptas while my parents went to see him.

When my parents finally got home that night, it was to tell me that Jack had died.

And just like that, this small thing—sitting around the kitchen table, talking about *2001: A Space Odyssey*—became one of my final memories of him.

"What about you, Caleb?" Mom said, pulling me out of my thoughts. When I blinked at her, she added, "What'd you get up to today?"

"Um . . . not much," I said. Ghost jumped up onto the chair next to me, where Jack used to sit, and made himself comfortable.

"Get any homework done?"

I hadn't, but I didn't want to admit that, so I shrugged. "Yeah, a little bit."

"How's that music project coming along?"

"Fine," I said. "Actually . . . I was wondering if Emmett could come over tomorrow so we can work on it."

Mom and Dad looked at each other. For a second, I imagined them saying that Emmett couldn't come over and insisting that I watch those videos with them tomorrow—but Mom just said, "How long would they stay?"

"An hour or two."

She nodded, taking a sip of her sweet tea. "And you'll be in your room?"

"Yeah, probably."

Another look exchanged. Mom said, "Well, all right, but I

want you to leave your door open."

Embarrassment flooded me. "Mom!"

"What? You're sixteen. Things can happen!"

My cheeks were flaming. "Mom, that's not—you don't have to worry about that, okay? That's not gonna happen, it's not like that," I stuttered.

She gave me a long look, and I knew I wasn't fooling her. I hadn't told either of my parents that Emmett and I were dating, but I got the feeling that she somehow knew anyway. I wondered if I'd said or done something to tip her off, or if it was just her parental intuition.

"Well, just leave it open for *me*," she said. "I'll feel better if you do."

I sighed. "Okay, yeah, I can do that."

Dad cleared his throat. "There was something else about tomorrow, too. . . ."

Mom nodded. "Oh, yes. Your dad and I were planning on getting some more work done in Jack's room tomorrow morning, packing things up. . . . Did you still want to join us?"

The way she asked it—it didn't seem like she was trying to make me feel guilty. It didn't even seem like she wanted me to answer one way or another. But I couldn't help the way it tugged at something in me, pulling on the guilt and shame and sadness and anger and emptiness I'd been feeling.

I suddenly didn't want to be home. I didn't want to think about this. I didn't want to remember that we needed to clean out Jack's room because he was dead, because he had been dead for almost six months now, because he had overdosed, because he had been addicted to heroin, because he had been trying to live with something so painful that he never even told me—

"I don't know," I said.

Mom didn't seem surprised by that answer. She just smiled a little. "That's okay. If you want, you can go through his things after we've finished cleaning the room out, if that's easier."

I wasn't sure that it *would* be easier. The idea of having to clean his room out made that ache in me grow, but the idea of *not* helping made me feel like shit, too.

But I couldn't help now. Not right now.

I just couldn't.

"Maybe," I said. "I'll—I'll think about it. But . . . just . . . probably not tomorrow."

She nodded. "There's no rush."

But I couldn't help feeling like there was.

Like they said they would, my parents spent Sunday morning cleaning out Jack's room.

I stayed in bed for an hour after I woke up, scrolling through Instagram on my phone as I listened to them through the walls. I could just barely make out their conversation, but I heard Mom say things like "Caleb might want that one day" or "Do we really have a use for that?" There were the sounds of furniture being moved, boxes being filled and set on the floor, and I imagined, for a second, that it was Jack in there, cleaning out his own room, packing up his clothes to be worn again one day. It wasn't as comforting of a thought as I wanted it to be.

Emmett came over that afternoon. I'd texted them the night before, apologizing again before I asked if we could talk in person.

Once we were safely in my room—my door open just a tiny crack—we sat on the rug. I'd been formulating what I would say when I saw them all morning, and now, I took a deep breath.

"I owe you another apology for—for what happened on Friday," I managed. "I know I said it already, but I'm really sorry for how I acted, and for making you take me home, and for ruining our night together, and just . . . for everything."

They nodded. Today, they were wearing a thick knit sweater, and their hair was a little damp, like they'd showered before coming over. We sat cross-legged on my floor, our knees touching.

"Thank you for saying that," they said. "And, for what it's worth . . . I wasn't mad at you. Just really, *really* worried." They frowned, and, since we both could hear my parents watching TV downstairs, they reached for my hand. "Caleb . . . what's been going on with you lately?"

Maybe it was the way they held my hand, or their voice when they said my name, or the sounds of my parents cleaning out Jack's room this morning—or maybe it was this ache in my chest that had only gotten bigger, the look Ghost had given me from the side-view mirror as Emmett drove me home, the memory of Jack and Dad talking about films across the kitchen table—

Whatever it was, I felt something in me crack, and before I knew it, thick tears were dripping down my cheeks and off my chin, and I dissolved into shaking, hiccuping, and Emmett pulled me into a hug.

We stayed like this for what felt like hours. But when I was sure the tears had stopped, I pulled away and wiped my cheeks. "I—I'm sorry, I don't know why I started crying like that."

"Do *not* apologize," Emmett said, with more force than I was expecting.

I tried for a smile. "Well, can I at least apologize for getting snot on your sweater?"

They glanced at the wet spot my tears had left behind on their shoulder, then flicked their wrist as if to wave it off. "It'll dry."

We were quiet for a moment. I wasn't sure when exactly Ghost had showed up this time, but when I glanced around my room, he was perched on the windowsill.

"It's about my parents," I finally said. "Or, really, I guess, it's about Jack. They told me something about him, about his addiction and his past, that really shook me up, but I don't know if I can really . . . talk about it in detail yet. I'm sorry, I know we're supposed to be able to tell each other everything, and I swear I'm not trying to keep it from you, but . . ."

"Tell me when you're ready," they said. "And in the meantime, if there's anything I can do to help, let me know, okay? I want to be here for you."

"You already are," I said.

They smiled at me, and I wanted it to wipe away all the bad—I wanted to be able to melt into Emmett's grin, shed all the layers of anger and sorrow that wrapped around me and replace them with my bubbly nerves, the giddy joy of a new relationship, the warmth that their smile spread through my body.

But, even though I still loved their smile, it didn't alleviate the other feelings. We were dating, and they cared about me, and I cared about them, and they were being such a kind and supportive partner—

And it still didn't fix everything. It didn't change what had happened.

Emmett left an hour later. We didn't get any homework done; we spent the rest of our time talking about the Christmas play that their little brother Jonathan was going to be in and the latest anime Logan had convinced Emmett to watch and anything else that wouldn't lead us toward a heavy conversation. I was grateful for the distraction.

With not much else to do for the rest of the day, I sat on my bedroom floor and got my guitar out, thinking maybe I could try to write another song.

Ghost came down from his perch and joined me on the rug, lying with his paws tucked under him as I warmed up by playing a cover. I wasn't sure why, but I had Nirvana's "Something In the Way" stuck in my head, so I looked up the chords online. I played through the song awkwardly the first time, trying to find the rhythm, and then one more time, hoping I would improve. The second time, it still sounded clumsy, off, and it frustrated me.

I looked at my phone; it was six p.m. now, and soon my

parents would probably call me down for dinner. I scrolled mindlessly through Instagram for a little while, but I didn't follow that many people, so it wasn't long before older posts popped up in my feed, including something that Tanya had uploaded a week ago. It was a time-lapse video of her painting the portrait of her mom, and I watched it three times before I switched to my text messages. I opened my text thread with Tanya and began typing.

Caleb

how was ur weekend?

It read as delivered. I stayed on that screen, waiting for her bubble to pop up, but nothing. I eventually set my phone to the side and turned back to my computer, still open to the song's chords.

After a while, I looked through the notes I'd written for another Holden song I was trying to write. The only thing I kept returning to was that one moment in the book where Holden asks Allie for help: *Allie, don't let me disappear.* I wasn't sure why, but that sentence stuck with me, and I just kept thinking about Holden holding on to the memory of his brother to help him, calling out to Allie.

I thought about Jack's voice when he told me, *I've been through some shit. And I hope you never, ever, ever have to go through that.* I thought about my mom's voice when she told me Jack had been sexually abused. I thought about Emmett telling me they were *really,* really *worried* about me. I thought about the way it felt to sit in my car, smoking Jack's cigarettes. I thought about Holden writing about Allie's baseball mitt, covered in poetry.

I managed to write only a few verses, and by the time I gave up, I was over it. Over everything. Nothing I wrote felt adequate. Nothing seemed to be okay.

Fuck this project. Fuck songwriting. Fuck my music.

What did any of it even *matter*? What was the point in this—in passing songwriting, in finishing this project, in writing about some fictional characters—when my brother was dead? When my brother had been abused for maybe *years*, and I never knew until now? When I was still being haunted?

What was the fucking *point*?

I thought I would feel better after talking to Walter; I thought I would find answers. I thought that he'd tell me something about Jack, something about their relationship, that would make it all make sense, that would clean out these feelings I had, that would fix everything.

But it had only made everything worse.

I deleted what I'd written.

I couldn't sleep that night.

I stared at my clock: 1:05 a.m. Floating up from downstairs was the sound of someone watching TV. I imagined my parents on the couch, some late-night talk show host laughing on screen. I wondered if it was one or both of them down there, and why they were up at all; my parents had never been night owls, so there had to be a reason. Could they not sleep? Had they woken up from a dream about Jack, the way I sometimes did?

I wondered if they'd watched home videos without me this weekend, or if my absence had stopped them. I wondered if Dad was hurt when I said I didn't want to watch any with them. I wondered if they were disappointed in me, if they thought I was a bad son. A bad brother.

Ghost sat on the windowsill. I stared at his form, although I wasn't sure what I was looking for. I wondered if he'd understood what I said to him on Friday night, and, if he did, if he was upset with me, too.

I kept returning to that feeling I'd had earlier—*what was the point?*—and it circled around my brain like a vulture. It was a different kind of despair than usual. A sharp, acute feeling. All encompassing. Loud. Overwhelming.

I wanted to escape it.

I remembered the bottle of vodka Nathan gave me, now tucked under my bed and hidden between boxes and books I'd pushed under there. And there was that other thought, the same one I'd had earlier in the week—*maybe that could help*.

I held on to that hope as I got out of bed, crouched on the floor, and dragged the bottle out from its hiding spot.

I thought it again and again—*maybe this will help*—as I drank from it, the liquor burning on its way down, and it warmed me from the inside out, the blissful carelessness on its way.

I felt it rush through me. I felt my thoughts start to spin.

From his place at the window, Ghost watched me drink, alone, in my room, and I watched him right back, taking drink after drink until my eyelids grew heavy.

My head spun as I clumsily shoved the bottle back into its hiding spot and crawled into bed. The last thing I saw before I drifted into sleep was his dark form blurring in my vision, silhouetted by the moonlight.

19

THAT MONDAY MORNING, I WOKE up on edge.

I didn't say much to my parents as I left for school, although I heard worry in my mom's voice when she told me to have a good day. Ghost followed me silently.

At school, I had a hard time paying attention in class. I didn't feel entirely there. My mind was stuck on that feeling that had overcome me last night, that I had tried to avoid: What was the *point*?

The alcohol had distracted me from it temporarily, but now it enveloped me again, and I just kept thinking about that as I walked through the halls, as I felt Ghost trailing behind me. What was the point in any of this? Why was I even bothering to come to school? Why did I even get out of bed—why did I try to live my life normally again? Nothing was normal. Nothing was okay.

At lunch, Tanya wasn't there, once again in the art room. At the realization, I felt it all rushing to me at once—my fear that she was still mad at me, my hurt that she might have been hiding something about Nathan. She never responded to my text last night, and we hadn't been carpooling to and from school. I was suddenly hit with this wave—I needed to talk to her, and *now*.

Before I knew what I was doing, I stood up from the lunch table, swinging my backpack over my shoulder, and said, "I'll be right back."

When I got to the art room, Tanya was sitting at her table, eating a granola bar and painting details on one of her pieces. She looked up at me when I entered.

"Hi," she said. "What's up?"

I stood at the edge of her table, my hands in my hoodie pockets. From here, I got a better look at what she was working on: another self-portrait, but this time based off a photo of her taken at her cousin's wedding, dressed in a pink sari and looking somewhere in the distance, a genuine smile caught on her face. I remembered that photo; it was taken last year, and Tanya had told me how happy she'd been, how beautiful she felt, and I could already see that on this rendering of her face, the joy caught on canvas. It took my breath away.

I was hit with how talented Tanya was, how amazing, how special, and the fear slammed into me full force—fear that I was losing her, that we couldn't return to normal after I messed up.

"Uh, nothing. Just wanted to talk to you and see what's going on," I said.

She put down her paintbrush. "Just working, mostly."

"Right." I nodded, but I wasn't sure what to say after that.

After a pause, she asked, "What did you *actually* wanna talk about?"

"What?"

"There's something going on," she said, "so, just, go ahead. Let's talk about it."

I crossed my arms over my chest. I should've known that she'd pick up on my bad mood, my restlessness. I took a breath, and then, in a rush, I said, "Did something happen between you and Nathan that you haven't told me about?"

She blinked at me. "What makes you think something happened between me and Nathan?"

"You left your phone face up on the table during lunch a while ago, and I saw that Nathan had been texting you . . . stuff," I mumbled.

"What stuff?" she demanded, and I wasn't expecting the seriousness in her voice.

"Just flirty things, like 'I miss you' and 'let's watch a movie together' and heart emojis, and I saw his contact name, and it didn't seem strictly platonic to me, but when I asked you about romantic stuff with Nathan the other day, you acted like I was crazy for thinking that," I said in a rush.

She sighed. "Caleb . . ."

I couldn't help it; my frustration built.

"Don't try to tell me that there isn't something going on between you two because we both know that's a load of shit," I snapped. "Why won't you just *talk* to me about it, Tanya? Is it because you're still mad at me for what happened the other weekend? Is that why you didn't respond to my text yesterday?"

"I haven't told you about the stuff with Nathan because I *can't*," she said, meeting my exasperation. "It's not my place to tell you other people's personal business—and no, it's not about what happened the other weekend, but if you wanna talk about it, then yeah, we can do that! Let's talk about how much you've been drinking lately!"

I was too stunned to say anything, just blinking at her wide-eyed. She took the opportunity to continue.

"I'm not mad at you for getting us home late," she said, a little calmer now, "and I'm *not* keeping something from you out of spite or whatever else you think is going on, and I didn't mean to not respond to your text last night, I just got busy, but Caleb . . . I *am* worried about you."

Her words washed over me—*worried about you*—and I thought about what Emmett said yesterday. It seemed like everyone was always *worried* about me, even when that was the last thing I wanted, even when I tried my best to seem okay.

She kept going.

"You've been acting so out of character lately, and just taking all these risks that aren't *you*—I mean, taking that vodka home with you? Drinking so much at the show that we couldn't even get home? And Emmett told me about what happened on Friday—"

"*What?!*"

"Please don't be mad at them—they were just worried about you, and they wanted me to know something had happened so I could be there for you—"

"Oh, come on!" I threw my hands up. "Everyone is acting like *I'm* the weird one for drinking when *all of you* drink, too! And so what, Nathan gave me some alcohol? How is it okay for *him* to have all that shit in his house, but I have, like, a *fourth* of a bottle and suddenly it's this huge deal? Why is it fine when your boyfriend does it, but when I do it, suddenly everyone is 'worried' about me?"

"He's not my boyfriend," she said, much quieter than before.

"Well, clearly he's not just a friend!"

She rolled her eyes. "Okay, fine! Yes, Caleb, you caught me—we liked each other! But it didn't . . ."

She turned her face away from me, and I realized she was tearing up. All my anger dissipated into guilt—and God, I felt like shit. I hadn't meant to come at her like this.

"It didn't work out," she finished, and I saw her wipe a tear away before it could fall.

"I—I'm sorry, Tanya. I didn't realize. . . ."

"I know you didn't. You weren't supposed to."

And I knew she was only saying that to be honest, but I couldn't help the sting I felt. We were supposed to be best friends, and yet, she intentionally left me out of this part of her life. I wasn't *supposed* to know about this.

"I'm sorry I didn't tell you what's been going on," she said, "and I'm sorry if you thought I was keeping something from you. But, Caleb, you're seriously worrying me, and I . . ." She looked down. "I don't know how to help you. This whole time—with Ghost, with Jack's death, with your parents . . . I haven't known how to help. . . ."

I thought back to this summer: the sweltering heat combated by blasting air-conditioning as I lay in my bed, unable to do much but cry; Tanya's persistent invitations to go out with friends, and my constant replies of *no thanks, sorry*; the way we avoided talking about Jack, leaving holes in conversation where acknowledgment of his life or death could've been, how the closest we ever got was talking about Ghost—and, even then, when we both knew that Ghost *had* to be connected to Jack's death somehow, we never discussed what that really meant.

Maybe neither of us knew how.

"I just want you to be okay," she said. "And this new interest in drinking clearly *isn't* you *being okay*, Caleb. Honestly, it scares me."

"You don't have to worry about me," I said. "I'm fine."

She frowned. "But you aren't, Caleb. Emmett told me they had to take you home, and—"

"I said I'm *fine*!"

I hadn't meant to yell, but I suddenly couldn't take it—the concern, the way everyone around me didn't want me to look away. They didn't understand why I couldn't think about this. Why I couldn't handle it.

"I'm fine," I repeated, quieter this time.

She looked at me, but I couldn't meet her eyes. I couldn't face it.

"Anyway, I'll—I'll just let you get back to painting. I'm sorry to distract you," I said, already heading toward the door. "I'll see you later."

If she responded, I didn't hear it.

I didn't go back to the cafeteria. Instead, I went out to the parking lot through one of the back doors without any alarms, and escaped to my car. I didn't care if I got caught skipping. I just wanted to get out of here.

I texted Emmett before I left.

Caleb

hey, i just wanna let u know im not gonna be in class today

i went home early

Before they could respond, I turned my phone on silent and started the engine. I didn't want to be here, but I didn't want to go home, either, so I put my music on shuffle and drove around the city. I pulled a cigarette out of the pack and lit it, rolling the windows down. I felt the smoke enter my lungs, tasted the menthol.

In my rearview mirror, I saw Ghost in the back seat, pacing around. He seemed upset again.

"You and me both, buddy," I mumbled to him.

That evening, after both my parents got home from work, they called me into the kitchen.

I was greeted with my mom's crossed arms and my dad's stern expression, the vodka bottle Nathan gave me sitting in front of them on the table. *Shit shit shit shit shit—*

"Caleb," Mom said, "would you care to explain?"

Panic crowded me, and I struggled for something to say. "I— Where did you get that?"

"In your room," Dad said.

"Why were you going through my room?!"

"That's *not* what this is about," Mom interrupted. "This is about why you would think this behavior is okay."

My argument with Tanya swam in my head, and I suddenly felt dizzy with anger, with pain—and then Ghost was there, blinking into the world, and seeing his faceless form, I felt that same thing crack inside me.

I was suddenly exhausted. All my anger waned, only leaving behind that ache that I knew couldn't be dulled.

"I'm sorry," I whispered.

I couldn't look either of my parents in the eye. I couldn't handle what I would see. Disappointment. Judgment. Anger. Concern.

They were both quiet for a moment. Then, I heard my mother sigh, and her chair scrape loudly against the tile floor.

She walked over to the kitchen sink and poured what little was left down the drain. Once it was completely empty, she threw the bottle into the recycling bin and came back over to the table.

"Talk to us, Caleb," she said, her voice catching on my name, and I realized she was tearing up. "Help us understand what you're feeling. Why you're doing these things."

But I couldn't find the words. All I could do was look at the table, staring down at the wood, and for some reason, I just kept thinking about the dream I had about Jack the other night, where he told me he would leave me one day, and I thought about his body at the funeral, his friends who shuffled past his open casket, the way I sat on the porch in that rocking chair and stared out into the trees until Ghost appeared like a vision.

"We want to help," Dad said.

My vision blurred from tears. "But you *can't*," I said. "No one can help. No one can bring him back."

Silence again. But Ghost seemed to respond to what I said, and he was suddenly getting up from his spot near my feet and circling around my parents, weaving between them, something desperate in his movement. What was he trying to do?

What was he trying to tell me?

"You're right," Mom whispered. "We can't bring him back. But you're not alone in this, honey. We're right here with you. And maybe that won't change what happened or magically make everything okay, but . . . at the very least, we can help each other through this. You don't have to do this alone."

The tears I had been holding back spilled out of me, and suddenly I was heaving, weeping, shoulders racked with sobs—and then my parents were next to me, their arms wrapped around me in a hug, engulfing me.

I leaned into them, letting it all wash over me, and although I couldn't see him, I felt Ghost's presence. I imagined the line connecting us, shrinking and expanding like a lung.

20

AFTER SCHOOL THE NEXT DAY, as I was heading to the parking lot, I got a text from Emmett.

Emmett

meet me in room 204?

It was the same room we'd worked on our songwriting project in, and Emmett was already there when I arrived.

"Did you get permission from Mr. Russak for us to use this room?" I said, once the door was closed behind us.

They grinned a little. "No, but I figured you'd want a private place to talk, and the door was open. Besides, this is better than a bathroom."

I snorted. "Yeah, I guess that's true."

We sat down on the floor in a corner, angled so that if someone walked by, they wouldn't immediately see us.

"Tanya told me you two had a . . . rough conversation," they said.

I laughed. "You can just say 'fight.'"

"Okay, well, in that case, she told me you had a fight," they said. "She asked me to check up on you, but I told her I was planning on doing that already. So, what's going on?"

I stared down at the floor. I remembered what Tanya had said—about Emmett filling her in about last Friday—and I suddenly felt anger spike at the both of them.

"Why did you tell her what happened on Friday?" I said. I tried to keep my tone calm, but some of my anger still snuck in.

Emmett's eyes widened. "Oh . . . I'm sorry. I guess I didn't realize that was something you wanted to keep private. . . ."

I was silent for a moment.

"Are you mad at me?" they asked carefully.

I sighed. "No, it's just . . ." When I imagined Emmett and Tanya talking about me behind my back, saying how worried they both were for me and exchanging stories about my latest fuckup, it made me feel small and ridiculous and judged. "I didn't realize you guys talked about me like that."

"We don't usually," Emmett rushed to say. "That was the first time. But, Caleb, you have to admit, things were getting out of hand—"

"I know I fucked up, okay? You don't have to remind me," I grumbled.

They blinked at me. I rubbed my temples.

"Sorry, it's just . . . Tanya and I had that fight yesterday," I said, "and then last night, my parents found vodka in my room, and they're already disappointed enough in me as it is, and . . . I guess it just feels shitty to imagine you and Tanya both looking down on me, especially after everything with my parents. . . ."

"We aren't looking down on you," they said.

"I know. I mean—logically, I know that. But I guess that's how it feels."

They nodded. "I get that. And . . . you're right. I'm sorry. I should've checked in with you first, to see if you wanted to talk to her yourself. It wasn't my place to tell her. But for what it's worth, I only did it because I care about you. . . . I wasn't sure how else to help."

"I know," I repeated. "It's okay. It just caught me off guard, I guess."

They reached a hand out to me. I took it and squeezed gently.

"So . . . your parents found alcohol in your room?" they asked.

I nodded. "Nathan gave me what was left of a bottle a while ago, and I'd hidden it under my bed, but I guess my mom was going through my room or something, and she found it. They grounded me until Christmas."

They winced. "Oof."

"They said they'll make some exceptions so we can finish our project, though, so at least we can hang out then. . . . And part of my punishment is that I have to attend group therapy meetings, at least for the next couple of months."

"Well, it could be worse?" they offered.

"Yeah. The group's kind of okay. I've gone a few times since August, and it's not *horrible*, so at least there's that."

Emmett nodded. We were both silent for a moment, and I

looked down at our hands, our fingers entwined. I leaned my head against their shoulder.

"Do you think I'm a bad friend?" I asked.

There was no hesitation. "Of course not. But I *do* think you and Tanya need to work some things out."

I groaned. "I know, but I don't know how to talk to her. Or if I even *can*."

"You can," they said. Not harshly—just like it was a fact.

"You have way too much faith in me," I said into their shoulder.

They chuckled and put their arm around me, pulling me closer. "I think I have just the right amount of faith in you. Friends get in fights, apologize, and then get over it. Nathan and I have done it a million times."

"Wait, really? But you two seem so, like, chill. What's there to even argue about?"

"Last year, when everything with Mallory was still really fresh," they said, "I lashed out at him more than I'd like to admit, and he took some stuff out on me, too. But then we talked about it, both apologized, and tried to do better next time. And now we're just as close as before. Maybe even more so, honestly."

"Do you ever struggle to talk about Mallory with your friends?" I asked. "Like, does it ever feel too big, or too painful, to talk about it directly?"

"Sometimes," they admitted. "But . . . I think it gets easier with practice."

I thought about that—the idea that you could practice talking about grief. Since June, I'd spent a lot of time thinking about it, sitting in the ache, running memories of Jack through my head, staring at Ghost's silhouette, crying alone—but I'd only ever said a portion of it out loud to anyone.

I thought about the song I'd started writing about Holden's brother, Allie. I thought about what Emmett said when we sat in the bathroom at the SALINE show, and about what Candi said in the parking lot.

"I wish I could just be happy with you and not have to feel all these bad things," I said quietly.

"Me too." They squeezed my shoulder.

"But I guess that's not how the world works, right? I can't run from it forever?"

"Not forever," they agreed.

We were silent again. After a moment, I lifted my head from their shoulder and pressed a kiss to their cheek. "Thank you," I said. "I'm glad you're in my life, Em."

They smiled. "I'm glad you're in mine, too."

"Who wants to start us off?" Tom asked, laying his clipboard in his lap.

It was the first support group meeting of December. I sat on the couch, and today was one of the rare times where everyone was here. I noticed that Garrett's hair was shorter and Candi had gotten a nose piercing. Two weeks was somehow so far away, and yet no time at all. I wondered what had changed for everyone in that time.

"I can start," Katherine offered. Tom nodded and gestured for her to continue.

She told us about the past two weeks—how her mom and stepdad took her to a concert, how December first was the nine-month anniversary of her best friend's death, how she was coming up on finals at school. As she spoke, I imagined what it would feel like to lose Tanya—and not just grow apart from each other, although that scared me, too, but I imagined what it would feel like if I woke up one day and she was gone, an unfillable hole in my life. Just the thought opened an ache in my sternum, and I remembered her voice when we fought—*it scares me.*

Ghost, as I expected, had joined me for this meeting. He sat outside our circle, curled up on the rug with his paws tucked under him as we went around and talked about the updates in our lives. Not for the first time, I wondered if Ghost could understand what we were saying.

"And what about you, Caleb?" Tom said, pulling my attention away from Ghost. "You've been quiet all session. How was your Thanksgiving?"

I wasn't sure what to say, where to even start, but I thought about my mom and dad hugging me the other day, and about how Emmett had gone to Tanya because they were worried about me, and about Tanya's face when she looked at me and said, *I just want you to be okay.* I thought about practicing.

"It was . . . a lot," I finally said.

Before I knew it, I was telling Tom and everyone else about my parents cleaning out Jack's room, about finding his cigarettes and his annotated copy of *The Catcher in the Rye*, about my dad's insistence on watching old videos.

I told them about how hard it was, going through the holidays without Jack, and about Walter—how I'd just wanted answers, how I hadn't meant to yell at him, I hadn't meant to blame him, but in the moment . . . I'd really meant what I said.

"I get what you mean," Candi said. "There was a point where I wanted someone to blame. It felt almost like I *needed* it in order to be okay, you know? Like if I just had a clear answer, if I just knew who was at fault, who had caused it, then . . . it would make everything better."

"Did it?" I asked.

She smiled sadly. "No. 'Course not."

I nodded. I'd expected that, but I still had to ask.

"Is it wrong to want to escape these feelings?" I asked after a moment. I stared down at Ghost as I spoke; I knew I couldn't say this and look at anyone at the same time. "Is it wrong that I want to find ways to . . . numb it? Or try to avoid it?"

I felt Tom's eyes on me. "I think it makes perfect sense that you would want an escape from such heavy emotions. But I think a better question is: Do you think that the way you've been doing that lately is healthy?"

"No," I admitted, and when I finally looked up at him, there was understanding on his face, something like recognition.

After the session ended, we filed out into the lobby. I heard Katherine and Jewel talking about some musical they both liked, and Ghost followed with the crowd as we all headed out to the parking lot.

I remembered how he'd behaved at the other meetings, following Candi almost as if he'd wanted me to approach her, and

I thought about how he acted around Emmett—his sudden calm when Emmett and I spoke on Nathan's patio, the way he'd inadvertently gotten us to partner for the songwriting project, the liking that he'd seemingly taken to them.

What was his goal? To get me to talk to people? And if it was—why? So I would make more friends? Why would a ghost cat care about me making friends?

Mom's voice from Monday flashed through my mind.

We can help each other through this. You don't have to do this alone.

I thought about how it had felt, talking during the session today. It was by far the most I'd ever said, and although it hadn't completely erased my bad mood, I felt . . . a little lighter.

As we were heading to our cars, Ghost started to swerve and follow Candi. Instead of ignoring it this time, I followed him.

"Hey!" I called, coming up to her.

"Oh, hey, Caleb!" she said, turning around. "What's up?"

Anxiety kicked in my stomach, but I rushed, getting the words out before I could change my mind.

"I really appreciated what you said today in the meeting," I said, "and—I hope this isn't weird—but would you wanna hang out sometime? I can give you my number, or if you're on Instagram or something, we could follow each other? It just seemed like maybe we have stuff in common, and I've been doing this thing lately where I try to make more friends and—um—yeah."

For a terrifyingly long second, I thought she was going to wince and say, *Sorry, no, that's kind of weird*, and I worried I'd just looked like the biggest buffoon in the world—but she smiled and pulled out her phone. "Yeah, for sure! What's your IG handle? I'll follow you!"

I told her, and when I checked my phone, it said I had a new follower. She told me she really only used Instagram to keep up with friends and watch cute cat videos, so she didn't post much, but that I was free to message her whenever.

"Awesome," I said, maybe a little too enthusiastically. "I'll do that."

We both went to our cars after that, and when I got in, Ghost was sitting in the passenger seat, relaxed and comfortable.

"Was that what you'd wanted this whole time?" I asked.

He didn't say anything, but I got the distinct feeling the answer was *yes*.

When I got home that evening, my parents were sitting on the couch in the living room, Mom typing something on her laptop as Dad flipped through channels. It smelled like apple cider, and I realized it was because they'd made a batch; two steaming mugs sat on the coffee table in front of them, sticks of cinnamon poking out of the top.

"How was the meeting?" Dad asked as I came into the room, stopping at the doorway.

"Um, it was fine." I shifted my weight from foot to foot. "There was actually . . . something I wanted to say to you guys."

Mom looked up from her computer screen, and Dad muted the TV.

I took a deep breath. "I . . . I owe you both an apology for . . . for everything. Not just for the alcohol stuff, but also for not talking to you . . . and for getting so upset with you the other day, Dad. I don't know why I snapped like I did. You weren't doing anything wrong, and I'm sorry."

Dad nodded. "Well . . . thank you for the apology, and I'm sorry if I made you feel pressured. It's just that you've been distant lately, and I know some of that is because you've been busy with school and your friends, but . . . we miss you. I thought spending some time together, all three of us, might be nice."

"I know," I said. "I'm sorry I've been distant."

"Come here." Mom scooted over and patted the space next to her. As I sat down, she asked, "Why *have* you been so distant?"

I looked down at her mug of apple cider, staring at the cinnamon stick. "I think because . . . you both want to talk about Jack and process his death with me a lot of the time," I said. "And it's felt too overwhelming to really deal with, so . . . I guess it seemed easier to avoid you."

Mom pulled me into a hug, and I hugged her back. I heard her sniffling, and when we pulled away, she wiped a tear away quickly.

"But I—I don't know that I want to do that anymore," I continued. "I think I'd like to watch those home videos with you guys, if we can."

Mom and Dad exchanged a look that I couldn't quite parse, but after a moment, Dad nodded. "Okay. We can do that."

So, after dinner, Dad connected his laptop up to the TV, displaying his computer screen. I got my own mug of apple cider and cradled it in my hands as he pulled up a folder titled "Videos 2009-2017," meaning Jack would be between the ages of six and fourteen in the videos, while I would be between one and nine.

Anxiety thrummed through me as we looked at the files, searching for ones to put on first; I couldn't stop fidgeting. Ghost sat at my feet, his head turned toward the TV as if to watch with us.

The first video Dad played was titled "Easter 2012," and in it, Mom followed three-year-old me as I toddled around the backyard looking for plastic eggs, my pink basket matching my frilly dress.

Eight-year-old Jack ran ahead of me in a yellow button-up shirt and dress pants, collecting eggs easily. Seeing Jack in the video wasn't as strong of a punch to the gut as I thought it would be, maybe because I didn't have many memories of him as an eight-year-old, but I still felt a pang of grief.

"Jack, make sure you leave some for your sister," Mom said behind the camera. I internally winced a little, but I tried to not let my dysphoria interrupt.

The video lasted thirty minutes, and it ended once I collected the final egg, which Mom had instructed Jack to leave for me to find, much to his annoyance. He stuck his tongue out at me as I triumphantly held up the egg, oblivious to his frustration.

"Jack really did not like me when I was little," I said as the video ended, and Mom chuckled.

"Yeah, he was pretty jealous when you first came along," she said.

"It took a few years, but he came around eventually, didn't he?" Dad said with a small smile.

I nodded.

"Oh, let's see what this one is," Mom said, pointing to a file titled "4-29-09."

The video started off with a shot of Jack sitting at a small, plastic kids' table, a Spider-Man action figure in one hand and a mermaid Barbie doll in the other. Behind the camera, Dad asked Jack questions about what he was doing. They were in a living room I didn't recognize, but with the same couch that we currently sat on—so this was at the old house, I assumed.

"Playing," Jack answered plainly.

"Who've you got there? Is that Spider-Man?" Dad asked. He sounded the exact same as he did today, except his Southern accent was a little stronger.

As Jack started explaining to Dad who Spider-Man was, baby me wandered into the room. Based off the video's date, I would've been almost one. Dad cooed my deadname at me, and I giggled and tried to crawl into his lap. The camera tilted, and the frame was covered by my open palm as I tried to grab it by the lens.

"Oh no, let's not do that," Dad said. He picked baby me up and set me in his lap, turning the camera around to see the two of us. It was kind of a weird feeling—looking at a version of myself that was so unfamiliar, so disparate from the current me.

He grinned at the camera, and then poked my cheek, causing me to grin, too. "Smile for the camera, sweetie!"

Baby me didn't stay still for long, though. I crawled off him, and he turned the camera around, pointing again at little Jack. I waddled toward Jack's table, stumbling into it. As Jack fussed at me for knocking into his things, a small black cat strolled into frame in the background. Baby me spotted the cat and started wandering close to it, and Jack got out of his chair to follow me.

"Be careful," little Jack told me. "Let me show you how to pet him."

The cat sat down near the doorway, and Jack crouched on the floor as he demonstrated to me the correct way to pet an animal. Baby me did my best to mirror his movements.

This was the cat that passed away when I was a toddler, I thought. The one that Jack had apparently been close with. I looked down at Ghost, whose head still faced the TV.

It dawned on me all at once.

It was Ghost.

It had to be.

Except—he didn't look exactly like the cat in the video. That cat had a face, for one thing. And it wasn't completely black; on the screen, I could make out patches of brown on its back.

But when I tried to conjure an image of our family's cat based on my memories, those details became blurry, fuzzy—until he was just a dark form, the details of his face gone, smudged out.

What was left, I realized, was Ghost.

Not for the first time, I wondered why he was here. Why he always followed me. Why he appeared after Jack died.

I imagined that line connecting us again. I imagined him on the other side of some veil, some other plane, wherever living things went when they died—I imagined him peering through and seeing my vacant stare into the backyard, rocking in that chair on the porch alone, my brother's grave so fresh, and I imagined him remembering our family, remembering Jack, remembering this moment where Jack taught me the correct way to pet him, where he demonstrated so gently, with so much innocence, how to care for another living creature.

And I imagined, for the first time, that maybe Ghost had come to help me. Not haunt.

As I lay in bed that night, I opened Instagram and brought up Walter's account.

I looked at his profile for a long time before I clicked on Message. I spent even longer trying to think of something to say.

calebstone

hey, walter. i want to apologize for what happened last weekend. do you think we could meet up and talk sometime soon?

And, to my surprise, I got a response.

w.young.03

im working tomorrow at cafe coco until 3. stop by and we can talk.

21

THE NEXT DAY AT SCHOOL, I skipped my last two periods to meet up with Walter.

Cafe Coco was a coffee shop in Nashville, and, thankfully, it wasn't too busy when I got there. The building used to be a house, and the patio out front was decked out in fairy lights, although they didn't show up much in the daylight. Inside, I stood in line as soft rock played on the speakers, and I saw Walter at the register, wearing a black apron and green beanie as he took someone's order.

I stared at the huge chalkboard menu behind the counter, and tried to convince myself that this was still a good idea. When I'd messaged Walter last night, I hadn't really expected him to respond, let alone so quickly, and I also hadn't thought through how this was going to work, what I was going to say.

All I'd been thinking at the time was that I needed to talk to him again, and I needed to make this right—but *how* I was going to do that, I still didn't have a clear idea.

When I stepped up to the counter, Walter looked at me calmly and said, "Hey, Caleb."

"Um. Hi." I stuffed my hands in my hoodie pockets.

"Give me one second," he said.

I nodded. He turned around, said something I couldn't hear to the other person working, and then disappeared to a room in the back. When he came back again, he didn't have on the apron, and he stepped out from behind the counter.

"I only get a fifteen-minute break, so let's make this quick."

"Right—yeah. Um. Thank you." I scrambled to follow him.

Walter led me down a hallway and out to a deck at the back of the building with a large overhead covering. It was cold outside, but I didn't say anything about it as we sat down.

Walter looked at me, and I realized he was waiting for me to speak.

"Oh, uh, yeah." I glanced down, unable to meet his eyes. "Listen, Walter . . . I'm really sorry for yelling at you the way I did, and for what I said. Gwen was right; it wasn't fair of me, and I was just . . ."

"Looking for someone to blame?" he finished for me.

I nodded. "Yeah. That."

"Hey, I get it." He sat up a little straighter in his chair. "That's why I agreed we should talk. It's obvious that you're pretty torn up, and while I can't speak to what it's like to lose a brother, I *can* speak to what it's like to say and do things in the moment that you later regret." He smiled dryly.

"Yeah . . . I've been doing a lot of that lately," I mumbled.

We were both quiet for a second, just listening to the music from the speakers.

"You and Jack did a project on *Catcher in the Rye* when you were at Brentwood, right?" Even as the words came out of my mouth, I didn't know why I was bringing it up.

He thought about it. "I think we did, yeah. That must've been . . . what, our sophomore year? Junior year? God, it's crazy how fast I forgot high school once I was out of it."

"It was your sophomore year," I said. "I found a thumb drive of Jack's that he used for school, and that project was on there. I haven't watched it yet, though. . . ."

"Why not?"

I shrugged. "I don't know. I guess I didn't feel ready."

Walter took off his beanie, setting it on the table, and ran his hands through his red hair. "I don't remember everything from high school," he said after a moment. "Probably 'cause I was so excited to graduate. I hated Brentwood; I wanted to move on and forget about it as fast as possible. But . . . I do have a handful of good memories from that place. Most of them are because of your brother. He made my life a little easier. A little more fun."

"Do you ever wish that you hadn't grown apart?" I asked quietly. "Do you ever wish that you'd . . . stuck around? Stayed friends?"

"Sometimes, yeah," he admitted. "I've had moments of missing him since we graduated, and when you told me he'd passed . . ." He looked down at the table, which was covered in colorful, scribbled graffiti. "I would be lying if I said I hadn't thought that, maybe, if we'd stayed friends, his life could've turned out different. Maybe *I* could've made a difference."

"I don't want you to think like that," I said. "I—I'm sorry I implied that. I shouldn't have blamed you."

"But there's a little bit of truth to it, I think," Walter said. "He made his own choices, yeah, but I can't help wondering: What if I'd been there for him? Would that have changed anything?" He sighed and leaned back in his chair. "Maybe not . . . or maybe I just would've gotten more time with him. Maybe we *could've* stayed friends. But I won't get to know."

I felt a chill, and, instinctively, I glanced around to find Ghost. He was sitting on top of a table a few feet in the distance. To my surprise, I didn't feel a flash of anger or irritation at the sight of him. Instead, it was like his presence anchored me.

"What if they weren't really his own choices?" I asked.

Walter frowned. "What do you mean?"

"You said Jack made his own choices. What if . . ." I searched for the words. "What if the choices that led him to dying were in response to things that were out of his control? Things other people did *to* him? I can't blame other people for his death, but is it fair to try to blame *him*, either?"

"No. I don't think it would be fair to do that," Walter agreed softly.

Ghost hopped off the table he'd been sitting on and sauntered toward us. He stopped at my feet, making himself comfortable once again.

"Can I give you some advice?" Walter asked.

I nodded.

"Don't spend all your time searching for answers," he said. "I have a feeling you could dedicate the rest of your life to trying to break down and understand exactly why everything happened the way it did, and you still wouldn't be satisfied. At the end of the day, who's 'at fault' doesn't matter—neither does the 'why,' really. What matters is that he's gone, and now everyone else has gotta find a way to live without him. So . . . just don't spend so much time trying to make sense of it all that you forget about living, okay?"

I stared at him, and, suddenly, I was moved that he was here, that I'd run into him at all. We were essentially strangers, but we had this one thing in common, this one thread connecting us, and it was such a rare connection, one that would only grow rarer as time moved on—he'd *known* Jack, and now he knew how it felt to miss him. Maybe not as acutely, not in the same way—but still, Jack had been a part of his life, had left a mark on him. They'd been friends. How many people could say that?

"Thank you," I said. "I'll try to take that to heart."

He smiled a little. "I hope you will."

It wasn't long after that before he had to return to his shift, but as we were saying our goodbyes, he said, "Oh, and if you end up watching that project, do you think you could send it to me? I'm pretty sure my copy of it got lost when I switched laptops, and I'd kind of like to see it. For old times' sake."

I nodded. "Yeah. I can definitely do that."

"Good." He smiled one last time. "Take care of yourself, Caleb."

"I will."

And I meant it.

At home, I grabbed my laptop and Jack's thumb drive and went out to the porch.

I sat on one of the rocking chairs, looking out at the backyard with my computer in my lap. It was cold out, the trees barren, but I didn't mind the chill so much. Apparently, it was supposed to snow later this week.

Ghost followed me outside and jumped up onto the rocking chair next to me, his phantom mass making the chair rock just the slightest bit, almost as if by a breeze. He turned his head toward my computer, like he wanted to watch, too.

I eventually built up the nerve to plug in the drive and pull up the *The Catcher in the Rye* project folder, and I pressed play on the file.

In the video, Jack, Walter, and Brooke reenacted several major scenes from the book. Jack was Holden, Brooke alternated between playing Jane and Phoebe, and Walter seemed to play whichever characters they needed him to. It was surprisingly high-quality for a school film project, but I wouldn't have expected anything less from Jack.

I watched the outtakes next. There were dozens of video files, ranging from twenty minutes to only seconds, and they were so mundane, so casual, just a group of friends goofing around in the hallways of Brentwood High School, in an empty classroom, in Jack's room, in our driveway. At one point, Jack messed up a line for Holden, and he started laughing, Brooke laughing from behind the camera, and he looked so happy, so normal, so *himself* that I couldn't help it when I began to cry.

I realized, then, that this was how I wanted to remember Jack.

As the boy with a passion for filmmaking, who worked on his scripts constantly and gushed about film history; as the teenager goofing around with his friends, ditching school to sit in a parking lot somewhere just to talk; as the brother who kick-started my love for horror and watched more movies with me than we could bother counting; who sat with me when I was depressed and told me it would be okay one day, who came home and hung out with me just because I asked him to, who picked me up from the mall and called me by my chosen name with ease.

I didn't want to remember him as *only* his addiction or his trauma or his secrets. Those were parts of him, but they weren't everything.

They weren't everything.

This, I thought as I watched him grinning at the camera, *this* was the Jack I wanted to remember.

I drove to the cemetery in silence.

I didn't turn any music on. I didn't smoke any of those cigarettes, which I had decided to keep in my glove box. All I did was roll the windows down, letting the cold air in, and drive. Ghost sat in the passenger seat, seeming a little calmer, almost like he knew where we were going, and he approved.

I hadn't visited Jack's grave since the funeral. A part of me was afraid of what I would see. There was a knot in my stomach as I parked, growing stronger as I hiked up the hill to where I remembered his plot was. Ghost followed next to me, trotting on the grass silently.

My parents had decided on a spot near the back of the cemetery, and I remembered an angel statue standing high above it. It was a beacon for me—a signpost. I saw its wings in the distance, and as we approached, Ghost sped up, until he was running in front of me, leading me toward the one place I had been avoiding for six months now.

Then, we were there.

Jack's grave.

I felt dizzy. I felt gutted. I felt raw.

Ghost seemed, for the first time, to be completely at peace. I sat down on the grass in front of Jack's gravestone, and Ghost lay down next to me, so close that we were almost touching.

I took a deep breath and wrapped my scarf around my neck tighter. It was a clear sky, no clouds to be seen for miles. The trees around us were bare of leaves, and the grass was a washed-out green from frost. It was silent. Here, we were far enough away from the road that I couldn't even make out the cars passing. It was only Ghost and me.

"I miss you," I said out loud, looking at Jack's gravestone. I stared at the date of death—June 11.

"I miss you so much it hurts," I continued. "I don't know how to keep going. I don't know how to live without you here. I don't know how I'm supposed to just go to school and walk through the world when you're gone. How is anyone supposed to keep going when you're gone?"

The tears came then. And I wasn't sure why, but I looked at Ghost, and I suddenly realized—it was just me and him.

I imagined that line between us again, imagined him peering at me from another plane and choosing to step over, choosing to join me.

I touched his head. There was that shock again, that dream-like feeling, that flood of memories.

But this time, I didn't shy away from it. I didn't find it overwhelming.

This time, I leaned over and hugged him.

Ghost relaxed into me. And I saw everything—Jack's and my childhood, the fights he got into with our parents, the days he came home with bloodshot eyes, the songs he listened to in the car on his way to school, the first movie we ever made together and then all the dozens after that. I saw him laughing with Walter and Brooke, I saw him crying, I saw him angry, I saw him overcome with joy—

I saw him. I remembered him.

And that was when I realized.

All Ghost had ever wanted from me was to be acknowledged.

He'd just wanted me to see him.

To hold him.

"I'm so sorry it took me this long," I said, hugging him tighter. "But I'm here now. I'm here."

When I got home, I went to my room, pulled out my guitar, and started writing.

I wrote like I hadn't in months. Lyrics and melodies poured out of me, the next lines flowing easily, and suddenly I'd written the final song for our *Catcher in the Rye* project. This one was also from Holden's point of view, talking to Allie, begging him for help, and I titled it "Don't Let Me Disappear."

But I didn't stop there. Somehow, I had more momentum, and before I knew it, I was writing, I was creating, I was singing.

I wrote about Emmett and how I sometimes felt guilty for finding happiness with them, about how seen they made me feel, and about how in love I already knew I was. I wrote about how it felt to be drunk at SALINE's show, how mortified I was by what I'd done later but also how I sometimes liked being a different version of myself.

And I wrote about a ghost cat who was haunting a boy. I wrote about a connection between them—about a grief that felt so big, it could've swallowed the boy whole. I wrote about the cat's attempts to help him—nudging him toward people who could help, including someone who the boy would come to love—trying to guide him through the dark. Trying to help him find his way out.

22

Caleb

hey. wanna ride home with me after school today?

i was kind of hoping we could talk

Tanya

sure. i'll meet u at the usual spot

* * *

We didn't immediately jump into the hard stuff. When Tanya got into my passenger seat, the first thing I asked was how her day was, and we spent the first ten minutes of the drive home talking about the lab report she'd failed in chemistry. It was nice, just talking about school and grades—normal things. It felt like we were back to our old selves again. I knew we weren't, and maybe we never fully would be—maybe we'd both changed too much. But that didn't mean things couldn't be good between us again.

She seemed to realize where I was going when I missed the turn to her house and, instead, pulled into the parking lot of the playground we often walked to. She followed me as I got out of the car and headed to the creek.

Once we were both sitting on the bridge overlooking the water, I said, "I'm sorry—for everything. For pushing you about Nathan, for being irresponsible with drinking and blowing off your concerns, for yelling at you in the art room the other day, for not talking to you about how I've been feeling. . . . I should've just told you what was going on with me."

"Yeah, that probably would've helped," she agreed. "But I'm sorry, too. I really *did* want to tell you about what happened with Nathan; I just couldn't. And I'm sorry if it's seemed like I'm too busy for you or like I'm ignoring you."

"You're allowed to be busy sometimes," I said. "You're allowed to have your own life."

"Yeah, but still. I know you're going through a lot right now, and as your friend, I should've tried to be there for you more. I just got so distracted with Nathan and school. . . ."

We were quiet for a moment. I looked down at the water, clear and running. Ghost was down there, sitting at the edge of the creek. He still seemed calm after our trip to the cemetery. Happy, even.

"You really don't have to tell me if you can't," I said.

"No, it's okay. After we talked the other day, I told Nathan what happened and asked how they would feel if I told you what was going on. . . ."

"'They'?" I repeated tentatively.

She pulled her knees up, hugging them to her chest. "Yeah. I'll get to that." She took a deep breath. "So. Basically. We both liked each other, and we talked about it. . . . We actually kissed at one point. . . ."

"What? When?"

"It was after school one day, when I was staying late in the art room, and Nathan came to hang out with me, and we were alone, and . . ." She shrugged with a small, sad smile. "It just happened. But things got complicated after that because . . . well, they realized they aren't a boy."

I couldn't help it—I was a little surprised. In my head, I'd occasionally used Nathan as a yardstick for masculinity to measure myself up against, an example of what I used to think I needed to look and act like in order to be "a man." The news that they *weren't* that idealized version of teenage boyhood took me by surprise. Maybe I'd been projecting onto them more than I'd realized.

"They're still in the process of exploring," Tanya continued, "but they've expressed some feelings that seem pretty transfemme to me. I see a lot of myself in them, and we've talked a lot about gender. When you said you'd seen texts between us, I thought you meant you'd seen ones where they talked about being trans, so I was worried that I'd accidentally outed them."

"Is that why their name in your phone is 'Nat'?"

She nodded. "That's the name they're currently going by."

"All right. Cool. And they're okay with you telling me this?"

"Yeah. They're planning on telling the friend group sometime before the semester ends anyway, so they said it's fine if you know a little earlier. Plus, I think it helps that they know you're trans, too, so I think they have a little less fear coming out to you."

"Are they worried about our friends' reactions?"

"I don't know," she said. "I think it's more just that they feel kind of insecure right now. They didn't want to tell anyone but me until they were *positive* they aren't cis because I think they worried that, if they came out and then realized they didn't feel that way, people would judge them."

I understood that. I knew that there was no way our friends would react badly, but emotions didn't always catch up to logic, and I understood how nerve-racking and scary it was when you were first discovering your transness. I couldn't blame them for wanting to keep it private.

"Does Emmett know?" I asked.

She thought about it. "I don't think so. If they talked with Emmett about it, Nat never mentioned it to me."

I nodded. "Okay. So, Nat is trans. But why does that mean you can't be together?"

"It's . . . complicated," she sighed. "When we were first talking about it, they said that they *do* like me, and they *do* want us to date, but . . . I think things are just too much for them right now, and they wanted some space to figure things out before entering a relationship. I mean, I remember what it was like, dating someone right after I came out. I put a lot of my feelings about my gender and transition onto the relationship, and I sort of used it as the only validation that I was a girl, so when my ex ended up being an asshole, it didn't just feel like I'd lost a boyfriend, but like I'd lost a part of myself, too. . . . I can't blame Nat for wanting to avoid accidentally doing that with us."

"Shit," I said.

"'Shit' is right."

"So, what now? Do you just keep being friends, knowing that you both like each other?"

"Yeah, kind of," she said with a shrug. "I mean . . . they told me that I don't have to wait for them, and I don't want to make them feel this pressure that they need to figure everything out as soon as possible so we can start dating. So, I think we're just going to keep being friends, and Nat is going to keep exploring their gender, and if, a few months or so from now, they feel like they're ready for a relationship, and we both still like each other . . . who knows?" She smiled, bittersweet.

"I'm sorry things didn't work out how you wanted them to," I said.

"It's all right. And, you know, I'm not as upset about it as I thought I would be. I'm happy to have them in my life, and I'm happy that I get to be there for them as they go through this journey. I'm happy I get to be that person for them, the way we were for each other."

I wasn't sure why, but that made tears prick at the corners of my eyes. "I love you, Tanya," I said, pulling her into a hug.

She hugged me back. "I love you, too, Caleb."

We sat on the bridge for a few moments, just holding each other. "I guess I should explain what's been going on with me," I said eventually.

She nodded. "Yeah, I wouldn't mind that."

I took a deep breath and told her everything.

When I was done explaining, she wrapped me in another hug. "I'm so sorry you've been going through all that. I wish I'd been there for you more."

"It's okay," I said, once we'd pulled away. "I wasn't really *letting* you be there for me. But I want to now. Ghost helped me realize that."

From his spot lying near the creek, Ghost's ears twitched in our direction, as if listening to me talk about him.

"That reminds me—I wanted to show you something," Tanya said, pulling out her phone and opening up her photo album.

I watched over her shoulder as she scrolled quickly through her pictures, landing finally on the one she wanted. She held her phone out to me, and I took it.

It was a picture of a painting she'd done: an aerial view of her and me sitting in this exact spot, overlooking the creek, the playground just barely visible in the corner. Our feet dangled off the ledge, our shoulders pressed together, and although you couldn't see our faces, I knew we were laughing, smiling, happy. And there—in the distance—was a soft, catlike black smudge.

"Is that . . . ?"

"Ghost," she said. "I know I can't see him like you do, but sometimes . . . I swear it feels like I can tell that he's around. The last time we were at the creek and we talked about Ghost, I got the feeling he was there, so . . . I thought I would add him to the scene. I tried to paint him based on how you've described him to me before."

I couldn't have stopped the tears if I wanted to.

"Tanya." I wiped the tears away before they could fall onto her phone screen, beaming. "You're my best friend in the whole world, you know that?"

She smiled, too, a little watery. "You're mine, too. I hope you like the painting. I was planning on submitting it for the showcase, if that's okay with you. . . ."

"Of course it is." I tugged her into one last hug. "You're amazing."

We stayed at the creek for another hour after that and talked about nothing, the creek below us babbling, Ghost's dark outline against the pale green grass.

The following week was a blur of working on the songwriting project. I went over to Emmett's after school a few days in a row so we could record the remaining three songs. It was a lot more work than I'd expected, but it was also a lot of fun. Plus, I was grateful for the excuse to see them outside of school.

We decided to perform "Don't Let Me Disappear" at the showcase. I hadn't originally written it for two people to sing, but we workshopped it for a while, and eventually came up with harmonies that made the song sound so much fuller. I played banjo on it, including a solo after the bridge, while Emmett played guitar. They sang the verses and I sang the bridge, but we both sang the choruses.

That Friday, we were called out of class early so we could prepare for the show. In the auditorium, we met up with Tanya and Dima.

"I can't wait to hear your poem," Emmett told Dima while we were waiting backstage to be called for our turn at sound check.

"Thanks! I can't wait to hear y'all." She gestured to the banjo case I was holding.

"Yeah . . . I'm a little nervous, actually," I admitted.

"Aww, I'm sure all three of you will do great!" Tanya grinned, nudging me with her elbow. "Although, I can't say I envy you. I'm perfectly happy with just my paintings being up there while I watch from the audience."

The visual arts students had their work displayed on the stage and around the auditorium. Tanya's art pieces—the self-portrait of her at her cousin's wedding, the painting of her mom, and the painting she'd shown me at the creek—were propped up on easels on the right side of the stage.

Prep for the show lasted about an hour. As the rest of the school was finally filing into the auditorium, Mr. Russak pulled aside Emmett, me, and the rest of his students who were performing. There were five of us in total, four from songwriting and one from another class he taught.

He clapped his hands together. "All right, kids, the show will be starting in a few minutes. You're all gonna do great! And remember: if you mess up, don't let it stop you. This isn't about being perfect; this is about showing off some of the amazing work you've done this semester."

We all nodded, and Mr. Russak dismissed us to tune our instruments and do any last-minute run-throughs we needed. I clutched my banjo tighter. I'd had butterflies on and off since first getting backstage, but now that we were so close to performing, they were back in full force.

I peeked around the curtain to see the students getting settled in their seats and spotted Tanya sitting with Logan and Nat. Things had been more normal between Tanya and Nat since last week, although I could still feel some tension there. Nat had yet to come out to the rest of the friend group, but I knew they'd get around to it soon.

Tanya caught my eye and waved. I waved back, trying to not look as anxious as I felt.

"You ready?" Emmett said from behind me. I closed the curtain and turned to them. They had their acoustic guitar slung over their shoulder, already tuned and ready to go.

"Not really," I said.

They grabbed my hand. "We're gonna do awesome. We've run through this song so many times, I bet we could play it in our sleep."

"Yeah, you're right." I nodded. "We can do this."

"We can do this," they agreed.

A moment later, the lights went down.

Emmett and I watched the first half of the show from backstage. We were allowed to sit in the audience once we were done, but for now, I watched the back of Dima as she stood at the mic and performed her poem. That guy in her class really *had* just been a jealous asshole; I didn't know much about poetry, but even I could tell she was talented. The audience roared in applause when she was done. As she walked by us, Emmett and I both gave her quick hugs.

And then, before we knew it, it was our turn.

"Please welcome to the stage Emmett Carpenter and Caleb Stone!"

The spotlights were bright as we stepped out onto the stage. It took a moment to plug our instruments in, but then I was staring out into the faceless audience. I looked to Emmett, and they nodded, a small smile in place.

I took a deep breath and started playing.

Our three-and-a-half-minute performance was a blur. One moment I was plucking the opening notes, and the next, we were walking off the stage, loud applause at our backs while my heart pounded in my chest. It had felt like a dream, being up there, the way that the music and the lyrics flooded from me, the way it was over before I could even process that we'd done it.

Emmett and I scurried off to get our instruments put away so we could join the audience. We sat with Tanya, Logan, Nat, and Dima, and they whispered their congratulations as we sat down.

From this angle, I could finally see how Tanya's paintings looked to the audience; they were vibrant and beautiful. I couldn't see the details well, but I still made out the catlike smudge.

Emmett leaned into me. "We did it," they whispered.

"And now we're *finally* done with that project," I whispered back.

They pouted. "But now how will we find an excuse to hang out?"

I stifled a laugh, and they bumped their knee into mine.

"Maybe we could write music together again sometime," I suggested.

Emmett grinned. "I'd like that."

We stopped talking after that, turning toward the stage to watch the rest of the show. I thought about the moment in *The Catcher in the Rye* that inspired "Don't Let Me Disappear," how it had stuck out to me even before Jack's death. I thought about the cat in those home videos, about how it felt to hold Ghost in the cemetery.

That night, after my parents and I were all home, I came into the living room where they were both watching TV.

"Hey," I said. "Can I join you guys?"

"Of course, sweetie." Mom scooted over, making room for me next to her. I sat down.

We watched TV together for a little while, none of us saying anything. Once a commercial break came on, I took a breath. "I think I'm ready to help clean out Jack's room."

Mom turned to me, her smile bittersweet.

"All right, well . . . we were gonna get some more work done this weekend if you want to join us?" she asked.

I nodded. She pulled me into a hug, kissing the top of my head, and I leaned into her. While we waited for the show to start again, I asked what I'd missed, and Dad caught me up on the plot so far.

Ghost sat at our feet in front of the couch, head turned toward the TV, too, but I didn't mind his presence. It was nice, almost comforting. In a way, it felt like Jack was with us.

March

23

DECK OF FOOLS'S FIRST HOUSE show of the new year wasn't until the beginning of spring, and it was hosted, once again, at Nat's house.

Tanya, Amy, and I showed up early to help set the equipment up. Deck of Fools was going to be performing their latest EP, *I Am Learning How to Live Again*, for the first time since it had dropped in February. It was a Friday night, and everyone seemed restless, rowdy, more excited than usual; it would be spring break in a few weeks, and we were all ready for the time off.

Last semester, Emmett and I got a ninety-eight on our songwriting final. That, plus the extra credit from the showcase and the late assignments I made up, ensured that I passed songwriting with a C plus. And I started writing again, albeit slowly. It was still hard, most days, to force the words out, but I got better at accepting that my songs weren't going to be perfect right out of the gate, and I started a writing routine, encouraging myself to keep going even when I didn't feel like I could. Since the project, Emmett and I had written a few songs together, too, and we planned to record them sometime soon.

I'd also started writing songs about Jack—a lot of them. I thought of it as practice talking about my grief. I was opening up more—not only to Emmett, but to other people, too, Dima and Logan and Nat and Amy, and, to some extent, the people at Tom's group, including Candi, who I now exchanged the occasional DMs with—but it was still difficult to talk about sometimes. Writing was a way to get it out. It was, all things considered, the healthiest coping mechanism I'd found so far. I'd shied away from alcohol and weed in the following months; I was much more careful now about when and why I chose to drink or smoke.

Nat came out to the friend group as nonbinary and transfeminine the day after the showcase, and since then, they'd seemed happier. More hesitant, maybe, but as the days went on, and as they settled into this new version of themself, I noticed how much more joyful they seemed. They'd always been smiley and laid-back, but now they seemed genuinely *happy*. It was nice to see.

This Deck of Fools show drew a bigger crowd than the one for their anniversary. People trickled in, and I recognized a lot of them from Williams—kids from theater and the music conservatory, acquaintances and friends-of-friends. While they were getting finished setting up, Walter and Gwen entered, and when they saw me, Gwen smiled and waved, and Walter gave me a polite nod.

I nodded back. We hadn't talked one-on-one since that day at Cafe Coco, but we saw each other every now and then at events like this, and things were all right.

When it looked like Emmett had a free moment, I walked over to them. They were at the makeshift tarp-stage, tuning their electric guitar and laughing at something that Dima had said. Logan was behind the stage, plugging something in.

"Hey," I said, coming up behind Emmett and sliding an arm around their waist.

"Hey, babe." They turned around and leaned into me in a hug, planting a quick kiss on my cheek. I'd started getting used to things like this, pet names and casual displays of affection, but it still sent a little jolt of joy through me every time.

"How's everything going?" I asked.

"Almost ready," Dima said, tapping her drumsticks against her thigh. "Maybe ten more minutes."

"Which is code for twenty," I said.

Emmett grinned. "You know us too well. Could you do me a huge favor?"

"Sure."

"Grab me a slice of pizza from inside?" They clasped their hands together, batting their eyelashes at me with a wide, charming smile.

I snorted. "Yeah, no problem. Be right back."

"Thank you, love you!"

"Love you, too," I said, before heading inside to the kitchen. We'd first said "I love you" to each other a month ago, when we were hanging out after we finished watching *Bride of*

Re-Animator, and ever since, I couldn't get enough of it. I told them I loved them whenever I could, and then some.

I'd also told them about Ghost. It was on New Year's, and the whole friend group was sleeping over at Nat's house. Around one a.m., when we were all heading to bed, Emmett and I snuck out on the patio to talk.

Things with Ghost had been okay during the holidays. He was around a lot, but when I wasn't viewing him as a nuisance or a problem, it wasn't so bad. I started thinking of him as a reminder that Jack was still with me. That his life still mattered.

And that night, as Emmett and I sat on the patio, looking up at the dark sky and listening to Nat's neighbors set off fireworks, I felt Ghost's presence, and it gave me the courage to turn to Emmett and say, "You remember how I told you once that I believe in ghosts?"

They nodded. I told them everything.

I told them about the first time I saw Ghost, and about how he took a liking to them, and about how Tanya and I theorized about his intentions. I told them how it felt, hugging Ghost at Jack's grave, and I told them about the home videos I'd watched, the black cat at our old house.

"Do you think he wanted us to know each other?" Emmett asked.

"I'd like to think so," I said.

Since New Year's, Ghost had stopped showing up quite as often. It became a few times a week rather than every single day, and although things could still trigger his appearance—like someone bringing up Jack's death when I wasn't expecting it, or smelling cigarette smoke as I walked down the street—he was a comfort to me. I was finally refusing to run from my grief. I was trying to embrace it.

In Nat's kitchen, I grabbed slices of pizza for Emmett, Amy, Tanya, and me, balancing paper plates on my arms.

"Make way, make way, I've got food for the talent," I said as I returned to the stage.

Emmett laughed, taking one of the plates from me. "You're the best. Thank you."

"I should let you guys finish getting ready," I said, "but let me know if you need anything. Also, you're gonna kill it."

I leaned up on my tiptoes and kissed them one last time before I left to sit with Tanya and Amy. They'd claimed a few vinyl chairs to the left of the pool, and they were already sitting down, chatting about the trip Amy and Logan were planning for spring break. I set the plates down in front of them.

"Aw, thank you, Caleb," Amy said. "You didn't have to do that."

I pulled up a chair and sat down with a shrug. "I figured I'd grab you guys some before it's all gone."

Tanya nudged me with her elbow gently. "You ready for the show?"

I grinned. "Always."

The three of us sat together, talking and laughing, for another fifteen minutes before Emmett finally tapped on the mic, their guitar slung over their shoulder, and said, "Hello, hello, hello! How's everyone doing tonight?"

I turned toward the stage, hollering in excitement with the

rest of the crowd. Emmett caught my eye and winked, a wide grin on their face, and I grinned back.

As Deck of Fools started the first song, I caught a glimpse of Ghost, sitting at the archway leading out to the patio, head turned toward the stage.

I leaned back and let the music wash over me.

Author's Note

Dear Reader,

I came up with the idea for *The Ghost of You* when I was seventeen years old. Sitting in class at the arts school I attended in Nashville, I doodled a black, faceless cat in my sketchbook, and from there I developed the bare bones of Caleb's story: a grieving trans boy being haunted by a ghost cat, his artistic lifelong best friend, and the cute musician the cat draws him toward.

And, perhaps most important of all, I knew the ending. I knew that Caleb's story ended with him accepting his grief, with realizing that Ghost was not there to make his life miserable, but to keep Jack's memory alive. Because of that, I also knew that this was going to be an incredibly emotionally demanding novel to write.

I lost my oldest sister, Erica, when I was fourteen and a freshman in high school, only a few months after I came out as trans. She was twenty-six when she died suddenly. She had struggled with addiction for as long as I could remember, but, similarly to Caleb, I was in fifth grade when the word "addict" was first used in front of me.

After her death, the grief was all-encompassing. I couldn't understand *why*—why it had to be her, why it had to be then, why she couldn't have survived like some others had. I searched for answers, but nothing was ever enough.

At the end of my freshman year, I discovered spoken word poetry, and before I knew it, I was writing extensively about Erica, about grief, about mental health and transness—about everything. I left my public high school for the arts school where my mother taught. There, I was accepted into the literary arts department, and I pursued poetry along with my fiction writing.

Then, when I was a junior, I became the 2017 Nashville Youth Poet Laureate. In the final spoken word event where I was awarded the title, I performed "Sunflowers," a poem I wrote about Erica. It talked about her death and her life, and about the stigma around drug addiction and the way our society demonizes addicts instead of helping them.

Writing about my sister was cathartic, most of the time. It helped me move away from anger and depression and denial, and toward acceptance. But it was often also difficult, and sometimes I just wanted to avoid my feelings. I wanted to pretend I was a normal, happy teenager, with a normal, happy life and no yawning chasm where my sister should have been. This was the core of Caleb's struggle, I knew: that disconnect between *needing* catharsis and connection, *needing* to talk about it . . . and yet avoiding it at all costs.

So, I put off writing Caleb's story for many years. I knew that, in order to do this novel justice, I would need a lot more time to process my own grief. Now I would like to think that I have—in large part due to choosing to write this book, which I began working on in earnest in 2022 after finishing my first novel.

At the time of this book's publication, my sister has been gone for ten years. Somehow, ten years is forever and no time at all. I'm twenty-four now, and I'm still finding new ways to miss her, new ways to grieve. Most days, I think of this as a blessing. It means she's still with me.

Much of this novel is semi-autobiographical. If you know me really well, you can probably pick out the specific scenes, character details, or references that I've taken from my real life.

I chose to do this for multiple reasons. One, because I wanted to draw from my own experiences, growing up with drug addiction in the home and losing a sibling to heroin. Although I wrote many, many poems about Erica, fiction was a space where I had not yet explored questions of addiction and grief.

Two, because as a teen I struggled to find young adult novels that spoke to these experiences, and I hope to change that for others. Some of the topics touched on in this novel are not easy or pleasant to talk about, but that's why I feel so strongly that we *should* talk about them.

By the time I was seventeen, many of the LGBTQ+ and/or otherwise marginalized teens I knew—including myself—had experienced some form of sexual abuse, trauma, or harassment. It seemed like violations and violence were upsettingly common occurrences in my and friends' lives, and yet, when I turned on the TV or picked up a book, I didn't see many depictions of what we were going through. The few I *could* find often felt exploitative, or they excluded queer and/or trans survivors from the conversation entirely.

Luckily, this is changing. Publishing is slowly making more room for young adult novels that deal compassionately with sexual assault, abuse, and intimate partner violence, and that depict a diverse range of survivor experiences, rather than a monolith.

I hope this novel, even in a small way, can contribute to that change.

Thank you, Reader, for picking up this book. Maybe you see yourself in these characters; maybe, like I was as a teenager, you are searching for your life in these pages, trying to make sense of your heartbreak or trauma or grief.

If that's the case, I want you to know that there is power in finding the words for your feelings. Sometimes we need to be able to name our pain in order to heal from it. Whether it's a creative outlet, one-on-one counseling or group therapy, or coming to your loved ones for help when you need it—there are ways to make the load lighter, to cope with our grief.

You are not alone, Reader, and it's going to be okay. I promise.

With love,
Michael Gray Bulla

Acknowledgments

MY SOPHOMORE NOVEL WOULD NOT have been possible without the incredible help, encouragement, support, feedback, love, and critique of so many people, including (but not limited to):

Pete Knapp, my literary agent: thank you for always having my back and believing in my ideas. I can't express in words how much you've helped me in this book's publishing process, and I can't wait to continue working with you on future novels!

Karen Chaplin, my editor: thank you for your trust in this story and in my writing, and for helping make both *If I Can Give You That* and *The Ghost of You* the best books they could be.

Allison Weintraub, Erika West, and the Quill Tree publishing team: thank you all so much for your help on this novel.

Marcos Chin, thank you for the gorgeous cover art, and Neo Cihi, thank you for narrating the audiobook!

Adam Sass, Z. R. Ellor, Daniel Aleman, and Adi Alsaid:

thank you all so much for blurbing *If I Can Give You That*!

Mom and Dad: thank you for all your immeasurable love and guidance, and for your unwavering support in my writing career. Thank you for reading early drafts of my books, writing music together, watching *The Twilight Zone* with me, and much, much more. I'm who I am today because of you two. I couldn't have asked for better parents.

Marcie, my sister: thank you for brainstorming ideas with me, and for instilling in me your good taste in music. And Max, my brother: thank you for playing *Breath of the Wild* and *Pokémon* with me, and for keeping me up-to-date on the teen lingo.

Ian, my boyfriend: thank you for knowing me and loving me as well as you do, and for listening to me ramble about revisions for hours on end.

Hayden, my childhood best friend. Much like Caleb and Tanya, we've stuck with each other through everything. Thank you for always being my bestie. <3

Ally, Riley, and Bean, my *D&D* group. Your friendship means the absolute world to me, and I can't wait to visit the West Coast with y'all!

Sasha, Alex, Nash, and all my New York friends: thank you for all the Halloween parties and group chat memes and Letterloop questions. I'm so thankful we've stayed in touch after graduation!

Dan Rosenberg, Becca Myers, and Caroline Manring: thank you all for teaching me and making my time at Wells worth it, and for reading some extremely early versions of my books.

Hermes and Hera, my cats. Thanks for being perfect, sweet babies who hang out on the couch with me while I work—and for giving me lots of inspiration for writing Ghost!

And, finally, the person reading this: thank you so much for taking the time to pick up this book. None of us authors could do what we do without your support. <3